WHITE RABBIT

KATE PHILLIPS

Houghton Mifflin Company
Boston   New York   1996

XII

XI   I

X   II

W H I T E   R A B B I T
. . . .

IX   III

VIII   IV

VII   V

VI

For information about permission to reproduce selections from
this book, write to Permissions, Houghton Mifflin Company,
215 Park Avenue South, New York, New York 10003.

Library of Congress Cataloging-in-Publication Data

Phillips, Kate.
  White rabbit / Kate Phillips.
      p. cm.
  ISBN 0-395-74285-4
  I. Title.
  PS3566.H4798W48   1996
  813'.54 – dc20   95-31059   CIP

Book design by Anne Chalmers

Printed in the United States of America

QUM 10 9 8 7 6 5 4 3 2 1

For information about this and other Houghton Mifflin
trade and reference books and multimedia products, visit
The Bookstore at Houghton Mifflin on the World Wide Web
at http://www.hmco.com/trade/.

For my family, in memory of
Elizabeth Soyster Hammond,
Fred Hammond, and
Eric Phillips

I am grateful for the support and encouragement of Tim O'Brien, my editor Janet Silver, Wendy Holt, and my agent Anne Borchardt. Also, I want to thank Jessica Dorman, Larry Cooper, Lena Deevy, Jennifer MacFarlane, and Lina Lee.

Facing west from California's shores,
Inquiring, tireless, seeking what is yet unfound,
I, a child, very old, over waves, towards the house of maternity, the
          land of migrations, look afar,
Look off the shores of my Western sea, the circle almost circled;
For starting westward from Hindustan, from the vales of Kashmere,
From Asia, from the north, from the God, the sage, and the hero,
From the south, from the flowery peninsulas and the spice islands,
Long having wander'd since, round the earth having wander'd,
Now I face home again, very pleas'd and joyous,
(But where is what I started for so long ago?
And why is it yet unfound?)

                              —Walt Whitman, *Leaves of Grass*

XII

XI   I

X   II

P   A   R   T   O   N   E
. . . .

IX   III

VIII   IV

VII   V

VI

RUTH SLEPT on her back, face up, mouth open, eighty-eight years old. When she breathed — and there were times when she did not — she exhaled with a wheeze and a jerk and a long dry hum from the bottom of her lungs. She lay deep in her green sleeping bag.

"Henry, for God's sake!" she mumbled. "Henry!"

Even in her sleep, the old man gave her fits. Thirty-six years they had been married, thirty-six years he'd been upsetting the fragile order Ruth lived to polish and perfect. Now, in her tireless dreams, he stood at the kitchen sink, trying to skin a big yellow grapefruit with the carrot peeler. A great fire raged all around him; flames lapped against his collar, oily black smoke came from the cupboards and drawers, but even so Henry stood there calm and quiet, skinning his grapefruit with the rusty carrot peeler. "Yes, sir," he muttered, "damn thick skin." He blinked stupidly and shook his head and turned the grapefruit in his hands. His shirt was burning. "Boy oh boy," he said, "*too* damn thick."

Ruth grunted and rolled sideways.

"Idiot!" she yelled.

"Texas grapefruit. Got to be."

"My God, man, that's a *carrot* peeler!"

"Texas for sure," Henry said. His ears and nose were burning. "Yes, sir, bet your life, this here's one of them mutant Texas jobbies, I seen 'em before, buggers just don't skin right — never did, never will, and there's a fact."

"Boob!" Ruth yelled.

Her own voice woke her up. She opened her eyes, adjusted her glasses — she wore them even when she slept. For a few seconds, still half asleep, she peered into the shadowy early-morning dark. No fire, no grapefruits. No sound except for her old Emerson radio.

"Texas," she said. "What a boob."

She sighed, reached out, turned up the volume on her radio. It was always on; she hadn't switched it off since the day she and Henry moved to Laguna Beach.

. . . *So all you California dreamers, let's look alive! Out of the sack! Touch those toes! Another new day, and you've started it out with FM Ninety-seven, voice of the New Southland, and I'm your breakfast buddy Bruce Gentry . . .*

It had been Bruce Gentry for ten years now. Another bonehead.

Ruth turned her head toward the door, yelled, "Henry!" There was no answer. At five-thirty in the morning, the whole state of California seemed deserted. Marooned with a moron, she thought. Trapped three stories high in her Paradise Lagoon condominium.

"Henry! You awake?"

Again, there was no response from the room across the hall. Ruth rolled onto her side, pressed her toes against the zipper at the bottom of her sleeping bag. A light, almost buoyant sense of familiarity came over her; she'd spent every night of the past five years in the bag. Not because she liked the feel of nylon against her skin — she despised it — but because washing sheets struck her as a profligate waste of time and money.

For a while, lying still, Ruth listened to the drone of a half-dozen radio commercials. Saturday, she thought. December the first. A White Rabbit day.

Time to get on with things.

"Henry!" she yelled.

5:35 A.M.

Ruth pushed herself up. She sighed again, released a squeaky little fart, then inhaled to test the efficiency of her lungs. The world seemed oddly different today — the air, maybe, or the fluttery morning shadows, or the scent of her own gas. A new and unwholesome gloominess filled the room. Even the bed beneath her seemed sad and dreary; her yellow candlewick bedspread, folded down around the bedposts, had long ago turned brown with age at the top of each tufted cotton ball. Ruth knew this, didn't need to see it. But it didn't matter — no detergent on earth could remove the residue of all those long, slow years.

She reached for her bedjacket, which hung to her left over the bedpost. The jacket was light pink and embroidered with looping blue flowers, an old lady's design, and Ruth had been wearing it every morning for almost fifteen years. She slipped it over her flannel nightgown. The jacket hung loosely, a bag on bones. When, Ruth wondered, had she become so small? She pushed away the sleeping bag and bent her legs, one knee at a time, slowly shifting her weight to the edge of the bed. Her right knee made a sharp popping sound. Dr. Ash said she'd been born with the bad knee, an inheritance of sorts, and that it certainly wouldn't kill her. Still, the knee had never hurt like this before — maybe it had to do with that cheap safety rail they'd installed above the bathtub.

Two mornings ago, when Ruth reached for the rail, the stupid gizmo had slipped through her hands and sent her sprawling back into the water, her rear end slamming against the tile as the right knee buckled.

Ruth sighed.

Born with it my eye.

She'd always had good legs, pretty legs; like a ballerina, Hale used to tell her. But now the knee had swollen up like an eggplant left to rot in the sun — an ugly, purplish lump — and to make matters worse, Henry hadn't heard a thing when she'd taken the fall, hadn't come to rescue her until she'd called out at least a half-dozen times . . . Yes, gorgeous legs, my little ballerina, Hale would say, and he'd run a hand along the curve of her calf, and sometimes higher, and he'd do sweet tickling things that didn't really tickle, and he'd even lean down and kiss the kneecap . . . Amazing legs.

"Henry! You awake?"

Such a boob.

Probably still snoring away in the room across the hall in that big old double bed of his. Ruth could hear him now, almost smell him.

She slid down from the high mattress. She dropped to the floor with a little gasp, then tottered cautiously toward the foot of the bed. There on the rug was her sit-up pillow, an old white thing that she liked to slip behind her back for support. She leaned against it every morning as she put on her face, and she leaned against it every evening as she took off her face. Fluffs of cotton stuck out where the seams had split; it had served her very nicely for almost forty-two years.

She bent down for the pillow — one click in the knee — then hesitated and told herself to retrieve it later. The disorder irritated her, but it couldn't be helped, she'd have to let the creaky old joints loosen up first.

On the radio, Bruce Gentry was still doling out his greasy

nonsense: *So come on, California, let's get an early start! A beach day in December, how good to be alive!*

"Right," Ruth muttered, "unless you're some platitudinous bonehead."

Good to be alive — how could you argue? — but better yet to be alive and be a Caster. Ruth Caster Armstrong, never mind this second marriage to Henry Hubble; Ruth Caster Armstrong, and that was something she could take pride in forever. "Posture, boys!" she used to tell her two sons. "Stand up, kid!" to her only granddaughter. "Straight and solid, no hunchbacks in the Caster clan."

Ruth pulled her shoulders back and shuffled over to the bedroom door. Bad knee and all, she still had that erect Caster posture. She shut the door with authority and turned her back to it, lining herself up against its flat surface. Heels first, then bottom, shoulders, head. She sucked in her stomach, pressed the small of her back against the door, and held herself there for a count of ten.

"So *there*," she said. "Ha!"

Eighty-eight years old, yes, but nobody could ever claim she didn't have spine. That Caster backbone. Which was the whole secret to making it through all those years. One thing for certain, even the most ordinary, unremarkable life would finally wear a person down — the weight of marriage and children, the funerals and Christmases and Easters, the simple burdens of memory that kept accumulating and growing heavier with each tick of the clock — all that could turn you into jelly, drag you right down into the grave. Yes, it could. Unless you had spine.

"Ha!" she said again, louder. "So *there*."

A little tickle of triumph went through her as she moved away from the door and into the speckled shadows of another morning.

By habit she again glanced down at her wristwatch. Almost five forty-five. She didn't need to see the back of the watch to know what *it* said: "To Ruth, love Hale, 1938." And here it was now,

1995. Approaching the year 2000, and she was almost . . . Dear God, almost a full century on this earth.

The fierce, blurry speed of all those years amazed her. Impossible, she told herself, that she had lived so long without him. Hale had died in January 1944 — murdered by an evil, implacable, utterly invisible virus.

Bugs, Ruth thought. Vicious little bugs.

She pulled a loose thread from the hem of her bedjacket, inspected the stitching in each sleeve.

Just for an instant, a wave of speckly white light seemed to rush in on her, and then, just as quickly, the white speckles faded away. Ruth lifted her glasses and rubbed her eyelids.

Teetering slightly, she moved back to the end of the bed, bending down again for the sit-up pillow. Then past the slippers she'd left out the night before (her toes were freezing) and up to the head of the bed, to push the sit-up pillow against the wall. And then back onto the bed, back into the sleeping bag.

Ruth looked left toward the bedside table and stretched to turn on the table lamp. The little pillbox from Gump's (a gift from her son Carter, before he'd lost all his money — would he ever remake it before she died?) sat on the table, waiting for her.

One Mevacor to lower her cholesterol.

Naprosyn and Tylenol, for the knee and aching joints.

One Cardizem on waking, another at nine or ten, a third in midafternoon, a fourth just before bed. Four a day. Dr. Ash — he took over after Dr. Rhodes retired — Dr. Ash said it didn't matter how high her blood pressure rose. What mattered was blasting the arteries open, four times a day. At bedtime, arteries wide open, Ruth sometimes treated herself to a little pink tranquilizer to help her sleep.

Now, in the morning, it was one Mevacor, one Cardizem, one Naprosyn, one Tylenol. She washed them down with water from the cup she kept beside her pillbox. Again, almost instantly, the bedroom went dimly with that strange white light.

Curious sounds, too. Curious shapes here and there.

Ruth lay very still for a moment, a bit puzzled, then blinked and reached for the phone.

"Oh, my," she murmured.

Stiffly, with a bony index finger, Ruth dialed and cleared her throat and waited, still puzzled, watching the odd white shapes move about the room like the tracks of some living creature — a fat, furry bunny jumping here and there beneath a wizard's magic wand.

5:52 A.M.

"White Rabbit!" Ruth shouted. "Got you!"

"I'm sorry?"

Ruth jumped. The voice sounded peculiar. Too low, too deep — as if its owner had swallowed an avocado pit.

"I *said*, White —"

"Yeah, sure. White Rabbit yourself."

Ruth was startled. For as long as she could remember — and her memory was good — the Caster clan had played this little game on the first of every month. The idea was simple: get up early and place the call and draw in a deep breath and yell "White Rabbit!" into the mouthpiece. Whoever got the words out first became an automatic winner. Victory brought a month's worth of good luck; defeat meant you'd best watch your step. To Ruth, the contest was more than a diversion. In one form or another she had been playing the game since childhood, passing along the rules to friends and family, and over time it had become one of the solid cornerstones in her life, a source of order, a base ritual that somehow supported and justified a great many lesser rituals.

She took the game seriously; she required the same of others.

Ruth rubbed her eyes.

"Who is this?" she said fiercely. "Where's my grandchild?"

"Hey, listen —"

"No, sir, *you* listen. If Karen's harmed — if you so much as

looked at her — I'll have the authorities there before you can say
. . . Who *is* this?"

There was a muffled whispering on the other end. Ruth ran her
fingers through her hair, tried to remain calm. A hundred times
she'd told Karen to bolt her windows. Men were men, and L.A.
was L.A., and it was getting to the point where a woman had to
wear body armor in her own bed.

After a moment, her granddaughter spoke. "White Rabbit!"

Ruth snorted. "Nonsense. I've already said White Rabbit."

"Not to me you didn't," Karen said. "Rules are rules, Grammy.
I win, you lose."

"Oh poof, don't be silly, I most definitely said it first. Definitely
and absolutely. That rapist who answered, he heard me." Ruth
paused, collected herself. "So who is he? And why of all things is
he answering your phone?"

"Mike," Karen said gently. "The man I married?"

"That one?"

"Right, that one. Do you know what time it is?"

Ruth frowned. "I have no recollection of this individual, what-
soever. Far as I'm concerned, you were never married."

"Oh, come on now. The schoolteacher. *Mike.*"

"Schoolteacher? What's a schoolteacher doing breaking into
somebody's —"

"He didn't break in. He's my husband."

"Husband! Breaking and entering?"

Karen released a quick, shallow sigh. "Just stop it," she said.
"Hang on a minute — he's on his way out the door."

"And now he's abandoning you. Stays there all night, this sweet
Romeo, then skulks away at sunrise."

"Grammy, please. One second."

Karen pressed her hold button, leaving Ruth to listen to a
screech of flutes and harmonicas. Ruth shook her head. All that
grief, she thought, and the poor girl's just taken the louse right
back. It made her blood hot. Ruth had known only two trustwor-

thy men in her entire adult life. Her own father, Walt, and her own first husband, Hale. Both were dead.

After a moment there was a rattling sound on the other end of the line.

"Hi, there," Karen said, "I'm back."

"You and everybody else."

"Well, I know, but this time it's —"

"Always *this* time," Ruth snapped. "I'd just like to know one thing. If you let Mr. Wonderful stay there all night, why's he in such a hurry to run out now?"

"His name's Mike. And he *is* wonderful. He has things to do, is all — had to get going."

Scowling, Ruth drew the bedjacket around her shoulders and considered the situation. Karen seemed tense, a little defensive.

"Well, maybe so," Ruth said, "but it still strikes me as very, very peculiar. This revolving door of his. In and out. A word of advice — don't get too cozy — he may be up to something. Always was, if you remember. Probably a drug addict by now. And you know about these new diseases."

Her granddaughter groaned. "Please drop it, Grammy. It's too early in the morning."

Ruth ignored her. "I'll tell you this much. When I was your age, things were decent. I'd already been married seven whole years, almost eight — no, nine. The first time, that is. My real marriage."

"I know, Grammy. Really, you've explained it all a thousand times. Hale had this car, right? And he drove you the whole way from Los Angeles to the Grand Canyon for your honeymoon, and it rained like crazy, and the car broke down and the roads were terrible, but even so it was this genuine religious experience, perfectly thrilling and sublime and beautiful."

"I never said religious."

"Please," Karen said, "don't get started. I need some sleep."

"I can imagine. Kept you awake, did he?"

"The other way around."

"My God."

"Listen, why don't we talk later?"

Ruth shook her head sadly. Eyes closed, she found herself picturing Karen's face, the sunny brown skin and blond hair and green eyes, and it was a few moments before she realized that the face belonged to a twelve-year-old. Hard to believe that this lovely little girl was now a married woman.

"Well, in any case," Ruth said, "it's considerably more than I'll ever understand. The man runs off on you, who knows where, then one day he busts in again and has his perverted way with you and all you can do is . . . I mean, you *allow* it. One minute it's divorce, the next minute you're letting him . . . Honestly, I don't understand."

"I was only considering divorce," Karen said. Her voice had again gone defensive. "Thinking about it. Barely even that."

"Is that so?"

"Yes, of course."

Ruth sniffed. "Funny that I don't recall it that way. Anyway, when I was first married, divorce was the last thing on *my* mind, God knows. I was so busy just worrying about little things, like would Hale catch me plucking the stray hairs from my chin in the morning. And the two of us were such dodos! We both had the feelings and the urge, but we didn't quite know . . . Have I ever told you what he thought about my legs?"

"Look, not right now, okay?"

"Ballerina legs, that's what my Hale called them, and you should've seen his eyes, the way he'd lean down and put his tongue right up against —"

"Not *now*."

Ruth wagged her head from side to side. A few years with some fancy job, a little time in her apartment without what's-his-name — and now what's-his-name back in the picture — and Karen seemed to think she knew everything. The girl would be sorry soon enough, brushing her grandmother aside this way.

"I'll call you later, Grammy. Maybe even stop over, okay?"

"Fine," Ruth said, "if you want."

"I do want."

"Well fine," Ruth said, and hung up.

For a few seconds she stared down at the phone. The image of twelve-year-old Karen flickered up again, bright and clear, then gradually melted into twenty-nine-year-old Karen. Still blond, still lovely. But the lightheartedness was gone now. Snatched away, as usual, by a burglar dressed up as romance.

Ruth felt a powerful, inexplicable sadness, as if the day itself were somehow infected with the poisons of melancholy. The sun was up now. December the first, a very peculiar White Rabbit day in Southern California.

Ruth leaned back against her sit-up pillow.

"Henry!"

6:08 A.M.

It was Saturday, cleaning day, which meant Luzma would come breezing in just after three o'clock, late as usual. Meanwhile, Ruth had things to do, business to take care of. There was the letter to mail to Douglas, a bus to catch. All the way downtown and back — it might well take the entire morning. And only one bus, too. She'd probably have to wait an eternity while it made its loop and came back to pick her up. Of course that wasn't so bad. She'd wait on the bench by the curb, or in the library (everybody there knew her) if it started to rain. This early sunlight could be deceptive. She'd take her umbrella, just in case. First, though, breakfast.

"Henry! Would you come here, *please!*"

Almost instantly, as if he'd been lurking there, Henry appeared in the doorway, already dressed, wearing his usual brown corduroys and thin white shirt. Ugly, she thought. And the clothes, too. The shirt was always filthy at the neck.

Henry gave her his hopeful morning smile. "What's all the hollering for?"

He was tall, almost six three. His face was pinkish, splattered with tiny brown nubs. (Without a hat, he couldn't tolerate even twenty minutes in the sun — a high risk for skin cancer.) Henry Ho-hum Hubble. Who on God's earth would have thought she'd end up with *him?* Dropped out of school in the tenth grade. And that hair. Back then, in those high school days, the hair had been as red as a vine-ripe tomato and slimy as a clump of seaweed. His brother Bill hadn't been so bad — a good dancer — but Henry, unfortunately, was the one who'd finally worn her down. It was Henry's house that had lured her in the end; and now this, for almost four decades. The thought gave her cramps. She'd been married to him twice as long as she'd ever spent with Hale.

"About time," Ruth said. "I almost thought you'd stopped breathing, the way you don't hear a single blessed thing." She frowned at him. "I believe it's breakfast time."

"Right now?"

"Certainly now. When else?"

"Well, sure, but I was thinking —"

"Now," Ruth said.

It was Henry's responsibility to serve her breakfast in bed each morning, to carry it up from the tiny second-floor kitchen on her special red plastic tray. A simple enough job, really. Everything was always prearranged according to a strict set of rules; even an old goat like Henry could understand the basic system. Each evening, just before bed, Ruth would pour Shredded Wheat cakes — the small kind, the bran kind — into her blue porcelain cereal bowl: one-half cup exactly. Next she'd add a quarter cup of All-Bran pellets. (They *did* look like rat turds.) Then, with a practiced eye, concentrating, she'd place a medium-sized banana on the tray, three inches from the side of the bowl, to be peeled and cut on top of her cereal in the morning. Finally, she'd position a knife and an eight-ounce box of prunes beside the banana. Henry, of course, had his own variation on this procedure, preferring to pour his milk on at night so that by breakfast time each little wheat biscuit had dissolved into sodden nothingness.

Now, standing in the doorway, he reached into his mouth to straighten a tooth. "Seeing as how you're in such a hurry," he said, "maybe you ought to try my method. Saves all that milk-pouring time. Barely got to chew at all."

Ruth rolled her eyes. "Just bring up my carton of nonfat, like always."

"Sure, okay by me," Henry said. He tapped the tooth and shrugged. "But my way's quicker. Gentle on the gums, too."

Henry had ten teeth left in his head. Several of these were loose, and he lived in fear of swallowing one of them, of losing another precious tooth forever. Now and then Ruth would catch him standing at the bathroom mirror, squinting into his open mouth as he made a careful count. Since his gums were too soft for dentures, he was constantly forced to readjust the teeth he had. The canine at the top right side of his mouth dropped out at least twice a week, and turned one or two complete revolutions every day. In Ruth's opinion, the whole business was disgusting. *She* had all but one of her original teeth, and went for checkups at least twice a year.

"Forget your gums," she said. "I'm not worried about gums. Just bring me the milk carton. And please, please, please don't forget my cup of decaf."

"You're the boss," Henry said, stuffing his hands into his pockets and shuffling off toward the stairs.

Ruth rearranged her sit-up pillow and spread out a small towel across her lap to catch crumbs. For her, breakfast in bed was both comforting and essential, the only decent way to begin a day. Henry, thank God, kept his distance at mealtimes. He ate breakfast — as he ate every meal now — in his own room, at his desk by the window. From the desk he'd look out over the tennis court to a narrow strip of green grass, then to the iron fence surrounding Paradise Lagoon, then beyond to Coast Highway. He'd watch the passing cars, or the early-morning tennis players, or the Rain Bird lawn sprinklers going round and round. Most often, though, he just sat there.

It truly amazed her. How the man could stay utterly motionless for hours on end. If it was baseball season, he waited for the pregame show; if it wasn't baseball season, he waited for opening day.

He could wait for months.

"Don't matter none to me," he'd say. "One thing about baseball, Ruthie, you got to have patience to burn."

Sometimes he wore his Dodgers cap while he waited. Sometimes he took it off to scratch his head.

6:23 A.M.

The radio was still babbling, though Bruce Gentry had signed off with the rising sun.

The main order of business today was to mail that letter to Douglas, Ruth's eldest son, the retired cardiologist. It was a matter of financial urgency, right up his alley. Douglas had a knack for money matters: every April, he prepared her tax papers; during the year, as necessary, he handled her health insurance and Medicare and all the silly forms and documents that came crushing down through the mail. These days, Ruth thought, they didn't bury a person under dirt, they just held you below the mail slot and piled on the paper. Anyway, Douglas would know how to fix those idiots at the Blockbuster Book Club. Talk about paper — they were swamping her.

"I need action," she'd written her son last week, "and I need it now."

She'd been a club member for more than two decades, but a year ago, when her eyes could no longer tolerate the strain, she'd reluctantly informed the Blockbuster people that her membership was now null and void. A murderous phrase: null and void. Except the books kept coming. Sometimes two a month, sometimes three or four. Books she hadn't chosen, the worst sort of books: horticultural dictionaries and Italian sex manuals and low-fat Tex-Mex cookbooks. Rapidly, over the course of a few months, she'd acquired a large and expensive library, to which the club kept adding — volume after volume — thanking her profusely with each new shipment. "Our favorite Blockbusting customer," they'd declared at one point. "We remain confident that literature will bloom forever in the fertile gardens of Mrs. Henry Hubble." Ruth was not amused. Block*heads*, she'd thought. She'd taken to leaving the books in their cardboard mailing envelopes, stacking them unopened on the big oak dining table.

It was a nightmare, obviously, but somehow Douglas would get her out of it. Along with the letter, she'd enclosed her latest bill. Four hundred and fifteen dollars, for God's sake.

"I mean it," she'd written to her son, "these people have to be dealt with firmly. Make them do something. Number one: cart away their junk. Number two: a personal apology. Number three: ample compensation. I've suffered, haven't I? Yes, I have. And if those Blockbusters start to hem and haw — if they so much as make a peep — you have my authorization to drag the swindlers into court. Like that old Perry Mason show on television. A big trial, all the trappings." The idea made her smile. She could see it. How she'd wear a shabby dress to the courtroom — maybe that rose-colored jumper with the little mauve flowers she'd bought for Karen's baptism. Smear spit under her eyes and hobble up to the witness stand, give her bad knee a nice loud crack, take out a Kleenex and make a few old-lady moaning sounds as the bailiff used a wheelbarrow to haul in pile after pile of unopened books. Yes, and then she'd start reading aloud. Make the jury listen to all the claptrap these Blockbuster people were inflicting on her. She'd drone on for hours and hours — maybe weeks. Batter them with excerpts from *Cooking for the Single Parent Child*. Give them a good long sample from *Life Cycles of the African Violet* or *Dirty Mouths* or *Pagan Prayer for Pagan Protestants*.

And if all *that* didn't earn some pity, well then, she'd just throw an old-fashioned fit. The jury wouldn't have a choice.

Guilty.

Guilty as sin. Mr. Big-Bucks Blockbuster would end up paying through the nose.

Ruth peered around the bedroom, imagining how she'd spend the riches. A new wide-screen television, luxurious damask curtains, maybe an original Van Gogh. Those Blockbuster creeps had money to burn — a million dollars would do just fine, especially when she'd been getting by on those paltry Social Security payments. Yes, a flat million.

She grinned a thin little grin.

Two million.

Towel in her lap, eyes fixed on the sleeping bag, Ruth raised first her left foot, then her right, shaping the green nylon into an expanse of gently rolling hills where she might one day discover a world better than this one. A world where people got what they deserved, and where making ends meet was never a problem. A daydream, maybe, but why not? A safe, happy place where she could stop clipping coupons and stop cutting corners and stop nagging old Henry and stop dipping into Hale's veteran's pension, which she kept downtown at the Security Pacific.

She closed her eyes.

Yes, those gentle green hills, and a shadowy forest beyond, and a waterfall and a river and puffy white clouds. It made a pretty picture, which calmed her, but even then the morning's curious shades of melancholy did not quite vanish.

6:35 A.M.

"Hey, Ruthie, I said here's your breakfast. What are you, asleep?"

Ruth looked up and there was Henry, his nubby-red face hovering six inches above her chest.

Reality was irksome.

"No, I'm not asleep, I've been up forever. Just put the tray here on my towel."

Henry set down the tray and watched as Ruth poured milk on the cereal, peeled her banana and expertly cut it over her bowl. She took a swallow of decaf, scooped up a spoonful of Shredded Wheat and All-Bran. Henry waited. Ruth ate several bites in silence.

"Ready with the grocery list?" Henry said. "Ten minutes, I better slap pavement."

"I'm eating."

"Well, sure, but —"

"Oh, all *right*. Go get your little pencil."

Each day, after breakfast, Henry walked the six blocks to the Alpha Beta for their groceries, trudging out the Lagoon gates and straight across the highway, stopping traffic with a battered wooden cane he'd painted white. Though he'd been walking with more difficulty lately (too cramped to move at all on days he was constipated), his trips were by and large successful. Of course, there were times when he picked out the wrong label — Cherry Coke for Diet, white Wonder Bread for Farmer's Wheat — but the checkout girls gave him a hand with most major problems. And he carried home bags that Ruth could hardly lift.

"Back in a jiff," Henry said, and left to select a pencil from among those he kept neatly sharpened in his top desk drawer. Ruth took a few more bites of cereal, drank some decaf, chewed two prunes. Boring, she thought, and pushed the tray away. She closed her eyes, sliding down against her sit-up pillow. How in God's name could her life have turned out like this? A pile of shriveled-up prunes.

Nineteen twenty-nine, Washington, D.C., and she awoke with a start. A red mist had been swallowing her. Eating her alive: a hungry red mist.

She pushed herself up.

Hale was still there, buttoning the pants of his best wool suit, bags packed and ready to go at the foot of the bed. Saturday morning. Just like all the other mornings, really, except he was going away, and somehow the bedroom was already registering his absence — darker than usual, all those deep, shadowy holes; she could actually feel him leaving her.

There was still that red mist at the margins of her vision when Hale looked up and winked.

"So you're back among the living," he said.

"I suppose. Everything's ready?"

"Sure, just about. One more minute."

Ruth made herself smile. "Well good, but you'd better hurry," she said, barely managing it, then lay back and watched him insert gold cufflinks into his crisply starched white sleeves.

A heavy silence pressed up against her ears. More than a year of marriage, she thought, and not a single night apart, and here he was going away for weeks and weeks and weeks, and she loved him so much, and she didn't know how she could say goodbye or keep herself from crying or get through the rest of the day. It wasn't forever, of course; she knew that. And this was his job — the Geological Survey needed him out in Oklahoma — but even so, God, she *loved* him.

Right then she almost said it.

"Hale?" she started, then stopped.

He slipped a tie around his neck, knotted it with his usual precision, moved to examine himself in the mirror above the dressing table. He looked elegant and dignified. "One second, baby, and we'll talk about whatever you want," he said, glancing at his wristwatch. "Plenty of time still."

"Not enough."

"Sorry?"

"We can't even —" Then she was crying. Not loud, but it was crying.

And then Hale was there beside her, close. "Hey, you," he said, "stop it."

Ruth made a meaningless gesture with her hand. It wasn't just the leaving, it was something else, too. Like a pebble lodged somewhere in the deep folds of her brain, something half forgotten, something never completely known. "It's stupid," she said, "but I can't make myself feel right. Really, it *is* stupid." She pressed her whole body against him: toes, stomach, breasts. "Just this stupid, stupid dream."

"A bad one?"

"I'm not sure." She kept pressing against him. "Ridiculous, isn't it? I'm like some silly little girl, I shouldn't be acting . . . This *red* stuff, Hale. It was *eating* us."

"Ruth, come on now."

A red mist, she told him.

Bright red. Not a gas exactly — something alive, something wet and red and hungry — and it was chasing them across a huge red desert. Red dunes and red tumbleweed and that voracious red mist. They were running hard. Hale's feet were gone. He was hopping and laughing, and the mist was eating his ankles, and then suddenly they came up on a boiling red river — red water and red spray and frothy red waterfalls — and Hale laughed and hopped into the river and made a sound she couldn't hear. His face had turned deep red, and his skin, too, and he was hopping across the river on big red stones. The mist was eating his knee-caps. So she chased after him. She put her head down and closed her eyes and moved fast, stone to stone, except the mist was eating her own lungs — she couldn't breathe, couldn't keep her balance — and then things suddenly went upside down and she was tumbling into the hot red river. She was swimming now. Thick red water, like raspberry cement, and she couldn't keep her head up, so she let herself go down deep, to the bottom, where Hale sat calmly waiting for her on a red bench at a train station — red trains and red tracks and a small red depot. Hale's ears were gone. His skull was going. He laughed and pointed up at a giant red clock. "Easy!" he yelled. "Hold your breath, Ruthie! Watch that clock!" So, yes, she did it — she took a deep breath and watched the clock spin. It told time in years. One tick and it was 1930. Then 1930 ticked to 1931. The clock chimed on 1944. "Easy," Hale kept saying, "so easy!" Then the train was pulling out. Red steam and red noise. And Hale jumped aboard and laughed and reached up high and seized the giant clock and squeezed it to the size of a softball and threw it to her and yelled, "Easy! See there? Just keep watching, Ruthie." He waved at her. The mist was eating his hands, so he waved with his wrists, then later with his elbows, and all the while he kept laughing and yelling, "Easy!"

Henry prodded Ruth on the forearm. "All set," he said. "Let's get that list made."

The sound of his voice was uncommonly reassuring.

Ruth opened her eyes and wiggled to sit up straight. Just some silly old dream, she told herself, but the day was clearly getting off to a bizarre start. Her skin was damp with sweat.

"All right, take this down correctly," she said, and drew the bedjacket tight around her shoulders. "No mistakes for a change. One bran muffin — oat bran, like usual. One carton coleslaw, small. Put 'small' in parentheses. Two bananas, medium. Make sure they're not green this time, or mushy, either. Four TV dinners, turkey. Don't forget to use the coupons. And remember Luzma and Luis will be here for dinner, so get *four*."

"Four," said Henry. "Check."

They would have their customary Saturday night guests for dinner. Luzma was coming at three, with her son Luis, and at six-fifteen, when the laundry was done, they would all sit down for a meal of cottage cheese and turkey.

Henry stood working on the list, his nubbed face three inches from his little memo pad, tongue poking out from the space between his front teeth.

"Did you get all that?" Ruth asked. "Turkey, I said."

Henry grunted, held the list out at arm's length, and blinked several times. He made a few painstaking corrections, dotting *i*'s and crossing *t*'s, then tucked the pencil behind his ear and turned toward the door.

"Turkey! Did you write that down?" Ruth called after him.

Ruth wore two watches.

One was studded with diamonds — a gift from Hale. It lost several minutes a day, sometimes hesitating at the half hour, sometimes even clicking backward a notch or two, but Ruth worked hard to keep it running on time. She never took it off — never. Even before bathing, she was careful to wrap a plastic sandwich baggie around it, securing the bag with a pair of thick rubber bands. It was this old diamond watch she consulted for the purpose of telling time. The other, from Save-On across the highway, had cost her five dollars. She wore it under her sleeve, out of sight, using it only as a gauge by which to adjust the precious watch from Hale. The cheapie meant nothing to her: a nuisance more than anything, the first item she removed before retiring each night. It was one of those new digital gadgets with lots of fancy displays and buttons, like some silly computer game, the numbers blinking and flashing and zipping around as if they had their own crazy agenda. Ruth lived in vague but relentless terror that she would accidentally hit the wrong button, making it stick forever on Date or Second.

Now, according to both watches, it was five minutes past seven. She had to hurry — the Postal Connection would close at noon.

Each morning, Ruth put on her makeup in bed, a soothing ritual she'd carefully attended to for nearly fifty years, with only one brief period of interruption. But it was a period she'd never forget: those horrid newlywed days with Henry.

Even now she got a chill when she remembered it.

"If I marry you," she'd warned him when he proposed, "there's one thing you can't ever forget. Separate bedrooms. And I'm afraid that's final. Let's face it, we've both been through this marriage business before, we've both had enough poking around to last us a couple of eternities." She gave him a cool, frank stare. "I've been a widow fifteen years now, almost exactly, and I'll never get sexy again, not with anyone." She smiled charmingly. "That includes you."

Henry shrugged. "What the heck. Okay by me."

They were married two days later.

Bam, he was all over her, a sex boob, and for weeks he kept slinking into her room just after breakfast — slithered, actually, like a sex snake — wiggling his way under the covers and making those vulgar sizzling sounds in her ear. "I need you in the mornings," he'd hiss, one clumsy hand on his own private parts, the other reaching out to paw at hers. He'd fondle her ankles and knees, pry at her thighs; he'd slobber on her face and drool into her mouth and then finally shoot all his slimy sperms across her stomach.

One morning as Ruth sat in bed, toiletry kit in her lap, mirror in hand, applying lipstick, Henry crept in with that same perverted grin on his face.

"Out!" she yelled. "You promised!"

"I did?"

Ruth glared at him. "'Okay by me' — your exact words. Loud and clear. A promise."

"Well yeah. But Jeez, Ruthie, I'm in love."

"Love?" Ruth said, almost startled. "What does *that* matter?"

Henry took a slithery half-step to the side. He blinked, moved to the foot of the bed, ran a thin forefinger up and down the bedpost.

His shoulders slumped.

"But see, you're my cutie pie, Ruthie, you're my own little doll, especially when you rub on all that juicy lipstick. Makes a guy's heart go pitty-pat." He straightened his shoulders, reached out, pinched her toes through the covers. "It's like I told Bill yesterday. We're on the phone, my brother and me, and Billy Boy says, 'How's that wife of yours?' So I tell him point blank, I says, 'Big brother, I roped me one high-class woman. Woman knows how to do herself up right. Lips like red apples.' That's what I tells him.

'Big red apples,' I say, 'but not them crunchy kind. Ripe and juicy.'"

Ruth felt her stomach flop over. "I believe I'm about to be ill."

"Well, sure, except we're talking pie-type apples."

Ruth blotted her mouth with a tissue. "Henry, forget apples," she said. "And while you're at it, you can forget this sex nonsense, too." She pulled out her jar of liquid base and applied the ointment to her forehead and cheeks, smoothing it out with the tips of her fingers.

Henry kept circling the bed like some ravenous hyena.

"And that face potion, Ruthie, that's the killer. Awful artistic. Awful creative-like." He touched the bedspread, fingered the blankets. "Like I always explain to my barber. 'Jimmy,' I always tell him, 'Jimmy, what you need is an artistic-type wife, like mine. Wife knows how to decorate herself.'" Henry moved toward the head of the bed. His fingers skimmed along the sheets, circling in tighter.

Ruth flinched and closed her eyes. A moment later, when she glanced into her hand mirror, Henry loomed directly behind her, hand on his crotch.

"So I'm in the chair, getting my two-buck shave, and I'm telling old Jimbo how he ain't ever seen the likes of my Ruthie, all fresh in the morning, just putting on that nifty paint job of hers." He was smiling, unbuckling his belt. " 'Pretty as a picture,' I says, 'or like one of them Greek statues, except plenty of ointment all smeared —' "

"Stop!"

Ruth hurled her makeup bottle at the ceiling. "No more 'ointment'! No more nothing!"

Henry was fumbling to hold his pants up. "Hey now, Ruthie, you're my lawful wedded wife."

"Laws get repealed."

"Like how?"

"Like this instant."

Henry's eyes wandered off on a brief journey. "But I'm happy. I mean — God, Ruthie — I *need* you."

"Well, fine, you've got me."

"But you said —"

"Just keep your word. No more bedroom antics."

Henry bent down for the makeup bottle. A viscous brown liquid oozed from a crack in the glass. He wiped the bottle on his pants, used the palm of his hand to press the spilled makeup into the carpet, then stood up cautiously and placed the bottle on the bedside table. He murmured something to himself — something that sounded like surrender — then folded his hands and sat down gently beside her.

"Well," he said, "I can *look*, can't I?"

7:07 A.M.

Ruth moved her breakfast tray to the bottom of the bed and reached for her toiletry kit, which she kept on the bedside table near her lamp and pills. She pulled out a jar of facial cleansing cream and rubbed the cream on and off with Kleenex tissue; she hadn't washed with soap and water in more than fifty years. She held up a small, round mirror and tweezed the stragglers from her chin, then used a piece of black emery paper to smooth out the skin. Meticulously, with a piece of cotton, she spread on a brown base — "Indian Face," she called it — which gave her a deeply tanned look even in December. As a final touch, she applied a layer of bright red lipstick. The face took eighteen minutes.

According to Hale's diamond watch, it was now almost seven-thirty.

She swung her knees to the side of the bed, careful not to knock off the tray. With a quick, puffing gasp, she plopped to the floor, one hundred and eight pounds, stepping into her slippers and heading — one hand on the bed for balance — toward her walk-in closet.

. . . .

No, she thought, the bathroom first. And just in time. She sighed and settled down on the toilet.

Ruth kept her nitroglycerine in a tiny silver locket (souvenir from one of her son Carter's trips to Asia — would he ever have money to travel again?) that hung at the end of a blue silk cord. At night she left the locket in the bathroom, on a small table in front of and almost blocking access to the toilet. She stored the locket there as a reminder to put it on first thing after her morning b.m., and to take it off last thing just before bed. Of course, she also kept a few nitroglycerine pills in the top drawer of her bedside table, in case of nighttime emergency.

Leaning forward, Ruth picked up the locket and gingerly lowered its cord over her head; the pills made a sharp rattling noise that gave her the jitters. She hesitated for a moment, running a finger up and down the long cord, then closed her eyes and arranged the locket on her chest.

Surrender, she thought.

Head of the conservation branch of the U.S. Geological Survey, director of the Oil and Gas Leasing Division, Hale was at the height of his career when the Naval Reserve Board called him out to the Pacific. Nothing grand, not war or diplomacy or the exploding of nuclear bombs, just some ridiculous fossil-fuel study. He'd received his immunization shots and begun making his farewells when he was snatched up by a murderous disease.

Almost instantaneously, as if under the power of some evil spell, he fell apart. He couldn't keep his meals down. In the space of fourteen days he lost twenty pounds and all of his strength, his skin shriveling up like an old man's, downy clumps of hair falling from his head and body. "Something's missing," he kept saying, again and again, as he moved through the house, unable to remember why he'd entered a particular room or where he'd placed his car keys or whether he even owned a car. Soon he stopped trying to remember. He went to bed and simply lay there, dying. Even the best doctors weren't sure what it was. A virus, probably.

Maybe something he'd picked up from the immunization shots; maybe something hereditary.

The day after New Year's, his skin began to burn — he couldn't bear to have Ruth touch his hands or legs — and finally, when his breathing faltered, Ruth drove him to the hospital. The doctors hooked him up to a monstrous-looking machine, administered painkillers, then left the two of them alone in a small, brightly lit room. Ruth sat on the edge of the bed, a hand on Hale's chest as if to help him breathe. He kept asking her to take off his socks, then to put them on again: a man who had always known everything, he no longer even knew if he was hot or cold.

Every so often he pointed vaguely toward the blank white wall in front of him and said, "Something's wrong. Can you move it, please?"

"Move what?"

He waved at the wall. "It's wrong."

"The wall? Honey, I can't move walls."

"Not the *wall*," he said, and seemed to doze off. Then suddenly he tried to sit up. "Move it. Please, there's too much."

"Hale, I don't know what —"

"There," he said, "*look* at it."

"At what?"

"Time! Right there!"

Later he took her hand. She could tell it was hurting him, the touching itself, but he summoned up a weak smile. After a moment he shook his head. "God, all that *time*, Ruthie. I never *saw* such a mess."

"Yes, yes," she said.

"Just time and time."

An hour later his eyelids fluttered.

He breathed once or twice, waved at the wall, then did not breathe again.

Ruth remembered walking into their bedroom that evening. She remembered going to his dresser and pulling out a tie. She remembered wrapping the tie around her neck. She remembered lying face-up on the floor and kissing the tie and pressing it against her face and talking to it and smelling it and examining the incredible vastness of their white bedroom ceiling.

Once, turning her head, she almost strangled herself. Somehow that helped.

Death, she thought, was a baffling adversary. A capricious trickster. Like sorrow or disappointment or betrayal, its advance could not be checked by any ordinary means; sorcery was required. The ability to change the past, perhaps, or to endure the unendurable, or to conjure up a whole new life.

With a cluck of her tongue, Ruth released her grasp on the nitroglycerine locket, finished on the toilet, stood up to wipe herself from front to back, dropped her nightgown over her bare bottom, and told herself to stop dawdling. At her age, if you weren't careful, you could most definitely poop the rest of your life away.

7:59 A.M.

Moving briskly, Ruth went into her closet and picked out one of the several outfits she kept on separate hangers. She liked to prepare entire combinations in advance — pants, blouse, sweater, and belt, for example — an orderly bit of forethought that saved her time and exasperation. Today she chose her white-pants ensemble, the white pants with the seams down the front, which went so nicely with the pink lace-collared blouse and the blue pullover vest. The outfit would be ideal for dinner with Luzma, she thought. Plenty of color. Perfect for the Spanish eye.

She lay the clothes over the back of the big chair next to the TV, pulled her nightgown off over her head — the cord of the silver locket twisting uncomfortably around the folds of her neck for an instant — and then put on her camisole, panty girdle, garters, and nylons, which she'd left on the cushion of the chair the night before. Balancing in her underclothes, left hand on the back of the chair, Ruth looked down at Hale's watch.

Five past eight. In a hurry now, she fumbled with the hanger of clothes and managed to struggle into the pants, blouse, and blue knit vest in just under ten minutes. She fetched her best pair of white sandals (they'd lasted ten years) from their place on the closet floor, sat in the chair to strap them on, headed back into the bathroom.

She glanced at herself in the mirror on the medicine cabinet, took her comb and bobby pins from the top left drawer beneath the sink, and started in on her curls. In years past she'd pulled them straight back with a barrette to show off a strong forehead, but the new hairdresser had given her these shorter ringlets, and she struggled with the bobby pins now, to clamp them into place.

Her hair was so white it almost glistened.

"Sure to be a beauty when you grow up, honey, a real heartbreaker," Auntie Elizabeth had said on one of their innumerable shopping excursions — 1914, was it? — as Ruth stood in the corner of a dressing room at Hinkley's, watching her aunt try on a series of outlandish hats. "You'll find yourself some wonderful fellow, that's a sure deal, too. Just make sure he's got class, like my man."

Ruth frowned into the mirror. "What'd you say his name was?"

"Chahhl-ton," Elizabeth said, in the funny voice she used when she talked about her fiancé. "Chahhl-ton P. Hahhll, and your ahhn-tie is going to marry him and move to Los Ahhn-geles." Elizabeth placed an exotic silk bonnet on her head, stuck her nose high into the air, curtsied for the mirror. Then she fluffed her pink taffeta skirt and spun around in a graceful circle, sequins glittering from her neck and sleeves. To Ruth, at seven years old, Aunt Elizabeth seemed the most glamorous creature on earth.

Ruth slumped. Without her aunt, she thought, life would be so boring. No more trips to the opera house to hear Elizabeth rehearse; no more late nights in Elizabeth's room, listening to gossip; no more of these weekend shopping excursions or walks down to the marina for ice cream, just the two of them.

For a few seconds Ruth felt herself drifting, just bobbing along, carried like a cork on the flow of memory. Then she began to brush her teeth. "But if you marry him," she said, voice garbled by toothpaste, "you won't live with us anymore."

Elizabeth stopped spinning and turned to face her. "I certainly will *not*," she said, lapsing into her normal voice. "I'm not about to sit around that dark, flat old ranch house all my life, your grandpa telling me what to do all the time. Honestly, if I have to spend one more day looking at his stupid sawed-off arm, I'll go absolutely insane." She hung the bonnet on a hook, pulled on a small satin cap, looked into the mirror. "Anyway, please don't start pouting. You're supposed to be happy for me."

"Naturally," Ruth said, almost to herself. She peered straight into the mirror and tried to force a smile. Few other girls her age had such beautiful teeth.

Elizabeth straightened the cap, frowned, and shook her head. Then she grinned. "Now watch me," she said, her eyes glowing. "Who am I?" She tucked one arm behind her back, so it looked like it was missing, and brought her free hand to her forehead in a stiff salute. "Always remember your origins, young lady, and be prudent," she said in a low, growling voice. "Gettysburg. Massachusetts Second. Two days lying on the battlefield, arm shot up and not a soul around to give aid or succor . . ."

Ruth swallowed hard, frightened but in love with her aunt's daring — *nobody* was supposed to make fun of her grandfather.

"Not a soul around to dress my wound, young lady, and no one to weep for me." Elizabeth puffed up her chest and strutted back and forth, pounding her heels into the carpet. "The vultures were circling and I was wailing and praying and sure I was a goner —"

"Until you fainted and those bugs ate out the poison," Ruth said, beginning to giggle.

"Maggots, child," Elizabeth said in her deep voice. "Those

were maggots, and don't forget it. Maggots saved your grandpa's life, maggots let him keep fighting to save this great country of ours, maggots made possible your very presence on this earth."

Ruth laughed and took a step toward her aunt. She'd heard those same words a thousand times.

Elizabeth dropped her arms and became herself again. "The way he talks, you'd think those damn bugs were God's own hand-maidens. So self-righteous! And treats your mother just like a slave, ever since your grandma died — expecting her to do every little thing for him *and* your daddy. Which is another matter, why your mother ever got married so young in the first place. Right after we moved out here. Who would've guessed it back in Massachusetts, precious little Lydia married to that hardscrabble bore?" Elizabeth coughed and glanced away for a moment, as if she'd realized her words were scandalous.

Ruth studied the carpet, digging at it with the toe of her patent leather shoe, embarrassed but intrigued, aware that her aunt was being wicked, hoping she would go on.

"All I mean is, your mother's always so sensible and thrifty, always so *perfect*, but she never even gave herself a chance to really live." Elizabeth pulled off the satin cap and lay a handkerchief on her head so it hung down over her eyes. She folded her hands and bent her head. "And I made this hat with my very own pin money," she said in a soft, self-deprecating voice, Lydia's voice.

Ruth remained still.

"And your daddy, he's even worse." Elizabeth slid the handkerchief off her head and tucked it into her collar like a tie. "All his talk about respectable life and a person's duties. But I'll tell you a secret. He himself deserted his poor mother and sister back in St. Paul, Minnesota, and that's a fact." She put a hand on her chest and, pretending to wheeze and cough, turned to face herself in the mirror. "Rode the train out here all by myself," she said in her husky Daddy voice. "Only fourteen years old and full of tuberculosis, but found myself a steady job. Hardest work there is, being a teamster. But I scrimped and sweated and nearly broke my back until I'd saved enough money to deserve sweet little Lydia here."

Curtsying for the mirror and batting her eyelashes, Elizabeth pulled the handkerchief from her collar and held it above her head, becoming Ruth's mother again. "Oh, Walter," she said in her soft voice, "it truly wasn't your money that won me. It was your charm! Why, from the very first time you spoke to me, I knew you were the acceptable family type."

Elizabeth dropped her arm and began folding the handkerchief into a neat square. "You ask me, your daddy looks like some scrawny chicken. No different from all these other fellows with tuberculosis — you know the ones — filling up the whole city like it's a giant sanatorium."

Elizabeth straightened her dress, checked her makeup, reached for the silk bonnet and positioned it on her head. "Come along," she said. "I'll buy this one."

Ruth wasn't sure *what* to think. She'd never heard anybody criticize her parents like this, not even Elizabeth. She asked the only question she could think of. "You think Daddy's a *chicken?*"

Elizabeth rolled her eyes and, taking Ruth's hand, led her out of the dressing rooms. "I suppose I shouldn't have talked that way about your mother and father," she said. "All I mean is, for me it's got to be the real thing. I need excitement. You know, *passion.* Spotlights! Orchestras! Romance with a capital R. Extravagance and undying love and all that. Not this boring, comfortable, workaday-type thing. My God, I'd rather have nothing."

Worse than nothing, she'd gotten in the end. The affair with Charlton had ended in disaster.

Ruth shook her head gravely.

It was her sober parents, of course, and not her reckless aunt and the sophisticated Mr. Hall, who had made it to the end of their days together.

Pensively, even somberly, Ruth replaced her toothbrush in its cup and began to examine herself from head to toe, a preening habit she'd inherited from Auntie Elizabeth. She turned her back to the medicine cabinet and held up a hand mirror to see how she must appear to others from behind; she studied her bottom in the mirrors — sagging but not fat; she plucked off a few gray hairs that had fallen to her shoulders. Then she turned for a profile, lifting her nose high into the air and glancing to her left, into the mirror. What she saw was a bit of mucus, firm and greeny gray, dangling there like a filthy old barnacle.

The human body, she thought. Always ready with a disgusting little surprise.

Glad she was alone, Ruth reached for a Kleenex.

8:19 A.M.

Ruth had practiced the piano almost every day, sometimes twice a day, since the year she turned eight. Now she hurried to complete her morning agenda so as to get in at least a few minutes of practice before the next Laguna bus came, at ten past nine.

She went to the bed and rolled up her sleeping bag, tight as she could. She stuffed the sleeping bag into a plastic sack, tied the sack with a piece of yellowed yarn, and carefully balanced the finished bundle on the space heater next to her TV. She returned the sit-up pillow to its place on the floor and pulled up the bedspread. Then, humming quietly to herself, she started down to the second floor. She used the stairs, not the elevator; she almost always climbed from floor to floor by foot, and believed this policy to be in part responsible for that string of eighty-eight birthdays.

The piano was positioned diagonally across from the couch in the room adjacent to the kitchen and dining area, just three feet from the sliding door that led out to the balcony. It was the same parlor grand that had been in Ruth's family for well over a hundred years, the same piano upon which her mother had improvised dramatic background for those marvelous magic-lantern shows. Ruth sat down on the bench, brought her hands to the keyboard, and began to play. She played loudly. Good, hard, straightforward technique. Though she made mistakes here and there, the trick was to keep banging away and not waste energy fretting about things that couldn't be changed. Like life itself. Mistakes were part of the music.

For some time Ruth lost herself in the Sonata Pathétique, eyes closed, lips tight, and it wasn't until she'd entered the second movement that she became aware of a loud, rhythmic knocking against the wall.

Her glasses slipped down her nose, then dropped to the left of the piano bench; a ribbon of dazzling white specks floated across the room.

"Too early, Ruth! The weekend!"

The voice came echoing through the wall she shared with 23. The knocking sounds continued.

Oh brother, Ruth thought. Hassan didn't intend to be rude, she knew; the man liked to hear her play and he didn't mind mistakes. But she wished he would just listen quietly. His pounding was distracting, and had now made her very dizzy.

She groped for her glasses, pushed them up onto her nose, then sat still for a moment, collecting herself. Those bright specks were still twinkling around the room like a million tiny lamps.

The knocking on the wall of 23 was always loudest when she played especially well. It had started long before Hassan moved in, when the previous owner of the place — who had died mysteriously — decided to haunt her.

In life he had been a friendly man, if somewhat reserved, in his mid-fifties with three cats and an ugly German shepherd that he walked four times a day. Ruth had thought him quite a gentleman. He kept his dog under strict control when he walked it, never letting it off the leash no matter how much it yapped and bucked, and only allowing it to defecate in Doggie Canyon — a sandy, bush-surrounded area just behind the community trash dump. In any case, one evening the poor man in 23 led his shepherd down to the Canyon and never came back. The next morning, just after sunrise, a neighbor came across him in one of the bushes along the edge of the Canyon, shot in the head. The dog had vanished. No weapon was ever found, no suspects apprehended.

Ruth secretly suspected the White Rabbit, as the incident had occurred on or very near the first day of October. Or had it been September?

Whatever the truth, it was almost immediately after this incident that the knocking began in Ruth's wall. It happened only during her sessions at the piano, and it became loudest when she played well. For a long while no one wanted to move into number 23. Which made Ruth uneasy — no one living next door and the wall knocking like that.

Finally, in the twentieth year of marriage to Henry, her sixth year with him at the Lagoon, Hassan had arrived. He was new to the country from Iran, and had come to Paradise Lagoon in search of a beachfront property. But in the end he chose number 23, even though it was two blocks up the hill from the ocean, mainly because the unit came with a custom elevator. It was, in fact, the only place aside from Ruth's that had one.

Hassan paid cash for 23. He was not superstitious. Maybe in Iran, Ruth sometimes mused, *all* the houses were filled with mysterious knockings.

Ruth sat still, hands folded in her lap, gazing at the keyboard. All those separate little notes, black and white, interlacing and blending to make up eight octaves. Or was it fewer than eight? She squinted down, counting. And then suddenly, as if struck by a hammer, Ruth again felt the hard, abrupt shock of sadness, almost overwhelming this time. Eighty-eight years old.

"Don't," she murmured. Then she shook her head. "Keep playing, just don't give in. Fight the bad with the good." But her quavering voice belied all clichés of positive thinking.

She lifted her hands into position, her right thumb above middle C. Slowly, she began to play. The white skin on the back of her hands looked like wrinkled tissue paper. Beneath the skin, thick cords of blue vein seemed to strangle the tiny bones. Her fingers felt dull and dry, like little twigs: however hard they might work, they could never reproduce the sweet sounds of her youth.

Still, there was that peculiar, almost audible sadness all around her, but a moment later it was broken by the sound of the door-bell.

Irritated, interrupted for the second time in one session, Ruth slammed down the fallboard. Why, she wondered, were people forever intruding on her peace? Impossible to finish even fifteen minutes of serious practice. She pushed herself up and marched downstairs to what she called The Room. The Room, which had to be traversed in order to get to the front door, or even to the small bathroom beside the front door, held a tattered guest bed and couch, a TV, a washing machine and dryer, and several old wall calendars. Ruth passed through all of this to the front door, which she opened. She blinked against the sun — the morning was already bright.

Kaji stood before her in a white bathrobe. The robe was tied loosely, and patches of the woman's bikini poked out.

"Nice sexy swim?" Ruth asked.

Kaji blushed. "My husband sent me," she said. Kaji was only recently arrived, new to the liberated ways of the West. Small clots of mascara clung to the tips of her eyelashes; her dark eyes glittered with a moist concern. Her long black hair was tousled. "Hassan says if Mrs. Ruth so awake and noisy, does she want to come decorate the Christmas tree?"

Ruth crossed her arms. Like hell, she thought. She knew Kaji had really come over to make sure she was still alive. No doubt Kaji and Hassan had become worried when the music stopped so abruptly.

"And does Mr. Henry want to come?" Kaji asked. "Children want Maman Bozorg to help put on the tinsel. We got the rain kind."

("Maman Bozorg" meant Grandmother. It was supposed to be flattering, Ruth knew, never mind that it sounded God-awful.)

Ruth shook her head. "I'm afraid Henry's over at the Alpha Beta," she said, "and I have to go downtown. Life isn't all tinsel and sex swims, you know." She took hold of the girl's bathrobe belt. "Come in here a minute, I'll show you something."

Ruth led the girl into the bathroom. "Since you're all dressed up for the nudist colony," she said, "you might be interested in what the beach looked like when I was your age, even younger than you." She pointed to the photographs that covered every wall of the bathroom and surrounded the toilet down to its base.

Kaji blinked at the arrangement.

"Now, you see, we used to summer at the beach in San Diego," Ruth went on. "Of course my first husband —"

"Yes? I summer at beach, too." Kaji tested a short smile. "I winter at pool."

Indeed. Ruth had seen her there, lying for hours on a tinfoil mat, with little plastic cups over her eyes and cotton balls between her toes. The pool lay only a hundred yards from the window above Ruth's dining table. It was surrounded by glass panels and approached by way of an iron gate, which Ruth passed on her daily afternoon walks. Sometimes, feeling curious, she'd stop and peer in through the gate, but she rarely entered for fear she might end up locked inside.

"You like to go to the pool in December?" Ruth asked.

"Yes."

"And you don't find it a bit . . . a bit chilly?"

"No. Very nice."

Well fine.

Ruth nodded and adjusted her glasses. "Suit yourself," she said. "But look, dear, these pictures were taken ages ago, before you were even born in Iran, before you ever saw a pool in your life." Ruth gestured at a photographic collage above the toilet.

Kaji blinked several times, slowly. "We had good pool in Iran," she said. "Good big pool."

"Yes, but look closely. Things used to be so splendid, so civilized here in California. We lived in houses with names, not numbers. There were still cesspools, but there wasn't any smog. We had gas meters for the lights, not electricity, and we used to have to put quarters in them. And look here — I'll show you a secret."

Ruth took down one of the more recent photographs, less than fifty years old, that hung above the sink. "A picture of good old Frank Deeds," she said. "And look at this." She turned the frame and slid out the cardboard mounting. She stripped away a piece of tape from the back of Frank's picture.

Kaji tightened and retied her bathrobe belt. "What you have there, Mrs. Ruthie?"

"Just wait a minute."

"It looks like —"

"Patience, young lady. Keep your pants on."

Ruth peeled off a pocket-sized snapshot, which the tape had been holding to the back of Frank's portrait. She handed it to Kaji. It was a picture of Ruth, sitting on a rock by the ocean, her toes buried in white sand. "I was forty-five then," Ruth explained. "Hale had died, you know, and I was visiting my aunt in San Diego. Frank took this picture. He'd moved there long before I ever returned, after he was divorced. Read the back."

Kaji turned the picture over, squinting to read the faded writing. "'You will — always be close — to my dart,'" she read.

"No, that says *heart*. 'You will always be close to my heart.'"

"No, it says 'dart.'"

"It most definitely does *not*," Ruth insisted. "Look here, I should know, it's addressed to me."

"Oh. But that man is not Henry."

"He certainly isn't! This is a man who loved me, and wanted to marry me after Hale died. He used to carry this picture in the pocket of his shirt — so I'd always be close to his heart, understand? That's what he'd always say, those exact words."

Kaji looked confused. "But that man is not Henry."

"That's what I'm *telling* you. This man is *Frank,* and he was very well known, very successful, and he was in love with me. For a while I thought I might love him, too." Ruth cleared her throat, handed Kaji the portrait of Frank. "But then I realized it would never work."

"Oh, Mrs. Ruth," Kaji said, gazing sadly at Frank's face. "I feel so sorry. He was old? He was sick or something?"

"Not that. *That* worked just fine. Too fine, in fact, which is exactly the point."

"The point?"

"I couldn't trust him. The man had this very — you know — this terrible squirmy wormy."

"Wormy?"

"*You* know."

Kaji still seemed confused. She studied both sides of Frank's portrait, then held it up to the light and looked at it from every angle.

Exasperated, Ruth put her hands on her hips. "I didn't think I could *count* on him."

"Oh!" Kaji said, smiling and nodding.

Ruth suddenly felt exhausted. "I'll explain it to you another day," she said. "Maybe when Hassan's not waiting. He probably thinks I've kidnapped you. Anyway, you need to go put that rain on your tree. And *I* need to go to the bathroom."

"Sure, Mrs. Ruthie," Kaji said. "Maybe I see you later, at the pool? You're okay — you feel okay?"

"Just wonderful," said Ruth. "Hardly a day over eighty."

Kaji nodded again, began to turn away, then stopped and turned back. Her bathrobe had come undone to expose a pair of slim brown legs, tufts of crinkly black hair poking out from under the elastic of her bikini bottom.

"That man Frank, he your big love-love?"

"I should say not."

"Mr. Henry then?"

"Now you're getting ridiculous," Ruth said. "I've told you several times, my first husband, Hale —"

"But I thought he was very dead? A long time dead."

"What possible difference should that make?"

Kaji made a motion with her shoulders. "Well, big difference. No love, a woman shrink like dust and blow away. Hassan tells me that many, many times. Woman needs always a big love-love. A live one, Mrs. Ruthie."

"Hale was *extremely* alive."

"Not now. He is extremely not alive now."

There was a pause before Ruth's tongue caught up with her thoughts.

"My dear Kaji," she said crisply, "Hale gave me all the 'love-love' I shall ever require. Now, please, tuck in your hairs."

8:51 A.M.

Alone in the bathroom, Ruth smiled to herself: at her age, with a weak bladder, the call of nature always made a good excuse to slip away from people. The truth, of course, was that she simply wanted a little quiet time and privacy, and this tiny bathroom was her favorite refuge. She stepped over to the sink. Carefully, her hand shaking slightly, she secured the snapshot of herself to the back of Frank's portrait, returned them both to their proper position on the wall. Then she gazed at the surrounding gallery of photographs, running her finger across the top of each frame, as if to make physical contact with those early years in Southern California. Los Angeles had been *the* place then. She and her parents had moved there from San Diego, her mother shipping their things on the *Santa Maria*, to escape public embarrassment after Aunt Elizabeth's misfortune.

They moved into the Wilshire District, though there was not yet a Wilshire Boulevard, and they saw Hollywood people —

Charlie Chaplin, Mary Pickford — though there was not yet a Hollywood. It was only a neighborhood then, and the famed Hollywood sign was merely the marker for an enormous real estate development, Hollywoodland.

They cut out the "land" a few years later.

Ruth finished eighth grade at Virgil Intermediate, then entered the new Los Angeles High; hers would be among the first classes to graduate from that school, in 1924.

Now Ruth glanced at her finger. It was covered with dust. She sighed and bent over the sink and began to soap up her hands. *Some* people, she remembered, had not graduated. Certain incompetents. Certain mental indigents. It was at Los Angeles High that she'd first put eyes on Henry Hubble.

Chemistry class, sophomore year: even without a picture on the wall, she could still see it clearly. The whole class standing at their lab tables as Mr. Purdick outlined the day's experiment on the blackboard. "Nothing to it," he was saying, "but if there's a question, just raise your hand. And be careful with those burners." Right then, Ruth heard a curious whimpering behind her. A skinny red-headed boy was hopping up and down, hand in the air, a light, squeaky voice yelling, "Teacher!"

Mr. Purdick did not seem to hear.

"Teacher, sir! Question — over here!" The boy's fingers were wiggling. He was hopping from one foot to the other. "Mr. Teacher!"

Mr. Purdick still took no notice. He kept his back turned, erasing the blackboard.

"Right here, sir!" The boy was squealing and hopping and waving a hand. "Question! A nice one!" He dropped his arm and lit a match and turned his burner up high as it would go. "A pretty good question! Teacher! A real good smart one!"

Mr. Purdick turned slowly. "Any questions?"

"Me!" the boy screamed.

"Henry?"

The boy's face went blank. He looked at the ceiling and

moaned and then, with an angry, fumbling gesture, swept his test tubes to the floor.

"Crap," he muttered, "I *forgot*."

Ruth stared down at the shattered glass. She examined the boy's yellow socks, his scuffed-up shoes, his brown corduroys. The trousers were cinched above his navel, held tight by a worn leather belt; his shirt was filthy; his face was pale and damp and freckled.

Genuinely pitiful.

"Well, it *was* good," he said. "It was a *real* good question."

A week later Henry Hubble dropped out of school. His excuse was Spanish influenza, but in truth the disease was much grander: colossal stupidity. Now and then, over the next two years, Ruth bumped into him in peculiar places — a tomato stand, a horse auction — but after she started college, they did not meet again for some thirty-five years.

Shaking a few drops of water from her fingers, Ruth turned to dry her hands. There she was at her high school graduation, in the photograph above the towel rack. She stood in the middle of the second row. She was impossibly young, and pretty, and smiling.

9:00 A.M.

It was exactly nine o'clock when she stepped out the front door.

Another fickle Laguna morning. Still hazy — the fog had not quite lifted — but bright enough to make you squint. Ruth reached into her purse, pulled out her clip-on sun lenses, and snapped them into place over her glasses.

She paused for a moment on the front steps. Then she lifted the tip of her cane, took aim at a yellow fire hydrant across the cement courtyard, and set off with a determined stride. She felt solid. Eighty-eight years old, yet still independent, still taking care of her own daily business. She moved her cane forward and back, forward and back, her umbrella swinging gently from its strap on her left wrist. When she reached the fire hydrant, she again lifted the tip of her cane and, squinting ahead toward a sprinkler at the start of the path between the tennis court and pool, marched off fiercely.

Her lungs were aching by the time she reached the Lagoon gates, at the top of a short hill. She took a quick breather, stooping to examine a small bush that Rodrigo had molded into the shape of a dog. Rodrigo was the groundskeeper, and this was his hobby: like a gardener at Disneyland, he was steadily transforming all the bushes in Paradise Lagoon into animals of different types and sizes. This particular dog, standing guard just inside the gates, had perked-up ears and a full green tail. Its body was mostly bare wire — the bush was young and hadn't yet filled out — and as she studied it this morning, leaning on the cane, Ruth felt rather queasy. Like some weird doggie autopsy. That exposed chest cavity, the various organs and blood vessels. Quickly, eyes averted, she walked past the dog to the Pedestrian Passage.

No sooner had she stuck her Auto-Mate gate card into its slot, opened the Passage, and walked outside the Lagoon, than the bus pulled up. She flashed her senior card, climbed on board, and glanced around for a seat.

9:11 A.M.

The bus was almost full. Most of the passengers had hair as gray as her own, except for a young, pleasant-looking man sitting toward the back, wearing a Stetson. There was a space beside him, and Ruth moved down the aisle to fill it.

The driver started up and they were on their way downtown, past row upon row of Lego houses in the hills. Ruth took careful stock of her surroundings. The hills, which were usually brown, had a touch of green on them now, as sometimes happened with even a little winter rain. Most of the trees along the highway still had their leaves. The bus rolled past four Italian restaurants, two video rental outlets, three or four frozen-yogurt shops, a good half-dozen real estate offices. Ruth flipped up her sunglass lenses and turned toward the gentleman beside her.

"Well, good morning," she said. "Pleased to meet you."

The man spat on the floor of the bus and smiled. A brown plug of tobacco pressed up against his lower lip.

"Enchanted," Ruth said.

She moved her feet out toward the aisle, protecting her good white sandals, then lifted her gaze to the window. Something terrible had happened here in Southern California. In her childhood, and during the Washington years when she'd returned with Hale for summer vacations, and even later when she'd first moved back, alone, to stay, people did not spit at your shoes. Things were civilized then. No pizza joints, no trash in the streets. And not all of these tract houses, every fifth one alike.

The man hacked a few times and spat again. The woman to Ruth's right, across the aisle, at least as old as she, was busy fishing through her shopping bags. The bags seemed to contain all of the lady's worldly possessions, from an evening gown to kitchen supplies to a giant Random House dictionary. The woman was dressed for subzero temperatures, in frayed woolen pants and a long tweed coat.

Ruth smiled at her. "Moving here to Laguna, dear?" she asked. "A little overcrowded, I'm afraid, but I think you might find it interesting."

The woman looked up from the orange she was peeling, her eyes blank, and smiled without opening her lips. Her fingernails were yellow — from the orange, maybe, or from some mysterious illness — and her fingers were red and chapped. She looked back down at her orange.

"Well," Ruth said, "enjoy your stay."

She pulled a strawberry Twizzler from her purse. She thought of her own great-grandfather, her father Walt's grandfather, who had lived in the same house in Geneva, Illinois, for one hundred and two years, dying in the same bed in which he'd been born. This poor old lady moves around too much, Ruth thought. She sent a smile in the woman's direction, tried to shape her face into a welcome.

Her jaw popped audibly, as it did so often now, which was maddening. She opened and closed her mouth, listening to the pops. It didn't hurt, but it was annoying. She wondered if anyone else could hear it.

For a time the bus rolled along Coast Highway. Things were quiet except for the drunk man up front, who rode the little Laguna bus all day, every day. Ruth had seen him at least a dozen times over the past month. Today he was complaining about someone who had apparently cheated him, swearing violently, gesturing at the air. The man beside Ruth rustled his morning paper; Ruth turned to see what he was reading.

CANYON KILLER APPREHENDED, read the headline in bold black. From beneath the bold print, a pale man with small, pointed ears stared out at Ruth. The face looked strangely familiar. She'd heard talk of him before, how he'd gone on a rampage through Canyon Homes, in the hills outside Laguna. He'd killed four men, the *Sun Times* said, with a sawed-off shotgun. She peered closely at the picture until her neighbor cleared his throat.

"Terrible," he said.

Ruth pointed at the photograph. "That maniac — he reminds me of a man I used to know."

The man laughed. "Yeah, well. Don't we all."

Ruth ignored him. "My Uncle Stephen, I mean. The same pointy ears. Of course, Stephen committed only *one* murder."

The man gave her an odd look. "What a pity."

"But not with a shotgun, of course."

"Of course not."

"A revolver."

"Revolver. Right, what else."

Turning uncomfortably, the man shifted his weight away from Ruth. For a half block they rode along in silence.

"Anyway," Ruth said, "in Uncle Stephen's case it wasn't really murder, if you know what I mean. Nothing in cold blood, like our friend here."

"Lady, listen —"

"Certainly *not* murder," Ruth said firmly. "They *called* it that, but . . . I suppose now you'll want to hear the whole unfortunate story."

The man sighed and folded his newspaper. "I suppose so," he said dismally. "But start at the start. Who the hell's this Uncle Stephen?"

Ruth rearranged herself in the seat. People sometimes baffled her. The way they kept intruding on her privacy.

In a crisp, no-nonsense voice, sticking to the essential facts, she explained that Stephen had been the second important gentleman in Auntie Elizabeth's life. "What you have to understand," she said, "is that Elizabeth was a talented, gorgeous young woman. A voice like a bird. Back when we all lived with my grandfather in San Diego — Jonathan Huntley, that was his name — back then, Elizabeth was singing with the San Carlos Opera. I used to go and listen to her rehearse. A soprano, you know."

"Yeah," the man said. "Really."

"Yes, *really*. Do I give the appearance of a common liar?"

The man yawned.

"So it should go without saying," Ruth said, "that Elizabeth had the whole world at her command. That beautiful, beautiful voice. And a lovely figure, too — elegant legs — I suppose that part runs in our family." Ruth glanced at the man. "Her prospects, as we used to say, were unlimited. But then she met her *first* man, Mr. Charlton P. Hall, which started the whole terrible downfall."

Beside her, the man pulled his Stetson down over his eyes. Ruth nudged him with her elbow, hard, but he seemed to have lapsed into a coma.

No matter, she thought.

With a cluck of her tongue, she continued with the story, talking past her neighbor to the bus window and the passing storefronts and the vast Pacific Ocean.

Charlton P. Hall. Dapper and handsome, one of San Diego's leading lawyers. A typical sweet-talking attorney-at-law. Yes, and poor Aunt Elizabeth was doomed from the instant they glanced at each other across the aisle of the First Presbyterian Church. A short, familiar tale: after the service they had iced tea together, and that same night he kissed her on the lips, not to mention elsewhere. (Lots of elsewheres, Ruth knew, but this part of the story she did not feel it proper to tell.) For weeks afterward, Elizabeth and Charlton were seen together at the theater and at parties and on the sidewalks of San Diego, strolling arm in arm, in a rapture so sublime that passing strangers stopped to smile. In the evenings, as they walked along the marina, they played a little game called What If.

"What if I told you I wanted to sing in Vienna?" Elizabeth would start.

"Well, yes, but what if I could not afford to send you?"

Elizabeth would think for a moment. "In that case, what if I found a magic lamp that turned grass into money?"

"But what if I could not use the magic, because . . ."

The possibilities were inexhaustible and the game could go on forever. So Charlton invented a rule by which the process always had to lead to the same final question: "What if I asked you to marry me?" he'd ask.

"And what if I said yes?" she'd answer.

When the wedding was only a month off, Charlton moved his practice north to Los Angeles. All the up-and-comers were headed there, and it seemed just the place to raise a family. Elizabeth stayed on in San Diego, making wedding plans, bragging to everyone, preparing for the happy life that was to be hers.

Then a telegram arrived: "What if I told you we could not be married?"

Ruth made a sharp snuffling noise.

"Boob," she muttered.

Handsome or not, men were hopeless. Hale excepted, all they ever wanted was to get their paws on all the elsewheres.

The bus had entered traffic. Ruth settled back with a heavy sigh. "Well, naturally," she said, "poor Elizabeth was crushed."

Crushed, yes, because with that telegram Mr. Charlton P. Hall simply vanished. Elizabeth stopped singing, stopped sleeping, stopped eating. For many weeks there were serious questions about her sanity. But then a piece of fortune intervened — an accident, really. A small advertisement in the *San Diego Telegraph*: SINGERS WANTED FOR REVIVAL GROUP. YOU BRING THE VOICE, WE HAVE THE STAGE. The next morning, as eight-year-old Ruth watched, Elizabeth packed her suitcases.

Of course Ruth's grandfather, old Jonathan Huntley, raised all sorts of objections — even made a few outright threats — but twelve days later Elizabeth was in Clayville, Rhode Island, decked out in a black robe and a yellow sash, singing "Rock of Ages" and "The Old Rugged Cross" for a traveling religion show. She'd found the Lord. She'd also found Uncle Stephen.

Stephen MacLeod: King of the Boobs.

A preacher, of all things. A fire-and-brimstone bozo. With his squeaky voice and pointy little ears, but with an eloquence far beyond his twenty-three years, Stephen was already famous on the tent circuit for his frenzied two-hour sermons. Women had visions. Men actually prayed. Elizabeth fell in love.

Clearly, the man was mad, or on the edge of madness, but it was partly this that intrigued her. She loved the way Stephen waved his arms before the big crowds, the way he sometimes stiffened and jerked up and down and shrieked at the sky, the way he'd collapse after his spasms of boil-in-hell sermonizing. Over the course of that summer, as the show traveled up and down the eastern seaboard, Stephen's behavior turned increasingly peculiar. On stage he'd sometimes fall dead silent, peering off into space as if transported to some other world. Other times he'd be struck by quick, violent seizures. In the middle of a homily, for example, he might suddenly throw back his arms and begin howling — loud animal howling — then he'd lurch forward and whisper "Dear Jesus!" and savagely thump his head against the pulpit. Acute dipsomania, a couple of the singers warned her; once, just before a camp meeting, they'd found him skulking behind the outhouse, stealing furtive swallows from a thin silver flask. Brain-damaged, others claimed; as a child, they hypothesized, he must have suffered a terrible kick to the head. All of which only piqued Elizabeth's interest: she believed she could win power over him, that she could save him, that under her tender care he would soon recover his senses.

One hot afternoon in Trenton, New Jersey, she saw her chance and instantly grabbed it. Another on-stage seizure. More howling and dribbling and sputtering. But this time, without a second thought, Elizabeth took Stephen firmly by the arm, led him to his tent, clamped an icebag to his forehead, knelt down beside him, and ran a finger across his frothy lips.

Years later, Ruth would hear the intimate details from Elizabeth herself. How Uncle Stephen gazed straight ahead like a blind man. How Elizabeth placed one hand over his eyes and the other upon her own belly, which was round and swollen with the child of Charlton P. Hall.

How she was silent for a time, planning her strategy.

"What if I were to tell you," she said, "that I can end this suffering in an instant? That I can save you, bring you serenity and joy and lasting peace? That I can make miracles happen?"

Stephen squirmed. "You're a witch?"

Elizabeth smiled at this. "Oh, yes."

"You mean —"

"First, a child. A successor, to carry on your work and great name. I do believe, Stephen" — she paused for just an instant — "I believe, in fact, that I'm destined to bring you some prodigious delight."

Lifting a weak arm, Stephen grasped Elizabeth's buttocks.

"You have to *believe*, though," she said, submitting to the pressure of his fingers, even gyrating slightly at the waist. "Keep them closed, now," she said, removing her hand from his eyes, untying her yellow sash. "Don't peek."

"Like this?"

"Tighter. You're peeking."

So Stephen shut his eyes, tight, and Elizabeth wound her sash around his wrists, binding them together above his head. "After the child," she whispered, "nothing but rest and endless pleasure." She lifted her black robe. "Holy pleasure, you understand, nothing crass or unlawful. I'd be a mother, after all." She hesitated and said, "Your wife."

Stephen was quiet for a moment. He mumbled a few prayers and then grunted. "Yes, a wife, go ahead."

"A legally binding marriage," she said, to make sure he'd understood.

"Of course," he said. "On with your magic."

9:29 A.M.

Ruth snorted. Witch, for crying out loud. Pure trickery, nothing else, but Uncle Stephen remained a believer for years to come. Right up until the day of the murder.

The bus made a sudden stop, then turned onto Glenneyre Avenue. The man in the Stetson was still comatose beside her, lips ajar, snoring away. She had a good mind to shove a cork down his throat.

For several minutes Ruth sat rocking amid her memories. "Witch!" she muttered, then a block later she chuckled and said, "On the other hand, though, it landed her a father for the child. But not for long." Elizabeth and Stephen were married immediately. They gave up the revivals and moved back to San Diego, to live with Ruth and her parents and old Jonathan Huntley.

Elizabeth was no longer so arrogant and carefree as she'd been in her younger days, but she claimed she was happy — glad to have found a good man of God, she said. Within little over two years, Stephen's seizures seemed to disappear and he took on a small local ministry. Elizabeth had two lovely babies, Margaret and McGregor.

"So, yes," Ruth explained to the bus window, "they made a fine, respectable couple, and for all I know Elizabeth *was* in fact a witch — who really understands these things? — but eventually her spell was shattered in the most terrible way." Ruth wagged her head sadly. "That's how it happens. Spells come, spells go."

Leaning toward the man beside her, rocking with the movement of the bus, Ruth found herself slipping back to that disastrous evening in the winter of 1918. A quiet evening, actually, until Uncle Stephen came crashing through the front door, grunting like an animal and shouting hysterically. Ruth was in her bedroom at the time, getting ready for sleep, yet even now, all these years later, she could hear the sudden commotion in the kitchen — things slamming, Stephen's voice bouncing against the walls and floorboards. The words were mostly indistinct. Something about betrayal, something about trickery and revenge. "I'll *show* her," he'd yelled, then again his voice went blurry, and then a moment later he shouted, "Don't tell *me* to be calm! I am not drunk! And I'm not imagining *anything!* I'll show her what the Lord has in store for people who . . ." And then came a thumping noise, as if a brick had fallen, and then the measured sound of Jonathan Huntley's voice as he tried to calm the man down. Again, most of it was lost now; just bits and pieces — "Yes, but the child is still yours in all the ways that matter" — "Of course it is" — "Been drinking!" — "Don't be an idiot, that musket's been around since Gettysburg." A high laugh echoed down the hall. There was a muffled shout, then the clatter of dishes breaking. Ruth remembered hurrying from her room; she'd almost reached the kitchen when a single shot rang out. She paused, frightened and confused, then pushed open the door. Jonathan Huntley lay curled on the kitchen floor, blood gushing from his mouth and from his one good arm — the only arm he'd carried off the field at Gettysburg. Stephen sat slumped beside him, crying and praying, whispering, "Lord, our Lord."

Ruth remembered standing very still in the doorway. It seemed an eternity before her mother and father and Elizabeth came up behind her. Lydia screamed when she entered the kitchen, and dropped to Jonathan Huntley's side. For a while, no one moved. Then Walt left to call an ambulance, and Lydia stood up and hurried down the hall to the nursery, to quiet Elizabeth's two crying babies.

Staring down at Stephen, Elizabeth slipped her hands into the pocket of her apron and was silent for a long time. She didn't blink, didn't move, didn't even seem to breathe. When she finally turned to Ruth, her face was oddly serene.

"Never trust a smooth-talking man," she said. "And never think you can change a fellow's ways."

Ruth brought a hand to her neck, cleared her throat, and nodded at the bus window. "Then the police arrived and carted Uncle Stephen away. My grandfather was dead, you see. And five days later, my parents and I moved to Los Angeles."

Shifting in her seat, she glanced at the man beside her. He was still snoring, his head bobbing up and down. So why should she expect the sympathy of strangers?

She sighed and let her own head drop, to rest on his shoulder, beneath his broad-brimmed hat.

"Excuse me, ma'am, here's my stop." The man patted her on the shoulder — slapped, really — then pushed past her to the aisle, crushing her bad knee. "You take good care now, you hear?" she heard him say.

Disoriented, knee throbbing, Ruth opened her eyes. The bus had pulled up to her stop by the library, midpoint in its circular route, which took an hour to complete. Quickly, she glanced down at Hale's diamond watch. It was past nine-forty. Time for her heart pill, and she'd almost forgotten!

Furtively looking around her, she tossed her chewed Twizzler on the floor. She pulled her daytime pillbox from her purse and picked out a Cardizem. She didn't need water; she could swallow it right there by simply gathering enough saliva in her mouth. She'd learned long ago how to do without, in situations more difficult than this.

The drunk man up front was yelling now — he went purple in the face, punched his fist into his palm; he drooled and stamped his feet and swore at his invisible enemy.

Sick, Ruth thought. Sick and very peculiar. She swallowed the pill.

She stood and gathered her things and moved toward the door at the back of the bus. "Rear door, please," she called to the driver. Her voice came out weak and raspy. "Rear, please," she called again, but the door remained tightly shut. "Excuse me!" she called. "This is my stop!" She reached over to push the yellow signal tape, but tumbled forward as the bus lurched into gear. "Stop!" she shouted, reaching up toward a safety loop that dangled high out of her reach. Eventually, she caught hold of the back of a seat and steadied herself.

Somewhere in the bus, someone laughed.

The door sprang open.

Ruth took a few deep breaths. Then she hobbled over, planted her cane firmly on the first step, and eased her way down to the sidewalk.

Three kids knocked up against her. They were dressed entirely in black; they had headsets over their ears and large silver hoops through their lips and eyebrows and noses. Ruth couldn't tell if they were boys or girls. They pushed past her and into the bus, shouting, singing, laughing uproariously.

9:49 A.M.

Ocean Street was crowded. As always, Ruth paused to survey the people strolling by: lean young men in white pants and deep tans, fat middle-aged women in tent-shaped tropical muumuus, senior citizens in bright leisure wear with crooked limbs and pastel hair. Ruth blinked several times; the world had become a strange and difficult place. After a moment she slung her purse over her right shoulder. She grasped the cane in her left hand, letting the umbrella dangle from her wrist, and peered down the sidewalk toward the Postal Connection, two blocks ahead. The sooner this letter was safely on its way, she told herself, the better. She pointed with the tip of her cane, drew a bead on the mobile newsstand at the corner, and set out.

An airplane flew by slow and very low, trailing a banner over the water, parallel to Main Beach. Ruth watched it pass, squinting to make out its message: "Party All Weekend with Oldies 92 FM!" Why not? she thought, as she lowered her eyes; people flew around the moon now, and advertised in the sky. What a world.

She arrived at the newsstand and paused to catch her breath. From shelf upon shelf of glossy magazine covers, half-naked girls gaped at her, their pouting mouths wide open. Ruth stared back at them in disgust. The girls were very young, even younger than her granddaughter. "Lose Weight While You Sleep," read the cap-tions. "Eat Enough for Two and Still Keep Your Man." Ruth wondered if Karen read this kind of trash. The girl was certainly a pouter. She'd seemed awfully tense on the phone that morning, and she *was* very skinny. What's more, she was letting that Romeo sleep in her bed. How could she? Ruth wondered. It didn't make sense. That so-called husband of hers was not like any school-teacher *she* had ever known.

With a cluck of her tongue, Ruth lifted her cane and took aim at the Connection. The day was becoming warm and much brighter; she flipped her sunglass lenses down. Walking fast, she soon arrived at the edge of a fiberglass planter, brim full of wilted succulent plants, next to the Postal Connection's front door. The Connection was housed in a concrete building, circa 1950, newly refurbished with false wood siding and a roof of asphalt tile. A sign hung above the door: "Your Connection to the World: Swift, Safe, Sufficient."

Ruth stopped to set her purse on the edge of the planter, struggling to undo the purse's zipper with her right hand without losing her left-hand grip on the cane. Slowly, she worked the zipper open, right thumb and index finger pinching the tag, the remaining three fingers pulling from behind. She found the letter to Douglas, took it out and set it beside a succulent, and proceeded to close the bag as she had opened it, but with the three fingers pushing from behind this time. It was no easy thing. Exhausting, in fact. Ruth took a deep breath, removed the letter from the planter, brushed off some specks of soil, headed into the Connection.

The lobby was cool and shady. Potted palms and rubber plants stood in every corner; lush ferns and philodendrons hung in baskets from the ceiling. Rising onto her toes, Ruth reached up to touch a fern frond and discovered it was plastic.

"Naturally," she said. "And next it'll be plastic food. Then plastic people."

She stepped in line behind a barefoot girl wearing a beaded gypsy dress. The girl was staring up into the eyes of a much older man beside her — mostly bald, except for a stringy gray ponytail at the back of his head. At his feet sat a package addressed to the North Pole. Every few seconds the couple kissed, or he pulled on her beads, or she tugged his ponytail. Ruth watched them as she would a movie, waiting to see what might happen next. As she looked on, she absently opened and shut her mouth, cracking her jaw. What if strangers could hear the every move of her mouth, she wondered, without her even knowing? Ruth grew concerned, peering at the couple in front of her. She leaned in close, opening and closing her mouth several times in quick succession.

The girl glanced at Ruth, then looked back into the eyes of her lover. They kissed. A long one, tongues and closed eyes.

Ruth held a finger to her jaw, opening and closing her mouth, waiting patiently for them to finish.

The man began licking the girl's face. Hands on her shoulders, eyes closed, he enveloped her nose with his lips and sucked on her nostrils. Ruth gaped. She opened and shut her mouth with feeling, popping hard, and after several moments the man finally turned and glared at her with a beady right eye.

Ruth stared back at him. "May I ask what you're *doing* to that young lady?"

The man released the girl's nose, but continued to glare. "Hey look, Grandma," he said with two flicks of his ponytail, "what I'm doing is none of your beeswax. And about what *you're* doing, it's not like it's a pleasant sound or something, if that's what you want to know. Nasty as hell, actually."

The girl beside him smiled. Her tiny nose glistened like a wet pebble. Apparently, she'd been enjoying the sucking business.

Ruth stood silent. They were almost at the counter.

"Comprendes, Mendez?" the man said. "I mean, it's not like the end of the world or something. Just respect our space, is all. We're occupied."

"Oh, shit on you," said Ruth. "Just wait till *she's* almost a hundred, *then* see how you like sucking noses!" Ruth folded her arms tightly across her chest. Just then, as if ignited, a couple of flickering images sparked up: Hale dipping his nose into her hair, running a hand along her leg; Hale smiling down at her after they made love. "And besides, since you're obviously so nosy, it's not like I didn't have plenty of men eager to attack me back when . . ."

"What?"

"Hale," she said, then hesitated, her voice snagging. She looked hard at the man in front of her. "None of your beeswax. And go find a barber."

The man shrugged and turned away.

Beeswax, Ruth thought. The word had a nice solid ring to it. The next time someone started prying into her feelings, she'd just click her tongue and say, "None of your beeswax," and then she'd give a brisk nod and wait for . . .

Out of nowhere, a sudden chill swept through her. It made her gasp — a quick, icy freeze, cold like she'd never felt it before. With her free hand Ruth pulled down her sweater vest, half clutching herself, blinking, and then a moment later something white and furry seemed to bolt across the Postal Connection's tile floor. Ridiculous, she told herself. Impossible and silly. Except there it was, right now, a furry white creature that paused and studied her for a second before hopping toward the door.

"You?" Ruth murmured.

Then she said, "What *is* it?"

She squeezed her cane, shook her head from side to side. The couple in front of her were staring. The ponytailed man rolled his eyes. The gypsy girl started to reach out but then decided against it.

"Hey, listen," the man said, "you all right?"

Ruth nodded. "Perfectly. For a moment there I thought I recognized someone."

"Yeah? I don't see any —"

"Oh, just a face. Gone now." Ruth tapped her cane against the floor and straightened up her shoulders. "It *is* chilly in here, don't you think?"

"Sure," the man said. "Real chilly. Down to seventy-five, easy."

He turned away and took the girl's arm and moved up to the window. Ruth stood waiting for another four or five minutes, now and then glancing behind her, scanning the floor, but everything seemed back to normal. An extraordinary day, she thought. One thing after another. In a way, almost, it was as if all her routines were under attack by some insidious force of nature.

Enough was enough.

When the couple had finished at the window, Ruth marched forward and placed her letter firmly on the counter.

"Nice permanent, Root," the clerk said. "Brand-new one, I betcha."

At least that much was familiar. It was the Chinese clerk today, the one who worked there every Saturday, the one who had so much trouble with his grammar.

"Yes, well," Ruth said, "I do try to keep up repairs. Thanks for noticing. Many chi-chis, sir."

"Sorry, Root?"

"Chi-chi," Ruth said. "It *is* your language, I believe."

The clerk frowned, then broke out in a luxuriant grin. "Ah, I see, you mean thank you. And you are welcome! But you should say 'xie, xie' — like that. Where you learn speak Chinese? Pretty darn good, Root. And how about Henry? How he's doing?"

"Same old thing." She handed him the letter. "It's to my son, Douglas. The doctor."

"Yes, I know."

"You do?"

The man was still beaming at her. "Oh, sure, you talk about this son always. I know address by heart, and granddaughter, and other son, too." He weighed the letter, stamped it, placed it in a box beside him. "Fifty cent," he said.

"Fifty?" Ruth frowned at the man. "I was under the impression that a letter, just a regular old letter, costs exactly thirty-two cents."

The man pointed to a list of prices on the wall. "Not at Connection, Root. You want quality, you got to pay for it. Otherwise, you go to regular government post office."

Ruth felt her heart begin to palpitate. "But I can't make it over there. There's no bus."

The man nodded. "Okay now, Root, no worry. Fifty cent. He get it for sure by Tuesday."

"Well, I should certainly hope so."

Ruth passed a dollar bill across the counter.

"No problem. Okeydokey."

"Now what you may not realize," she said sternly, waiting for her change, "is that Douglas is an extremely busy man. Not rich, of course, not like his brother, Carter — you know, Karen's father, the one who's traveled all over the world. But that Douglas of mine, well, he was always the eager beaver. Very clever, too. Even when he was a boy, all those years ago, even then you'd never find him loafing or wasting time or . . . Just like his father, you could say. Have I ever mentioned my first husband, Hale?"

"Sure, Root. I guess maybe two thousand, three thousand times maybe."

Ruth blushed. "As he well deserves."

"A good man, you tell me. That Mr. Hale."

"Exceptional," said Ruth.

She put her change into her purse, thanked him, and moved off to the door. When she stepped outside, the ponytailed man was giving a long farewell suck to his girlfriend. Repulsive, Ruth thought. And Karen was probably subjected to the very same thing: that maniac husband wrapping his lips around her granddaughter's nose, clogging her breathing apparatus and spraying God knows what sort of germs right up into her head. Ruth clucked her tongue. Maybe that was why the girl had become so nervous and short-tempered — bugs crawling around her pretty little brain.

Pausing on the sidewalk, Ruth calculated the time that remained. She'd stepped off the bus at nine forty-two. With a half-hour trip back to the Lagoon, and then a half-hour trip from there back here, and the loss today of approximately two minutes for traffic in both directions, the bus should arrive at exactly ten forty-six. She could still do her math, all right.

It wasn't raining, so she would wait on the bench. She wanted to be early, just in case, so she started right away, lifting her cane and taking aim at a green mulberry bush and walking briskly down the sidewalk.

Almost immediately, from a bay window off to her right, a large red banner caught her eye: "Anytime Is Teddy Time at Intime!" Two mannequins in their mid-thirties, wearing red contraptions with black straps and black lace, posed provocatively beneath the banner. The brunette straddled a mutilated briefcase, its contents spilling everywhere, as she leather-whipped a half-open file cabinet while eyeing her next victim, a personal computer. The blonde looked calmly out the window past the fury of her friend, nursing a baby through the hole in her brassiere.

Intime was owned by Ruth's most Francophile acquaintance, Nora Gretts, and was managed by Nora's two assistants. Since 1924, when Nora and Ruth were freshmen together at UCLA, Nora had dreamed of owning just such a boutique. She had always been thin and high-strung, and wild in those days — always game to smoke in the bell tower or serve laxative-laced brownies for dessert or take the forbidden trip to Balboa Island. In their sophomore year, Nora and Ruth became sisters in Kappa Kappa Gamma. In their senior year, Nora was elected homecoming queen, and was the sorority's most-dated young woman. After graduation, she went off on a tour of Europe, and for many years afterward none of the sisters heard another word.

No one knew why Nora returned to California in 1953, looking a great deal worse for wear. Among those Kappa sisters still in the area, bizarre rumors began circulating. Some said it was syphilis, others that she'd lost a child. Whatever the case, in a matter of months Nora had opened Intime and was back in form — asking to be called Lady Soirée and boasting that she was the "première source of the latest modes, importées de France." Over the years, Nora's thinness turned to frailty, her wild exuberance to the realization — all the more bitter for its delayed arrival — that time passes and beauty fades. As her breasts and cheeks began to sag, she took to staying home, smoking and drinking coffee in bed, reliving her glory days in a scrapbook of yellowed clippings from the *Daily Bruin*. Except for holidays and weekends, when her assistants demanded time off, Nora ignored her duties at the shop. She kept careless records, avoided bill collectors, ordered shoddy goods from Korean catalogues. And when she did go to work, her behavior was more than a little erratic, and extremely bad for business. She would kowtow to customers, fawning over them as if they'd been friends for years; she'd sing and dance, twirling through the aisles and pinning discount tags on every item that had even a tinge of pink; she'd try on various new articles — an edible negligee, a high-tech chrome leotard — appraising her puffy flesh in the full-length mirrors; she'd stroll through the shop in a garter belt and bra, "soliciting customer opinions." But then, perhaps only an hour later, Nora's mood would suddenly turn critical. Grumbling that the stock was in a mess, she'd tear through the Korean nighties, spraying them with perfume, soiling them with her newsprint-stained fingers. Shocked at her own prices and scandalized by the merchandise she sold, she would shout, "There ought to be a law!" before stalking out in a huff.

Ruth hesitated for a moment outside the red-curtained door. Today was Saturday, one of those rare occasions when Nora would actually be here. Ruth straightened her hair and glanced at Hale's wristwatch — just enough time for a quick hello. She looked both ways, then slipped inside.

The room was stuffy, almost unbearable, and the overhead lights were dimmed. A scratchy recording of *Bolero* was playing, the volume turned high, but there was no one behind the counter.

Ruth moved up and down the short aisles, past fur-topped camisoles and gowns of imitation tiger skin. Twice she called out for Nora, with no luck, now and then stopping to peer through shelves of slippers and racks of bras. "Nora, yoo-hoo," she yelled. "I know you're here."

A squeal shot out from the back of the shop. Then a shuffling noise, then another squeal. "Don't you dare! What do you take me for?" It was Nora's voice — Ruth would have known it anywhere. And it was coming from the john, at the end of the panties aisle.

Ruth paused. "Hey, it's me, Ruthie." No answer. "Look, Nora, I don't have a lot of time here."

Nora squealed again: "Watch those hands!"

"Pardon me?" Ruth said.

"Your hands!"

Ruth gripped her cane tightly. "Listen, have you lost your mind? I'm not touching a thing."

Instantly, Nora let out a quick, shrill giggle.

Well fine. Ruth lifted her cane, drew a bead on the bathroom door, and advanced with determination down the aisle. She knocked twice, noticing that the lock was on her side of the doorknob. "I've had it, Nora, no more games. I'll give you a count of ten, then I'm afraid I'll have to make a forcible entry."

The laughter stopped. Ruth detected a rustling behind the door.

"One, two, three . . ."

"Now just a *minute*," Nora yelped.

"Oh, for God's sake, it's just me," said Ruth, and skipped the next several numbers. "Nine, ten! Here I come." She pushed the door open.

Nora stood on the toilet seat in a white peignoir and long lace gloves. A young man — very young, Ruth noticed, considerably younger than either of her own sons — stood facing Nora, with a camera. He turned toward Ruth as the door opened.

"My lucky day," he said. "A double feature."

"I'm sick," said Ruth.

Nora winked at her. "Well, that's your privilege," she said. "Just don't do it here." She lifted the hem of her gown, extended a gloved hand toward her companion, and descended daintily to the floor. Two circles of cherry-red rouge swung like gleaming Christmas ornaments from the tips of her pointed cheekbones. "Ruthie, darling, I should've known it was you. Always popping up to ruin someone else's good time."

"Good time?" Ruth stepped back, her cane extended in front of her like a rifle. "If you call this a good . . . Well, you obviously do, but this pervert's young enough to —" Ruth stopped as the boy crouched down to snap a picture.

"Great!" he said.

Nora smiled at the boy and threw out her chest. With one hand she hiked up the skirt of her gown, far above the top of her knee-highs; with the other she reached toward the sink and splashed water on her face and hair. "We'll go for that seaside look."

"You're eighty-seven years *old*," Ruth said. "I refuse to participate in this ridiculous spectacle."

"*Seventy*-seven," Nora said quickly. She glanced at the boy and cleared her throat. "One *is* as old as one *feels*."

"In that case," Ruth said, "I'm God's mother."

Nora made a huffing noise and let her gown drop back to her ankles. Then she pushed past Ruth and closed the bathroom door on the boy, locking him inside. "The lad's harmless," she said, and sniffed. "Like to try on a little something?" She glided over to a circular rack, plucked off a pair of bikini panties. "Maybe one of these gorgeous new garments? Except with the way you've let your midriff go, Lord knows if you'll fit a decent size."

Ruth held the panties out in front of her, pinched between her index finger and thumb, scowling at the foul smell she imagined they emitted. "Decent," she muttered. "What's decent about no crotch? Or about those goings-on in your bathroom?"

"Once the prude, always the prude."

"Prude my eye." Ruth dropped the panties to the floor. "I came in here to pay my compliments, such as they are, but it appears you're getting along just fine without me. Too fine, if you ask my opinion." She lifted her cane. The tip snagged on the panties, scraping them off the carpet.

Nora laid both hands upon her breast and said, "Dieu!"

Flushed, eager to escape, Ruth turned and hurried down the aisle toward the front door, nudging it open with her left shoulder. She paused at the threshold, blinded by the bright sun. "And you can tell that young man in there to go" — she searched for a proper phrase — "to go soak his pathetic apparatus."

10:36 A.M.

Her mind in a whirl, Ruth made it to the bus stop and collapsed heavily on the bench. She had to go to the bathroom. Badly, in fact — upsetting events almost always brought on the urge. Across the street was a Mobil station, but she didn't dare risk it. Only a single bus traveled the circular Laguna route — the same bus that had brought her downtown — and with the inevitable struggle to adjust her girdle, Ruth feared she might still be stooped over the toilet when the bus pulled up for its only stop that hour.

She felt a warm dribble against her thigh. Leaks everywhere, she thought. Fluids and words and ancient history, it all came spilling out willy-nilly, no control at all. She tensed herself, straining, holding on for dear life. It occurred to her that Nora might sell rubber panties. Probably with obscene little leopard-skin flaps.

When the bus pulled up at ten forty-one, five minutes ahead of her estimation, Ruth congratulated herself on the prudence and discipline she'd shown in not leaving the bench. She climbed on board, showed her card, and looked for a seat near the front. The purple-faced drunkard was still there, settled down now, asleep against a window. He burped as Ruth passed, and the smell — bourbon and bologna — reminded her of Henry.

She sighed and sank into an empty seat.

Henry had first been seduced by the promises of alcohol shortly after realizing that his marriage would be bone dry. For a time, at least, the booze seemed to offer comfort: a couple of martinis at lunch, a few more before dinner, then he was prepared to face another night alone. But after retirement and the move to Paradise Lagoon, boredom drove Henry to the bottle with a ferocious new thirst, something close to desperation. Part of the problem, Ruth assured herself, was purely physical. Henry was legally blind (though Ruth knew he could see just fine when he truly wanted to), and as a result he was hard put to find diversions of any kind. Listening to the radio, earplug tucked in tight, he'd spend hours staring blankly at the Lucky Strike thermometer above his desk, or he'd play long silent games of solitaire, or he'd just yawn and scratch himself and fiddle with his pencils. Some days, as second climbed over second, slow and empty, Ruth would overhear him counting aloud the minutes before he mixed his first drink.

One summer morning just before eight o'clock, she'd found him passed out on the floor beside his desk. He lay with his arms bent beneath him, his nubby-red cheeks crusted with dribble, sunlight washing over him in pale waves. His cereal bowl had fallen to the floor; dozens of mushy, swollen Shredded Wheats were pasted to the rug.

At that instant, Ruth recalled, something gave way inside her. The sting of a new affliction, perhaps; the pang of old disappointments that were best left unremembered.

She bent down, sniffed his collar. Whiskey, for sure. It was odd, though. She hadn't heard him open the liquor cabinet when he went down to fetch their breakfast trays that morning, and she hadn't heard him leave his room since then. For a while she looked him over, from the white socks to the floodwater corduroys to the dirty cuffs on his baby blue windbreaker. She frowned. Presently, she took note of a queer bulge near his left armpit.

In truth, she'd first noticed it long ago. For a month, at least, Henry had been wearing the same blue windbreaker day and night, elbows pressed against his ribs, hands entwined at the navel as if to cradle some private pain; more than once she'd found herself wondering about it all. The bulge seemed to move each time she looked. Not much, just an inch or two, like some sort of slow migration. What it was, however, she had not really hoped to discover. Maybe something he'd swallowed years and years ago, a giant artichoke or an undigested hamburger. Or perhaps benign cancer — a restless, wandering tumor.

She could no longer ignore it. She drew in a breath, lifted her chin, tore open his jacket. There, nestled inside the inner pocket, was a glass mouthwash bottle. "Well, so," she said.

Henry opened his eyes and grinned.

"Didn't know you was in here," he said.

Ruth snatched the bottle from his pocket. She held it up to the light, unscrewed the cap, and put it to her nose.

"Right," she said. "Jimmy Walker."

"That's Johnnie, hon."

Ruth narrowed her eyes. *"Degenerate."*

Sighing, pushing up to his hands and knees, Henry looked at her like a mangy pup begging for dinner. "Hey, just kidding, sweetie. I'm off to the bathroom, get the old teeth scrubbed up."

"Whiskey," Ruth said.

"The old breath potion, it keeps the kisser in order. My brother told me that. 'Lots of mouthwash,' Billy always says."

"Whiskey," Ruth said again, lowering her voice. "Not in this house. And certainly not at this hour."

Still on his hands and knees, Henry reached up for the glass bottle. "Well, you're right. Maybe one last splash, okay?" He scrambled forward. "That's class-A stuff, Ruth. Damn tasty over Shredded Wheat."

Ruth gave him a hard, level stare. Quietly, she put the bottle on the floor in front of him, straightened up, and turned to leave the room.

"Okay, okay!" he yipped. "Bad breath ain't the only problem!"

He panted and wagged his bottom, gazing up at her with huge moist eyes. For an instant Ruth had to fight back an impulse to scratch his ears.

Henry picked up the bottle.

"Listen, Ruthie, I ain't no saint." He burped. He shook his head. Slowly then, he hoisted himself up and stood wobbling in the sunlight, still gripping the bottle with both hands. "A man gets dull as dirt in his bedroom all alone, miserable lonely. No offense, naturally. Anyhows, I see the drift, so to speak. Won't do it no more — drinking on the sly, I mean — and that's for sure. Swear to God in heaven. Apostles, too, and all the martyrs."

He wobbled sideways again, and winked.

"Watch this."

He made his way to the window, pulled off the screen, licked his lips, and tossed out the bottle. There was a sharp shattering sound.

"Amen," he said.

Ruth walked over to his side. She gripped his elbow and made an effort to steady him. She peered out the window, down into the public courtyard below. "Go fetch the broom," she said, "before someone steps on all that glass."

11:12 A.M.

Dazed, blinking herself awake, Ruth looked out the bus window and took stock of her surroundings: more Italian restaurants and frozen-yogurt shops, more video rentals and real estate offices. Fast-breeding Salmon Estates covered the hills, smothering open spaces beneath their smiling pink façades. "Coming Soon! Seven New Neighborhoods!" said the billboards at the side of Coast Highway.

The bus pulled over briefly at a stop near Treasure Island. Ruth peered ahead, past the few remaining passengers and out the front window, looking for her palm tree. It was an advance warning sign that her own stop was approaching.

"I spy!" she whispered as the tree came into view, over sixty feet tall on the highway's ocean side.

The skinny palm stood on Paradise Lagoon's greenbelt. When Ruth and Henry were first moving in, bringing down carloads of things from Los Angeles each day, they had held competitions to "spy" the palm tree first. The earlier you saw it, the better your luck for the day. Driving south down Coast Highway, behind the wheel of her trusty Studebaker, Ruth sometimes had to let Henry win, his eyes were so much worse than hers.

Over twenty years had passed since then. Originally there had been three palms; the one that remained had been the runt of the three. Alone and badly weathered now, stripped bare except for a tuft of leaves at the very top, it held on stubbornly, proud to be the tallest living thing around.

To Ruth, the first sight of the tree brought on a warm, cozy sensation, like coming home was supposed to feel.

Behind the tree, the giant condominiums loomed. Slick and self-assured, almost pompous behind their half-million-dollar price tags, they stood row upon row on a slope facing the ocean. They were not worth their price, but unabashed they stood in ranks of muted green, one identical to the next. Had they always looked so frightening? Ruth wondered.

Number 24, behind the tennis court, was hers.

She gathered her cane, umbrella, and purse, and when the bus doors snapped back, she stepped down to the sidewalk.

She walked briskly over to the iron fence that guarded Paradise Lagoon. Today for some reason a snarl of six or seven cars was backed up behind the Lagoon gates. The new California, Ruth thought. Traffic jams in your own driveway — blaring horns and red faces — cars jerking forward as the twin gates slowly opened and closed like a pair of heavy steel curtains. Some of the drivers had Auto-Opens, which they aimed at the gates from behind their steering wheels; others were forced to lower their windows and reach out toward a black iron stand, to insert their Auto-Mate cards into a narrow slot. Several of the cars made false starts as Ruth looked on, and there seemed to be more than the usual confusion. Probably the gates were broken again.

"Cadillac quality" my eye, thought Ruth. Installing this fence had been just another ploy of the management to raise her monthly Association dues.

The Pedestrian Passage, which swung out to open like a regular door, was tightly closed. It had its own card mechanism; the slot sneered at Ruth now like some defiant hoodlum. She was the only pedestrian around, so she'd have to use her own card. Usually she kept it rubber-banded to the outside of her wallet, inside her purse, but today it wasn't there — she must not have put it away properly at the Postal Connection, after paying for her letter. Using her left hand both to balance on her cane and to hold her purse, she fumbled through the purse's contents with her right hand.

By now she desperately needed to pee. The gate, however, could not have cared less if she was stuck there all day.

Finally she dug out the card, hidden in a corner beneath a sticky wad of Kleenex. Bending down, reaching out toward the slot, she was about to slide the card in when the gate sprang open of its own volition.

She jumped, almost dropped her cane. But there was no time to consider the matter; right now, the whole world had condensed into a single hard pressure in her kidneys. She hurried past the sculpted dog, with only one glance at his perked-up ears; she hurried down the hill as fast as she'd ever walked in her life, then down the path between the tennis court and pool. Once at her door, she rang the front bell.

She glanced at Hale's wristwatch — almost eleven-thirty.

The pressure was intense now, almost unbearable. "Henry!" she cried. She rang twice more, but there was no answer. With a weak yelp, she opened up her purse and began digging again. This time she knew to go for the corners, and after what seemed an eternity she found the keys hidden exactly where her card had been. She unlocked the door with a shaking hand, hustled into the tiny bathroom.

"Thank the Lord," she said.

It was a lovely moment. The fine, warm spray reached out for her thighs, but she could relax now, no damage done. All the photographs looked down, proud of her. Not a single drop in her underpants.

When she was finished, she called again for Henry.

Asleep, no doubt. Or maybe still at the Alpha Beta. She started for the second floor. She was more fatigued than usual, and feeling a little dizzy, but she would still use the stairs, not the elevator.

"Henry!" she called.

Slowly, a bit wobbly, she climbed to the third floor. Her knee popped audibly all the way. They had always been so good, her legs. She moved into Henry's open doorway.

There he was — deaf as a stone.

Back turned, standing straight up at his window, he cackled to himself and looked out toward the condo gates, left hand on the windowsill for balance. In his right hand he gripped an Auto-Open, which he aimed in the general direction of the gates. He pushed the button randomly, absorbed in his game, obviously taking great pleasure in all the chaos down below.

Ruth watched as Henry refused assistance to a red Honda Accord. Next in line was a blue hatchback. The driver rolled down her window and began to reach out toward the slot with her card when Henry leaned forward and pushed his Auto-Open button and laughed as the gates rolled apart. The blue hatchback hesitated. Then it drove through fast, hitting the speed bump much harder than could have done the car good. Next was an old black convertible — pausing just long enough for Henry to beep the gates closed. The driver braked hard and reached out with his card, and Henry beeped the gates open; there was another short hesitation; the convertible edged forward and Henry beeped the gates shut. His skinny shoulders were shaking. He giggled and waited for a line to form behind the trapped convertible and then hit the button four times in rapid succession — open-close, open-close.

Henry's eyes were bad, it was true, but he clearly sensed the confusion he was causing. With each push of the button, he'd snort and slap his leg and do a little dance in his size-thirteen loafers.

A child, Ruth thought. Married to a twelve-year-old.

He jumped when she poked him in the back.

"Hey, you made it," he said. "Long time no see. I've been worried."

"Is that so?"

"Bet your booties." He slipped the Auto-Mate behind his back. "Just keeping my eyes peeled."

"Well, here I am," Ruth said, "but I could've drowned in my own urine out there. Don't think I'm not on to your foolish games."

"Games?"

"The gate," she said. "You let me in yourself."

"I did?"

She glared at him. For the second time in less than an hour, she remembered the day he'd thrown his booze bottle out this very bedroom window.

She sighed. "So where's the change from my groceries?"

11:45 A.M.

It was part of Henry's job, when he went to the Alpha Beta every morning, to pay for their food separately and return Ruth's share of the change, down to the penny. Each day before he headed out, he took ten dollars from Ruth's grocery money, which she kept in a pickle jar on the kitchen counter. When he got home, having made it one more time across the highway with no accident, he handed Ruth her own receipt and change, which she carefully counted before preparing her lunch.

Like the morning routine at 24 Paradise Lagoon, the midday rituals never changed.

At eleven o'clock sharp, without exception, Henry made himself a bologna sandwich. Or rather, two open-faced bologna sandwiches. He would toast two slices of wheat bread, spread them both with butter (lots of butter; so much, in fact, it made Ruth queasy to watch), and then pile on alternating layers of bologna and Chef Tooley's Famous Peanut Sauce. He would place the sandwiches on a flowered paper plate. He would drape a napkin over the sandwiches, pour himself a Diet Coke, position everything on his tray, and carry the tray up to the desk in his bedroom. Screwing in his radio earplug, he'd finally sit down to eat. As he munched the atrocious sandwiches, he liked to watch Rodrigo hose down the tennis court and then sweep off the water with his big push broom. Some days Rodrigo made elaborate and beautiful patterns in the water, which Henry would admire from the window. Huge spirals, for instance. And flowers. Once Rodrigo drew the wavy figure of a woman. Once he drew a flag. The patterns were clear from above — clearer than they could have been to Rodrigo himself — and Henry took special pleasure in staring down at the unfolding pictures as he ate his daily bologna.

Ruth, too, had her own rigorous lunch procedure. The same sandwich, without variation, each day: coleslaw and salami on wheat. And two bites of oat bran muffin. The muffins cost seventy-nine cents apiece, and they were huge; Ruth almost never finished an entire muffin in one day. She'd have precisely two bites at lunch and then, depending on what she was doing, nibble at the leftovers throughout the afternoon.

These habits were important to Ruth in ways she could never entirely explain, not even to herself.

All those years maybe. All the accumulated tastes and sensations that pile up over a lifetime — they could be overwhelming — they had to be sorted out and labeled and filed away in their proper mental folders. No choice really. If you lasted long enough, as she had, you could end up choking on the debris of your own life.

Not that she gave it much thought. What was necessary was necessary, it was that simple.

Ruth looked at Hale's watch. Almost noon. She was starving.

She made her way down to the kitchen, went to the counter, and pulled today's muffin from its crisp new bag. She took the first bite, holding her left hand beneath her chin to catch any crumbs. Inevitably, she missed a few — four little specks on the counter. She licked her index finger, pressed down on a crumb, brought it to her mouth. She called it The Index Test. If a scrap adhered to the index finger of her left hand, it was obviously safe to eat. Anything small enough to stick, she reasoned, could not possibly carry sufficient germs to poison her. She did not hesitate to perform The Test on the counter at the bank, for example, or even on the bench downtown, where she waited for the bus. Any crumb that did not adhere to her finger was to be picked up and saved until it could be properly thrown away.

In this case she knew the exact nature of the crumbs, and she finished them off: two, three, four. Then she took her second bite from the top of the muffin and replaced the leftovers in the bag, which would be dealt with according to another specific procedure later in the afternoon.

Next, she made her sandwich. She did not toast the bread, nor spread butter on it. She preferred cream cheese — light cream cheese, with half the calories. Methodically, concentrating on each step, Ruth dropped on three slices of salami from the processed roll that lasted her two weeks, then added a few spoonfuls of coleslaw. She cut the sandwich in half and arranged it on her tray with a glass of buttermilk. Then she carried the tray to her place at the dining table, to the one small space that she kept cleared of papers.

She slid into her chair and took a few deep breaths. At last, she thought. Life was exhausting.

12:20 P.M.

After lunch, Ruth began to sort through the day's mail, which Henry had carried up to the table when he got back from the supermarket. Today it was mostly catalogues. Buried among the catalogues was a slim cardboard mailing envelope addressed to Mrs. Henry Hubble. It was marked with red lettering: "Holiday Blessings from Your Buddies at Blockbuster." Scowling, Ruth grabbed the envelope and shook it from side to side; an unpleasant, fetid odor wafted up through the air. Probably some scratch-and-sniff guide to the animal kingdom, she thought. She leaned forward and placed the envelope atop a stack of similar envelopes piled high in the center of the table.

She sighed and looked about.

Normally, after sorting her mail, she also paged through the newspaper, but unless a sensational story jumped out at her, she never read much but the horoscope and the obituaries. She liked to check the astrological predictions for her two sons and her granddaughter, and she liked to search for death notices of people she had known. In the event she found one, she would cut it out. She kept her pile of obituaries in a tidy zip-lock bag, the most recent notice on top, in the drawer of her bedside table. She'd been doing this for years, and had a substantial collection. Lately, though, she hadn't found much: more people died in their seventies than in their eighties, she'd learned.

Her second clipping project was the television listings. Except for *Wheel of Fortune* and *Jeopardy*, between seven and eight in the evenings, she rarely watched television; still, it was good to have the listings, just in case. She would cut out "Tonight on TV" and "Tonight on Cable," and paper-clip them to the appropriate day in the TV guide that came in Sunday's paper. She had to fold the clippings twice to make them fit inside the booklet; though she struggled to do it right, they always stuck out the edges in a mess.

Today, though, Ruth skipped her entire clipping routine. Those peculiar white specks were back again, flickering here and there like some sort of television static, and she decided it might be best to lie down for a few minutes. She picked up her tray, carried it to the kitchen, added her plate and glass to the morning's dishes in the sink. On her way out she bent down to drop her napkin in the trash and stopped in her tracks.

"My God," she said. The plastic sandwich baggie, clothes-pinned inside a corner of the brown paper bag, was completely full. Overflowing, in fact.

Ruth stooped down for a closer look. This would not do, with Luzma coming to clean. If there was one thing Ruth could not tolerate — and there were many such things — it was a stinky, overstuffed garbage bag. Embarrassing, too. A maid should never have access to one's private leavings.

She left the kitchen, moved to the bottom of the stairs, and yelled up to Henry. It was a few moments before she heard his slow, lumbering steps on the landing.

"Henry!" she yelled again. "Garbage time!"

He stood looking down at her, frowning, then pulled out his radio earplug. "Cribbage time?" he said.

"No, I said *gar*bage."

Henry shook his head. "Well, it's your call," he said, "but I never even knew you *liked* cribbage. Live an' learn, I guess."

Ruth wondered if they electrocuted old ladies for murder. "Garbage!" she yelled. "You know perfectly well I despise crib-bage. I *despise* little games." There was a tinge of real disgust in her voice, which startled her.

Henry blinked, glanced at the ceiling, then shrugged. "You're right. Must've thrown it away."

"Thrown *what* away?"

"The cribbage board, sweetie."

Ruth was having trouble breathing. "Listen, Henry — the

trash. Take out the trash. Just leave me my View and Calendar sections, and take the rest of today's paper, too."

Henry shook his head as if perplexed and started down the stairs. "A mysterious lady," he said. When he reached the bottom of the stairs, he gave Ruth a sly, knowing look.

"What?" she said.

"Full of surprises, aren't you, cutie?"

"What?"

He flicked his eyebrows.

Suddenly, despite herself, Ruth released a quick snort of laughter. It was the first time she had laughed in days.

Henry did a little dance step, then turned and headed out to the kitchen.

Ruth stood there for a moment, quite still, looking after him. Remarkable, she thought. For a silly man, he could be singularly shrewd.

Though the Lagoon regulations did not require it, Ruth separated her trash in a most particular way. She called it The Arrangement. The process began with an ordinary brown grocery bag, with which she lined her plastic garbage bin. Before insertion, the paper bag had to be folded down one or two inches along its upper edge, so that it would remain upright even under the weight of some substantial piece of trash. Next, she would carefully attach a plastic sandwich baggie to one of the paper bag's corners, by means of three clothespins. The clothespins stretched the plastic baggie and held it taut, forming a triangular-shaped compartment for small bits of refuse. Finally, she would place a coffee can at the bottom of the brown bag as a third receptacle.

The question of what went where was complicated. If Kaji brought over some foreign dish in unusual wrappings, things could get confusing in the extreme. For the most part, however, Ruth and Henry ate the same meals every day, which made it possible for Ruth to establish certain rules. Most items went straight into the brown bag. Cottage cheese containers, TV dinner boxes and their plastic dishes, various aluminum cans, cereal and prune boxes — all these were deposited into the big brown bag. Peanut butter jars and yogurt cartons also went into the brown paper bag, but *not* the tinfoil yogurt tops. Certain bits of refuse required special treatment. Soiled wrappers of all sorts were to be placed inside the crinkled bags that Ruth pulled out of cereal boxes whenever she or Henry finished off their Shredded Wheat or All-Bran: these included greasy wrappers from Ruth's salami rolls, her cream cheese wrappers and muffin papers, and Henry's plastic bologna cases and coffee filters. Banana peels had to be stuck inside cardboard toilet-paper tubes. With two people in the house, a roll of toilet paper was normally finished off every three days; if constipation happened to set in, reducing the use of paper, it was permissible to stuff several banana peels into a single cardboard tube.

The triangular plastic baggie was reserved for chewed strawberry Twizzlers, hair balls, wadded-up Kleenexes, and little bits of rotten cheese. Also prune pits, lids from Diet Coke bottles, tinfoil yogurt tops, and candy wrappers.

The coffee can, finally, was exclusively for crumbs — those that had not passed Ruth's Index Test, and were thus not pure enough for consumption. Ruth would carry crumbs home inside her purse from the various places around town where they had failed The Test, then she'd use a pair of rubber gloves to transfer them into the can. It was among her favorite procedures. An act of environmental consciousness. And good fun, too. She liked to contemplate each crumb that found its way into her collection, and she liked to imagine the lives of the people who had dropped them.

For years Ruth had encouraged Henry to follow her system. She tried to teach by example, calling out to him from the kitchen each time she used the trash, letting him know which receptacle was about to receive which piece of trash. She watched over Henry like a hawk whenever he dumped in his own wastes, pointing out errors, scolding and cajoling and sometimes even begging.

At times, Ruth thought, the man seemed to be suffering from a learning disability. He simply couldn't catch on, tossing things indiscriminately, especially when Ruth wasn't watching, and as a consequence she was constantly having to rearrange his refuse. It was a wearisome and frustrating task.

In the end she did what she should have done from the start, writing down a complete list of rules and posting it on a cabinet above the trash. Even then Henry had trouble. "Greek to me," he'd say, and though Ruth explained and reexplained the rules, trying to persuade him of their simplicity and obvious merit, it eventually became clear that the man had absolutely no ability to recognize subtle distinctions. After Ruth realized this, her frustration — which had begun to manifest itself indirectly, in arguments over matters completely unrelated — settled into a steady, suspicious, resigned malaise. Though it piqued her, she lowered her expectations of Henry and handled the matter herself. She did insist, however, upon his correctly *distributing* the garbage among the various dumpsters down at the community trash yard, which Ruth called The Pig Pen.

He was to carry the whole Arrangement across the cement courtyard just as it was; the contents of the three receptacles were not to be mixed together. Once he'd arrived safely inside the fenced-off grounds of The Pig Pen, he was to remove the clothespins from the little baggie, seal it up tight, and place it inside one of the community dumpsters. Next he was to put the coffee can aside and deposit the brown paper bag inside a second dumpster. Then, as a concluding embellishment, he was to retrieve the coffee can and sprinkle its assortment of crumbs over each dumpster in The Pen.

It was, Ruth thought, an elegant ceremony. Logical and efficient. Of course, things did not always come off according to plan — but what in her life ever had?

Ruth stood at the kitchen counter, watching as Henry stooped to pick up the garbage. For him, she knew, the distribution process was humiliating. He grumbled about it constantly. He hated the clothespins. He hated the plastic baggie. He hated the coffee can and the brown paper bag and the toilet paper tubes stuffed with banana peels. It was demeaning, he kept telling her, to walk across the courtyard carrying it all, and he felt plain foolish standing there in The Pig Pen, separating his trash and scattering little crumbs around.

Right now, in fact, he was obviously stalling.

Drumming her fingers lightly on the countertop, Ruth spoke in her most commanding voice. "Now be careful. Let's not get things all jumbled up."

Henry lifted the plastic bin to his hip. "Right," he said skeptically. "Think I got the hang of it." He clamped his baseball cap securely on his head, lumbered past her, and started down the stairs.

When the front door banged shut, Ruth hurried over to the window. There he was, directly below her in the courtyard. Except he wasn't moving. He'd set down the plastic bin and was hovering above it, hand in his mouth, playing with the revolving tooth. He stood transfixed like that for several minutes. Then he lifted a hand and crossed himself. There was a short hesitation — knees bent, shoulders arched — then he swooped down over the bin. In three quick pinches, he released the plastic baggie from its clothespins and spilled it open into the paper bag. He pulled the coffee can from the paper bag and, turning the can sideways, scattered the crumbs as if from a giant salt shaker: some floated through the air like dandelion puffs; others fell to the ground, where Henry danced on them.

12:54 P.M.

Sabotage, Ruth thought.

To think — thirty-six years with a man like that. She turned from the window, shuffled over to the couch, and lay down. A clear case of sabotage. And if Henry was capable of one deception, he was certainly capable of a thousand. She fluffed and stacked two thin toss pillows and slipped them under her head.

With Hale, of course, life had been different.

Senior year at UCLA. The first night of spring vacation, a sorority party, honeysuckles and orange blossoms and streamers twisting from the ceiling and people dancing and flirting and full of the future.

Ruth stood at the hors d'oeuvres table, alone, trying to hide. She felt ugly. God, she *was* ugly. That afternoon she'd gone in for the first professional permanent wave of her life, but to say the least, the results were not what she'd expected. When they'd removed the clips, down at that fancy new salon on Seventh Street, her whole head was in need of salvation: a loathsome mass of waves and curls and tangled knots. Later, she wet down her hair a dozen times, used an iron on it, combed it and brushed it and soaked it in salt water. Nothing, though. Ugly wasn't quite the word. Freakish — that was closer. Especially with all the other girls in their impeccable bobs and fancy braids and perky ponytails.

Ruth glanced around the room, sighed to herself, and poured a glass of grapefruit punch. That damned hairdresser. In the morning she'd march downtown and give the woman a good —

"Well, darling," someone said behind her, "how incredibly pretty."

Ruth froze. It was Nora, of course. Ruth winced and swallowed hard.

"So *very* pretty," Nora said, coming to her side, plucking an asparagus spear from the table. She took a dainty bite and rolled her eyes. "So special-looking. So *interesting*. Just so absolutely and perfectly *you*."

Ruth pulled back her shoulders, ran a hand through her electric spirals. "Thirty cents a curl," she said bravely.

"Oh, it shows, and you clearly got your money's worth, every penny." Nora's lips settled into a smirk; her own hair had been sculpted into a rock-hard bob. "Hear about my Easter plans?"

"A date?"

"Be gone for three weeks — invited out to Atlantic City."

"Wonderful," Ruth said. Her heart sank as she pictured Nora gliding down the boardwalk along the sand, fancied-up in fringe and sequins, swarms of hungry men nipping at her heels.

Nora smiled. "Oh, and listen to this. Judy Snyder and Edith Tumay just got themselves suspended — stayed overnight at Balboa Island last weekend. Not alone, either. With the boys from Alpha Delt."

"Really," Ruth said.

Christ, what next? All she needed was one more success story, somebody else's grand adventure. Again, despite herself, she ran a hand through her hair. What she should do, maybe, was just disappear. Run away to the Philippines. Albania, maybe, or China or New Guinea or some other exotic spot. A place where the natives wore bones in their hair.

"Well, Nora," she said, "I guess I'd better wander over —"

And then he tapped her shoulder.

A crooked nose. Flecks of brown in the hazel-green eyes. A pinstriped seersucker suit. Far too young for the balding head. But even that — especially that — was beautiful. The way the yellow light glanced off his forehead.

Ruth smiled as a streamer blew across his cheek. Suddenly, ridiculously, she felt an urgent need to put a hand on that fine shiny head.

"Dance?" he asked.

Nora leaned over to whisper in her ear. "Petroleum engineer. Nine hundred a month."

Ruth would have no memory of walking to the dance floor.

She *would* remember glancing up at the man, positioning her feet, sliding her hand into his. Then they were moving — a windy kind of moving. Her legs felt like wheat. There was a dampness under her arms, warm and clammy; she hoped it didn't show through her silk dress. She could feel the man staring at her, a kind of ticklish heat, but she kept her eyes fixed on the knot in his tie.

"Beautiful hair," he said. "Adorable."

She wasn't sure she'd heard him correctly. She was sure she *hadn't*, the music was so loud.

"Your hair," he said, "it's gorgeous."

"Oh, don't."

"Perfect."

She glanced up at him — he didn't seem to be joking. She lifted her chin. "Well," she said, "that's a generous thought, but it's a wreck."

"No, I love how it fluffs up that way. All these women here, they look like peas out of the same boring pod. I bet they're all jealous of you." He smiled at her. "And now every man's jealous of me."

"Well, I like yours too. The hair, I mean."

He laughed. "Not much to like."

"But I mean . . . You know, how the light sparkles off your forehead."

"Mr. Mirror?"

"Just like my father," she said. "Sometimes his whole head starts to —" She sucked in a breath. Idiot, she thought. "I meant — you know — bald isn't *old*."

He was smiling at her in a funny way. She could smell his shirt and skin. They were barely moving, ignoring the music. Briefly, as Ruth closed her eyes, it occurred to her that maybe the new permanent wasn't so terrible after all. At one point he seemed to dip his nose into her hair — like a honeybee, almost — and a moment later, when he stroked the curls at her neck, Ruth tried to recall whether she'd left a decent tip for the hairdresser.

Chunks of blurry time went by. Music and party sounds, and awkward silences too, and after four dances Ruth found herself searching for something to say. Work, she thought, then blurted it out. "What about work?"

"I'm sorry?"

It was hard to make her tongue move. "Do you work here? In town?"

"For an oil company. Graduated from Berkeley two years ago. My name's Hale."

"Dale?"

"*Hale*. With an H."

"H," she said. "H is nice. I'm Ruth Caster."

"Yes, I know."

"I'm a senior here, I'm about to —"

"I know."

"You know?"

"Oh, sure," he said. "Lots."

When the band stopped for a break, people began drifting off the dance floor; someone turned up the lights. Ruth stared at the knot in Hale's tie. She hoped they'd keep talking — his eyes were so pretty to watch — but again she had trouble coordinating tongue and brain. Nothing came to her. She glanced over at the hors d'oeuvres table. Nora looked up and waved and blew a kiss.

"Hungry?" Hale said.

"Oh, no."

"What about air?"

"The air's perfectly fine, thank you."

"No, I mean do you *want* some? Outside."

She nodded stupidly.

And what now — reach for his arm? Yes. Grip it hard? Be brave? Yes, just this once. And she did it: she even smiled. She raised her eyes, kept her spine straight, allowed him to lead her out to the back porch.

Again, there was that blank, blurry feeling. A cool, windy night. A bright half-moon. Many stars. The physical universe seemed to press against her skin.

"So," he was saying, "when's graduation day?"

"Soon enough. Two more months."

"Plans?"

"Yes, well —" She let herself look up at him. "Not yet."

At ten o'clock he offered her a drink from his flask. At ten-fifteen the moon slipped under clouds. At ten-twenty he was explaining the oil business, his voice slow and deliberate, and Ruth smiled and nodded and watched the flecks in his eyes; she studied his hands and lips; she felt a peculiar calm. Not much later, he kissed her. Then he kissed her again. Around eleven, when they returned to the dance floor, he took her by the hand.

His expression was almost somber.

"Well?" he said. "How do we firm up those plans of yours?"

They saw each other every night.

Hale had his own car, which was rare back then, and in the evenings he'd drive over and pick her up and take her back to his place on Heliotrope Drive. Of course there wasn't any real hanky-panky — Ruth remembered her Aunt Elizabeth's misfortunes, and was careful to look behind Hale's flattering words, to get to know him before doing anything she might regret. Almost immediately, though, she realized there would be no trip to the Philippines after all.

And then one evening, when Hale proposed, she also gave up on the idea of graduation itself.

They were married, in a chapel with loud brass bells, just six weeks after they had met. Ruth vowed to take the name of Armstrong and she kept that vow; and after their honeymoon trip to the Grand Canyon they moved into a house on Santa Barbara Avenue, out by Exposition Boulevard.

Ruth remembered the first months well, as if they were only yesterday. She and Hale painting the walls of their very first bedroom, and ending up painting each other. Driving out by the ocean, stopping along the road, climbing up into a tree to watch the sunset. The day a bird got trapped in the kitchen and Hale rushed home from work to perform a rescue operation. How at night they shared secrets in bed, and how Hale murmured "Yes, I know" to everything she said, and how he really *did* know. The morning they had their first fight. The night they made up. The tuneless tunes he used to whistle as he washed dishes, which at times almost drove her crazy, but which now ran through her head whenever she was lonely.

She remembered Hale's laugh, his bushy eyebrows, the smell of his undershirts. The funny faces he made to cheer her up before he got out of bed in the morning. The strange searching smile he gave her as they made love. The big vein that ran back along his bare, broad forehead, and how very soft his skin felt for a man so strong.

After fourteen months in the house on Santa Barbara Avenue, Hale took the job with the U.S. Geological Survey and they moved to Washington, D.C. That winter, Ruth became pregnant with Douglas, the future doctor, and Hale took his first trip out to the new oil fields in Oklahoma, leaving her behind. Ruth missed him desperately, but it helped a little that his letters were loving and indulgent. "My Darling Girlie," they'd always start, and he wrote her almost every day, even when nothing at all had happened.

Years passed. Carter was born, a child with a rhythmical bounce who would one day become an artist. Hale's responsibilities increased, and he received regular promotions; soon he was staying in Oklahoma for months at a time. He continued to write regularly, and his letters were consistently kind: they described Ponca City, where he had a little house, and the men and women at the Indian reservation, where he did his work.

Once, for Hale's thirtieth birthday, she visited him at the little house in Ponca City.

It was a big surprise.

For over a month, back in Washington, she'd made secret arrangements for the trip: the children were to stay with the Deedses, and she taught them to behave as proper guests; her parents wired money for the train ticket, despite believing her plans too extravagant. And then one evening, exactly a week after Hale boarded the train for Ponca City, Ruth herself boarded the same train, and followed him. June 16, 1935: she had never before traveled by herself.

The journey lasted two days and three nights — three hot, exhausting, unnerving nights. At one point, rather late in the course of the final night, just as she was drifting toward sleep, Ruth was roused by the sound of a woman's loud pleadings and protestations in the neighboring berth. She heard a drunk man's steady, insistent drone, then a woman's — it hardly sounded like the same woman — muffled shriek and giggle and groan and a strange, quick thumping noise that sounded like somebody bouncing a ball. There was passionate talk — "That's right, honey, now, yes, that's right!" "Please, honey!" "Yes!" — then, suddenly, quiet. An imploring, drawn-out sort of quiet. Intrigued, filled with a vague but real desire to be nearer the disturbance, Ruth slipped from her bed, pulled a robe over her nightgown and, stepping out into the corridor, almost bumped into a very young, diminutive girl — she couldn't have been older than sixteen — dressed in an expensive, silky black cocktail dress, with lace sleeves and a low-cut neck. Her chest, Ruth noticed, was almost as flat as a child's. Her hair was reddish, long and curly and damp, several matted clumps slicked flat against her neck; her eyes were dark and tired; her tiny face was glowing. She was, Ruth thought, disarmingly beautiful. The girl leaned against the wall with the languid, complacent grace of a creature immune to love.

She twisted her red lips into a serpentine grin. "Silent suffering," she said, gesturing toward the closed door of her berth. "Don't *we* do enough of it?"

"We?"

"You know, *we*," the girl said, moving forward and dropping a hand on Ruth's forearm. "We women."

Speechless, Ruth stared down at the hand: an immense white stone sparkled from the wedding-ring finger. Ruth wondered if it was real, the stone, and if it was really a *marriage* stone. More likely, she thought, it was just some ruse devised by the girl's desperate lover: the shimmering, immodest jewel seemed to wink at all conventional notions of propriety. Ruth looked into the girl's face. The lips were too red, she thought; wet and smudged with excessive kissing, probably, or red wine, or fruit punch; they both fascinated and unnerved Ruth, as if they might swallow all her secrets in one giant gulp, then spit them back out into the mocking night.

Ruth said, "I'm not sure I understand."

"*You* know." The girl rearranged her posture. "A woman needs to take charge once in a while, don't you think? Make him pay attention."

Ruth said nothing. Briefly, she was reminded of her Aunt Elizabeth. The same immodesty, the same sexual flippancy. Ruth felt a familiar mix of admiration and envy and fear.

"Well?" the girl said. "Cat got your tongue, lady?"

"My what?"

"Your tongue," the girl said. "You got one?"

Ruth hesitated, stepping backward into the threshold of her little sleeping chamber. It wasn't that she didn't want to talk. She did, but she was unaccustomed to discussing personal matters with anyone, let alone a half-naked stranger. In the Caster and Armstrong clans, public mention, indeed any mention, of private emotions was considered unacceptable, a sign of bad breeding and bad taste. Still, there was something alluring about the girl, something unfettered and innocent, and Ruth could not quite bring her usual judgments to bear. She felt an intense curiosity.

"Well, I," she stammered, "I heard some noises. But so long as you're okay —"

The girl hooted and gave Ruth's arm a squeeze. "Marvelous," she said. "Even better." She glanced into Ruth's berth, looked her over from head to toe. "And you?"

Abruptly, rather painfully, Ruth was struck by the prudery of her own neat comportment, her thick green robe and cool skin and tight curlers and delicately scented ointments and upright, honorable behavior. She forced herself to make the conventional response.

"Fine," she said.

"*Fine,*" the girl repeated. The expression on her face was irreverently reverent.

"You see, Hale —" Ruth's voice was strained. "He's in Oklahoma, you see. Working there."

"*Oklahoma.*"

The girl released her grip on Ruth's arm and began to twist a strand of wet red hair around and around her finger. "Well, Oklahoma." Was she laughing? She was certainly smiling an unsettling smile. "Well, now, lots of time before Oklahoma. Must be ten stops before then." Her red lips puckered with compassion. "Ask me, you're liable to get a trifle bored all alone in there by yourself, Miss . . ."

"Mrs. Hale Armstrong," Ruth said.

There was an awkward silence. A question was on the tip of Ruth's tongue, and she finally asked it.

"What about you?" she said.

"Me?"

"Yes. Well, your name. And your . . ."

Her voice sounded nervous, she realized — she wasn't used to being nosy — and she struggled to appear more composed.

"Your destination."

The girl only stared.

"I mean, well, as for myself, it's my husband's birthday, his thirtieth, so I'm going out to Oklahoma. A surprise."

Still no answer.

Ruth took a step forward. "And you?"

"No destination," the girl said at last. "Wherever the train takes us." She laughed. "Wherever I want."

Suddenly, a kind of growl came from the girl's berth. They both turned as the door opened and a man stepped out — middle-aged, for sure, though his sand-colored hair and puckish, delicate features gave him an oddly boyish air. He wore a black satin robe;

he had fine pale skin and dark, exhausted eyes. Absently, he nodded at Ruth. Then he put one hand on the girl's waist and, squeezing her there, pulled her back toward their berth.

"See?" the girl said, slowly closing her eyes. "Isn't it nice?" She reached for the man's hand. With a faint moan, she pressed his fingers into the flesh of her tiny left breast.

Ruth glanced away. Countless thoughts — a vast tidewater — flowed through her brain. At one point it occurred to her to wonder about the status of her own marriage. But she dismissed the question: she was in love.

Then the girl spoke.

"Sorry, Oklahoma." She made a little curtsy, closed the door in front of Ruth's face.

Alone in her berth again, Ruth lay face-up on her cot, sleepless, gazing at the images that danced before her eyes: red lips and tired eyes; her breast, his fingers. She was filled with a new kind of wonder. What *were* the ingredients of physical intimacy? How could they be measured and combined? Spontaneity and unabashed attention-grabbing were required, that much seemed clear, and she vowed that she would be more demonstrative with Hale. More daring, more expressive.

Her love for her husband would never diminish. It would grow with the years, become more fervent, more sensual, more alive. Yes, she would make sure of it.

She twisted on her side, all desire and anticipation, desperate to arrive in Ponca City. "Oh Hale," she whispered, "I love you, I —"

"Hey, no sweat," a voice said.

He touched her.

"We're shipshape on the garbage front. Everything in its right place, just like the doctor ordered."

"Yes?" Ruth blinked and looked up from the corner of an eye. She lay curled on her side, warm and sticky, clutching a toss pillow tight against her stomach.

"Trashwise, I'd have to say we're —" Henry gave her a worried look. "Hey, you okay?"

"Yes, fine," she said, lying. "What else?"

"All right, but you seem a little — what's the word? — kind of worn out. Kind of daydreamy." Tenderly, with palpable concern, his hand found a resting place on top of Ruth's head. "Guess I'll just go on up to my desk now." He hesitated for a moment. "Course, you need anything, just holler."

Ruth reached up and pushed his hand away. She ran her fingers through her hair: it was cut very short, the curls neat and tame.

"Yes, go on then," she said, "I've got things to accomplish here."

"Righto," he said.

"So many things."

"Absolutely."

Henry was still gazing down at her, his eyes troubled, hand in his mouth now, twirling the loose tooth.

"Well?" she said.

"Right as rain. I'm on my way."

He turned and shuffled toward the stairs. After a few steps, though, he stopped and grinned back at her like a little boy.

"Didn't mean you aren't cute," he said. "Just tuckered out."

"*Henry.*"

"Holler loud, I'm always there."

Ruth watched him trudge up the steps.

Cute, she thought. An utterly preposterous notion, of course, but somehow the sound of it gave her a moment of quiet, almost indecent pleasure.

She looked at Hale's diamond watch: already past one-fifteen. Normally, on the afternoon of a White Rabbit day, she'd spend at least an hour calling relatives and friends, never mind the cost. But this was cleaning day, and Luzma was due in less than two hours. Ruth yawned. The thing to do, she decided, was to get in some exercise right away. Once the girl left, it would be too dark to venture outdoors.

Sometimes the days seemed very full.

"Cute." She sighed, and pushed herself up.

Ruth stood on the steps outside her front door, sunglass lenses clipped into place, umbrella swinging from her wrist. It was becoming warm now: silvery waves of heat seemed to snake up from the cement. She lifted her cane, aiming across the courtyard toward the yellow fire hydrant, then lowered her cane and struck out, moving fast. At the hydrant, she took a short breather before aiming the tip of her cane again, drawing a bead on a lemon tree at the end of the path between the tennis court and pool, and continuing on her way. It usually took Ruth forty-five minutes, propelling herself in this cane-pointing fashion, to complete her daily exercise.

Destination Zigzag, she called her walking game. The object was to move from point to point like a boat tacking across the wind, changing course every fifty yards or so, stopping to catch her breath at each Destination along the way. The word "Destination" seemed essential to her; it implied purpose and meaning and maybe even adventure; a simple exercise walk became a daring little voyage. Though Ruth played the game often in the course of each day, the Destination Game had special meaning on her afternoon walks, because these walks began and ended without interruption at her own front door. If, as she stood at her penultimate Destination, Ruth spotted number 24 in her exact line of vision, approximately fifty yards across the courtyard, she could point to her door with relief and resignation, knowing that it was the proper Final Destination.

She almost always followed a route around the same two rows of condominiums, which jutted out from the pool yard like a skinny thumb and index finger rising from a knotted fist.

Alongside the first row, on a strip of land between the condominiums and the visitors' parking lot, was a garden. The garden was done in mixed Spanish Revival and Oriental styles. At its center stood a plaster mission church, about five feet high, surrounded by bamboo fronds. Rodrigo watered the garden twice a day, which kept it a nice lush green; there were a few small palms, a few small bush-animals — elephants, giraffes, flamingos. Rodrigo had been training the animals on molded wires. Like the dog at the front gate, they were flimsy and full of holes, so that as Ruth walked by she could look not only through their bodies, but also straight through their heads.

Swinging her cane with a nice rhythm, feeling jaunty, she made her way past eight front doors to the end of the first row and circled around the last condominium. The road on this back side was a mess. That whole week, men from the gas company had been digging it up, leaving chunks of asphalt and pieces of pipe scattered all over the place. Ruth picked her way cautiously through the debris. Another waste of monthly Association dues — she'd have to help pay for this unsightly and unnecessary project, one she'd never wanted undertaken in the first place. Sighing to herself and shaking her head, she lifted her cane to skirt a deep hole, then walked around an orange plastic warning cone.

Three steps later, she came across a snail in her path. She stooped to examine it for a moment, then squashed it with the end of her cane. Brown and green and slimy, the crushed slug oozed out from its broken shell. It gurgled and frothed, shimmering as it expired in the afternoon sun.

Death: the aftermath was never pleasant.

Ruth winced and resumed her walk.

Only a few months after Hale was buried, she began making preparations to return to California. It was nothing like her dreams of moving home with Hale and the boys. Douglas had already started at a private high school and wanted to stay there, and Carter, a precociously artistic youth with the temper to match, demanded that he be allowed to join his older brother.

"You should leave the boys right here in Washington with me," Mr. Squib, Douglas's headmaster, told Ruth; he added something about talent and stability and decent father figures. And so, one August morning, Ruth said goodbye to her two sons.

She packed all of her things into a trailer, the Mullen's Red Gap luggage trailer that Hale had bought for summer vacations, and set out across the country, alone. She hadn't shed a tear since the day of Hale's funeral. Already she'd discovered both the power and the solace of routine — death had its own relentless requirements — and the journey west was one more bit of business that had to be transacted. So don't think, she told herself. Just drive. Pick out a target on the map and point the car and then later pick out another target farther down the road. In any case, the driving was all she could handle. The heavy trailer terrified her, always swinging wide on turns, and there was no choice but to concentrate on the physics of velocity and mass. She locked both hands on the wheel; she took her time, resting every two or three hours, buying meals in roadside diners and staying in cheap motels at night, where the bath water came out brown. Mile after mile, it was all routine. The tires beneath her, the horizon ahead. Don't think, she'd remind herself, but now and then she'd find herself thinking. Hale lighting the barbecue. Hale talking on the telephone. Hale coming out of the bathroom with a towel around his waist. Hale playing catch with Douglas and Carter on the beach at San Diego. Hale running his fingers through her hair, kissing her on the neck; Hale lifting up her skirt and pulling off her stockings and saying, "Pretty legs, pretty legs." Hale dancing and Hale dying.

One afternoon, somewhere in the flats of New Mexico, she felt a sharp jolt at the back of the car. In the rearview mirror she could see the trailer wobbling back and forth like an untracked roller coaster. Ruth squeezed the steering wheel and tried to brake gently, but after a second the car jerked hard to the left. Almost instantly there was a loud pop, then a grating sound, then something snapped and the trailer went careening into a ravine at the side of the road.

Somehow, struggling, she brought the car to a stop. For a moment she sat perfectly still. There was no traffic at all. No houses or restaurants or gas stations — no one to know whether she lived or died.

All alone, she thought.

No Hale, no God. Just an expansive white nothingness.

The desolation was startling. Sand and mountains and empty road. Sweat dripped from her curls; her blouse stuck to her skin like a piece of damp plastic. Slowly, not quite conscious of her own movements, she reached into her purse for her sunglasses, slipped them on, blotted her face and neck with a tissue. She told herself to stay calm. Sooner or later help had to come — a public highway after all, and things could be worse, and all she had to do was be patient and wait for . . . Right then something seemed to spring open inside her. Partly sorrow, partly rage. It all came out at once: a loud howling sound from the bottom of her lungs. She dropped her forehead against the horn and let it blare.

For the rest of her life it would lurk on the edge of her dreams. A blaring horn. The sound of her own ferocious howling.

"You *idiot*," she wailed, "I *loved* you."

It was her greatest secret: the hurt and horror.

Actively, with startling self-discipline, she purged this anger from her thoughts. She would not remember it again.

She would remember a stretch of empty time passing by, a bland nothingness. Later, when she sat up, absolute silence filled the car. Permanent silence, pure and thick and mortifying. "Well," she murmured, "now what?"

But still only silence.

"Hale?" she said.

She opened the door, stepped out, walked around to the front of the car, and lifted the hood. A plume of steam curled up, licked at her nose and eyes. She leaned back, fanning the air with her hand, then studied the maze of machinery parts: little red wires and little blue wires and several black caps that sizzled when she touched them. For a moment she stood sucking at the tips of her fingers. Then she scowled, pushed the dirty curls from her forehead, backed away from the car, and sat down in the middle of the road.

She didn't budge. Legs crossed, hands folded, she stared willfully at the endless white stripes unfolding toward the mountains.

Ruth would not remember how long she sat there. Maybe two hours, maybe longer. All she would remember with any certainty was the scorching sun, the asphalt burning through her skirt, the long empty desert road. Later, probably much later, a car appeared on the horizon like a tiny sailboat on the waves of a great white ocean. Ruth sat still as it approached. Only when the car had come to a stop did she stand up, straighten her blouse and skirt, and walk over. A man and a woman and three children and a dog were crowded together inside, as cozy and secure as anything Ruth had ever seen in her life.

The man smiled at her. "You okay?"

Abruptly, for the very first time since Hale's death, Ruth permitted herself the great luxury of sarcasm.

"A widow," she said. "I'm just *fine.*"

1:51 P.M.

A plane flew overhead, dragging a banner: "Rock Around the Clock with AM 660!"

Ruth had completed her first loop. She was feeling lightheaded, much more tired than usual, so she paused to catch her breath. Her current choice of a Destination had landed her on the second of three steps that led up to the pool.

The pool yard was surrounded by large glass panels draped with vines of hanging ivy. Fiery red bougainvillea bushes grew just inside the glass; quite often, the midafternoon sunlight reflected off the glass at just such an angle as to cast the red from the bougainvillea up into Ruth's eyes like some great forest fire.

Though anybody could look through the glass as into a giant

fishbowl, to see who was swimming or lying by the pool, the area could be entered only through a black iron gate at the top of the three stairs where Ruth now stood. The gate opened with the usual Auto-Mate card. When the management had campaigned for increased monthly Association dues, they'd promised that this gate, like the fence that surrounded the whole Lagoon, would offer "Cadillac quality" protection. It would keep unwanted lechers from the pool, they said, just as the fence at the highway kept out unwanted vehicles.

Now a hand-printed sign hung from the gate: "Members! We don't Swim in our Toilets. Let's not Pee in our Pool!"

Ruth climbed to the top stair to see if Kaji was inside. She raised a hand to her eyes, shading them from the bright sun, and peered through the iron bars. She saw the figures of several women — hips and halters — but couldn't quite make out who they were. She would not enter to take a closer look, however, since she lived in dread of somehow ending up locked inside. For not only did you have to insert a card to get in, but you had to insert one to get back out — and what if she dropped hers in the water as she walked beside the pool, or what if someone took it from her by mistake as she sat watching the people swim? She worried about this constantly: locked up in her own pool yard, dying of sunstroke or starvation.

Behind her, a horn suddenly blared. Ruth cringed, thrown off balance. For an instant she was transported back to that empty desert highway. "Help," she said quietly, to nobody but herself, "I'm a widow."

"Hey, Grammy!" someone yelled.

Ruth teetered slightly, pressing her nose between two of the iron bars and looking slowly from one sunbathing figure to the next. Then the voice came louder:

"Grammy! Over *here*, in the parking lot. Hang on a minute, I'll drive over."

It was Karen. Ruth's heart leapt.

The girl was driving a white convertible; as she pulled up alongside the curb, Ruth noticed that her hair was a mess, as usual, and still that terrible silver-blond color: she'd taken to dye since turning twenty-nine. She was wearing bright red shorts and a green tank top, which reminded Ruth, in a flash, that it was almost Christmas.

Ruth walked down to the bottom step, leaned into the car to offer her cheek, then tapped at the white door with the tip of her cane. "Where'd you get *this* contraption?"

Karen reached out for Ruth's hand. "Bought it myself, just last week. Mike helped, of course."

"Mike?"

"Oh, stop that. Mike-the-husband — you talked to him on the phone this morning."

"Well, yes, of course," Ruth said. "Him." She saw no point in pursuing the subject. "I guess you're sorry about this morning."

"Sorry?"

"You know, Karen."

"What? I was a little sleepy, that's all." She tucked her hair behind her ears, pulled a long strand of neon-green gum from her mouth. "I mean, really, it was barely sunrise, for Pete's sake. What do you expect? Anyway, I tried to reach you later but nobody answered."

"Tried when?"

"Around ten."

Ruth thought it over. She'd been downtown then. And Henry, no doubt, had been asleep — he wouldn't have heard a siren, let alone the phone.

"Well, I accept the apology," she said. "But in the future, you might try to remember an old lady like me needs all the good luck she can get. I would have won, you know, if you'd answered the phone yourself."

"Won?"

"You know."

"What? Oh, right." Karen laughed. "White Rabbit."

Ruth cringed as if the blow had been physical. "Fine," she said. "A repeat offense." She stared into the space behind Karen's head. Then she tapped the car door with her cane three times. "Go ahead and park, and come walk with me. I've got one more loop."

Karen bit off the strand of gum, rolled it into a little ball, flicked it over the windshield. "Can't stay," she said. "I'm meeting Mike down at Five Crowns. Just wanted to let you know I'll be stopping over later — be back as soon as we're done with lunch."

Ruth raised her eyebrows. "Five Crowns? Just how does the maniac make a living these days?"

"A schoolteacher, Grammy."

"Schoolteacher? At Five Crowns?"

Karen laughed and rolled her eyes. "He's been saving it up or something, Grammy, I don't know. The point is, I'll be back in a couple of hours. Can you remember *that?*"

Ruth clucked her tongue. The girl had always been wiry and nervous, but today she seemed particularly tense. "Just asking, sweetheart, no need to get excited." She gave her right knee a pop, squared up her shoulders. "Anyway, why meet him way down here? Aren't there enough overpriced restaurants in Los Angeles?"

"We'll talk about it later, okay? I have to run — supposed to be there at two, he'll be furious if I'm late."

"Furious?" Ruth said.

"Well, I didn't mean —"

Ruth snorted. "What is it with this man? After all that non-sense he's been up to lately, running away on you like that, you're awfully eager to accommodate his schedule, not to mention his other requirements. If you want my opinion, you should just —"

"Not now," Karen said. "I already promised you, I'll be right back."

Ruth shrugged and adjusted her glasses. "Fine then, it's your life," she said, "but I've had some experience with men myself. Remember what I told you about old Frank Deeds? Used to work myself into quite a tizzy, trying to be all gussied up and punctual for those shabby weekend trysts of ours. And you know what good it did me."

"Frank Deeds was an ass."

"I beg your pardon?"

"You heard me."

Ruth forced a small, threadbare smile. She stared down at the curb, tapping the cement with her cane. What was the point in talking if the girl was so closed-minded? Frank had *not* been an ass. Thirteen years older than Hale, a man full of worldly news and advice, he was one of the best-known lawyers in Washington, D.C. Ruth and Hale had met him their first year there, when they had their place on Nevada Avenue and Frank and his wife were living up the hill on Oliver Street.

Still gazing at the curb, Ruth shook her head. "Hardly an ass, dear. Quite a catch, in fact."

"Oh, right," Karen said.

Ruth ignored her. "Very debonair and quick-witted, if you follow my meaning. Not to mention expensive suits. He used to come over, bottle of Scotch in hand, and he and Hale would be up half the night, trading silly stories from work or chortling about the latest antics of Frank's wife, Myrna. I used to overhear them, you understand, I never got involved directly —" Ruth felt herself slip away for a moment. Like switching TV channels, like plucking ancient reruns from some swirling electric time-air — *Time!* Hale had cried. *Right there! So much time!* — and the time-screen lighted up with ghostly speckled static, then shapes and voices, then grainy episodes of a sad old comedy that kept spinning itself out forever — Frank stealing glances at her ballerina legs, Frank opening doors for her with a gentlemanly flourish. The night she'd accidentally overheard him discussing his thoughts on love, and how he'd given her a wink and a wide rakish smirk that made her turn away. And then of course the time when he tried to put his tongue in her hair, and the time he almost . . .

"Grammy, are you *there*?"

"Pardon me?"

"Welcome back."

Ruth pretended not to hear. "In any event," she said, "the man did have his faults. Too many hormones. But he was earnest in his own way — and he saved my life the winter your grandfather died." She tapped the car door. "Which, I do believe, is more than we can say about this flashy man of yours, who almost kills you himself, deserts you, runs off in the middle of a marriage, and then thinks he can make it all up with a fast car or two."

Karen laughed. "Volkswagens aren't exactly hot rods, Grammy." She started the engine.

Ruth stepped back and rearranged her shoulders. She didn't want to make the girl angry or press her too hard — she might not return at all. The thought terrified her.

"All right, sweetheart," she sniffed, lifting the tip of her cane and turning to pick out a Destination near the row she was about to circle. "I do miss you."

It hadn't been necessary for Frank to confess his marital problems a great many times before Ruth began to feel awkward when she met Myrna at the market, or when the four of them went out for dinner together. "How lucky we are," Ruth would whisper to Hale, nudging him under the table with her foot while Frank and Myrna argued over what wine they'd order or who would drive home at the end of the evening.

Later, predictably, Frank and Myrna ended up in divorce court, and Frank left his firm and moved out to San Diego. He went on Ruth's recommendation, or so he'd said when he left. He never wrote. At one point, Hale heard word that the man's life had gone downhill a bit — too many women, too much gambling, too many drunken jaunts down to Mexico.

In any case, Frank returned to Washington the winter Hale died. The day after the funeral, feeling like wood inside, barely able to function, Ruth had phoned him on impulse: she remembered picking up Hale's address book and reaching out to dial the number in San Diego. "I'll be there," he'd said. "Day after tomorrow, I'll be there."

Day after tomorrow.

That was Frank.

To his credit, of course, he did eventually take charge of things. Escorted her to dinner. Made her eat and talked reassuring talk and encouraged her to wash her hair and change her clothes and pluck the stray hairs from her chin. That first evening he helped her draw up a budget, went over Hale's investments and property holdings.

For nearly three weeks Frank stayed on in Washington just to keep her company. Or so he claimed. Motives aside, Ruth couldn't have made do without him. It was touching, really, the way he sat comforting Carter and counseling him about school; he began looking into prospects for selling the house; he spent whole afternoons listening to Ruth's worries, sipping coffee and nodding thoughtfully and coming up with crisp, lawyerly suggestions. At the same time there was a funny feeling to it all. If, as he often did, he took her hand as he tried to console her, he would squeeze her fingers a fraction too hard. He seemed overly eager for her return to California. And once or twice, in the middle of the night, she'd opened her eyes to find him standing above her, mumbling to himself and gesticulating.

Finally, one rainy afternoon, Frank made his position clear. The roof above Hale's old office had begun to leak, and water was streaming across the cracked ceiling, dripping off at various places to form puddles all over the floor. Ruth scurried about the room, strategically positioning buckets and bowls. She gathered together some sponges and rags and was just bending to mop the hardwood paneling when she felt Frank's fingers on her back.

The skin seemed to curl around her bones. "I thought you were spreading that tarp on the roof —"

"My love," he said, "my great dear love —"

" — cleaning leaves out of the rain gutter —"

"It's been love, Ruthie, from the moment I first put eyes on you. Knock-down hammer-hold love."

Ruth knelt there on the floor, her bottom in the air, drips of water splashing against her forehead. "Me and fifteen other women," she said, and tried to laugh. "Maybe *fifty* others."

Frank shrugged his shoulders. "Very true," he said. "I've had my share, that's for sure, but now it's different. I mean, I've never felt like this before, not even close. It's love, Ruthie. The kind that wakes a tired man up."

Ruth turned to look at him, startled but also half amused. Carter was due home from school at any minute.

"Frank, be serious," she said. "I have two grown children. And you're practically old enough to be their grandfather." What she did not say, of course, was that he'd been her husband's good friend — maybe best friend — and that Hale had been in the grave barely a month.

"You're right," Frank said, "except I've felt this forever. Known this forever. I was born knowing it, and I'll always know it. Can't you even . . . Can't you feel that?"

Ruth could not even *guess* what she felt, let alone know it forever. Beyond a certain point she simply wasn't capable of thought. Frank was a good man, no doubt, and if he really meant any of this, he'd wait for her. She stood up and pulled away from him, moving to another puddle across the room.

"Back to work," she said.

She was panting as she passed a diamond-shaped orange construction sign next to number 39, the last condominium in the row. She felt terribly lightheaded — her vision had gone fuzzy at the edges — and for a time she could not recall how she had arrived at this particular spot on the planet. Her internal compass seemed out of whack. No true north. She put one foot in front of the other, watching her sandals trudge along like a pair of separate creatures; they no longer seemed attached to her feet, and as she rounded the corner of number 39 there was the queer sensation that she'd lost authority over her entire body — everything. The past seemed to steer her. She walked slowly, trying to regain control, wondering if it was even worth the effort, until suddenly, inexplicably, a white chalk circle appeared on the asphalt before her. She took a half-step forward. Inside the circle, at its very center, was a soupy pile of dog feces. Ruth stared for a moment, surprised. The management had *finally* done something useful with her monthly dues. A brilliant idea, actually, to send someone out to draw a warning circle around this mess. She smiled to herself, making a mental note to congratulate the managers, then she lifted her cane and gingerly navigated around the circled-in poop.

In a way this incident reassured her. There were real things in the world, things you could touch, things the imagination could never distort. Things that demanded attention, even action. Things that — whoever saw them, from whatever angle — always looked the same.

Ruth took another breather after arriving at the rear of number 39, placing her hand on the condo's wall, swinging her right knee in and out, loosening it up. She blinked several times to be sure her vision had cleared. Then stiffly, feeling the heat, she pulled back her shoulders, aimed fifty yards ahead toward the bumper of a silver BMW, and continued down the smooth black asphalt.

Arriving in Los Angeles, that summer after Hale's death, Ruth moved in with her mother and father, into the same upstairs bedroom she'd used as a girl. Nothing at all had changed. The same quilted bedspread, the same white dresser with pink knobs, the same wooden trunk below the window. Fresh poppies and marigolds peeked up from a vase on the windowsill. Something about the flowers, and the unchanging sameness of things, made Ruth cry.

At dinner that night she was still crying. It went on through the main course and into dessert — she couldn't stop — and then her mother began crying too, sniffling and dabbing at her eyes with a napkin.

Ruth's father tapped a plate with his fork. "What *is* this?" He looked at Lydia, then at Ruth. "All right, of course, I know it's an awful time," he said. "Hale's death and all. And I'm not opposed to regular sadness. Except it's been five months now. Almost six. Sooner or later people have to pull themselves together. The truth is — don't take this wrong — the truth is, you've got certain obligations. Responsibilities like everybody else. Your two boys, Douglas and Carter, sometimes I think you've completely forgotten them."

Ruth stared at her strawberry shortcake. "They're in school. They don't need me. *Nobody* does."

"Don't be ridiculous."

"But it's true, I'm just a —"

Across the table, Lydia released a loud, breathy sob. Ruth handed over a fresh napkin. Oddly, her mother's crying made Ruth feel firmer inside, almost hard, as if someone else had stepped forward to take up the exhausting burden of emotion.

"So right now," her father was saying, "right now you should try rejoining the world. Find things to do. A hobby, maybe, or a good job." He gave her a short, hopeful smile. "Think about it. Isn't there some — how do I phrase this? — some *interest* you've always wanted to pursue?"

Lydia blew her nose and looked up. "The piano," she said. "That's a possibility. More piano lessons."

"Great," Ruth said, "I'll play my own funeral march."

Tears bubbled up in Lydia's eyes again. "Don't even suggest such things. What about art? Watercolors? Ballet? Or maybe — maybe give gardening a try. That little patch out back where it's all weeds, I'll bet you could grow some absolutely spectacular tulips there."

"Or I could chop off my head."

"Darling."

"Eat steak knives."

Her father reached across the table and took Lydia's hand. "Ruthie, please. No need to take this out on your mother and me. We just want what's best."

"Water torture. Join a convent."

"Nonsense," her mother said. "You aren't Catholic."

Ruth looked down at her shortcake. What did they know? Her parents still had each other. More than anything now, Ruth was simply and crushingly lonely — that wild howling desert loneliness — loneliness that made her skin dry up and her bones go brittle.

Besides, a widowed woman in her late thirties should not be living in her father's house. She should die.

The idea tempted her.

In bed that night she tried to make it happen. Not one more breath — never. Her face went hot, her lungs itched, her throat seemed to clog up with a substance like thick wet tar. Don't breathe, she told herself. *Never.* A few seconds later, when the dizziness came, she found herself imagining her own pale corpse. Buried in Hale's coffin. Wrapped around him, snuggled tight, cozy and peaceful and happy and dead.

She woke up early the next morning. Alive, of course, which she took as an omen.

That same afternoon she enrolled at the Sawyer School, where for three months she studied shorthand and typing. In late October she secured a secretarial position at a doctor's office over on Figueroa Street. It was a godsend. To her surprise, she actually enjoyed the work, enjoyed fussing over patients, enjoyed the way so many people suddenly needed her — like that pregnant girl who came out of the examination room crying, like the poor vagabond who panicked when he saw his bill.

For half a year, Ruth was content.

Then Frank Deeds showed up again, with his absurd notion that happiness was always possible.

It was a pleasant time, for the most part. Like a convalescence. At least twice a month, Frank would come up on the train from

San Diego and take her out to lunch or a show. They laughed together, they talked, they had fun. Ruth could almost feel herself mending. The man was a little too smooth, maybe, but he was urbane and well mannered and handsome, even charming. A man who had once rescued her, who had literally led her by the hand out of that paralyzing depression.

Other things, too. Those wonderfully expensive suits. The way he used words. "The Lord's honest truth," he'd tell her, "you're like an aged French wine, perfect tannins, perfect nose, more exquisite with every passing day."

Talk like this made Ruth's stomach flutter — she couldn't help herself — but at the same time it bothered her when Frank issued his standard pleas before boarding the train to go back. Always the same lopsided grin, the same artful pitch: "Hop on, Ruthie, San Diego or bust, we'll have ourselves a ball." She'd laugh a little, and come up with an excuse, then go home to hide. The man scared her. He pushed too hard — too certain, too passionate. Now and then, though, she was frightened by her own late-night stirrings, certain needs and desires. She'd stare into the dark, feeling a vague guilt, remembering all the promises she'd made to Hale, things like faithfulness, and devotion, and how she'd love him forever.

There was also the problem of Frank's reputation.

"Don't fool yourself," her father warned her one evening. "I know the type. Jetting down to Mexico. Drunken binges and dice tables. Probably dilly-dallying with every female in San Diego."

"Well, I suppose," Ruth said quietly. "But he loves *me*."

And that was something.

Yes, it was.

Her father huffed. "Then why doesn't the man act like it? Straighten out and stop splashing money around like toilet water? Because he's an ass, that's what. He's Frank Deeds."

"Listen, Daddy, you don't even —"

"A donkey. A downtown dandy."

Ruth inserted some stiffness into her voice. "You're not even listening. I'm the one who's stalling. I'm the one who can't agree to a serious commitment. If you want the truth, the real truth, he's crazy about me. Wants me to visit him in San Diego."

She hesitated.

"And if you want more truth, I'm going."

2:07 P.M.

Ruth leaned heavily on her cane, feeling faint. She'd made it around the second row of condominiums and was back at the pool. Yet something wasn't quite right — her heart was pounding, filaments of sparkly white light moved in ribbons across her field of vision. For a few seconds she wondered if she might pass out, or something worse, but then, just as suddenly, she felt perfectly fine again. Her pulse slowed, the waves of light were gone. Never mind, she thought. She could walk farther than people seemed to realize. Despite prevailing attitudes, especially here in California, old age did not necessarily equate with infirmity. Even Henry still managed to cross and recross the highway each morning — with an armful of groceries, for God's sake. And she could certainly outwalk *that* fumblebum. She'd do an extra loop, this time on the path that circled the pool. She raised her cane, squinted at a lamppost near the far end of the pool, set off with a clipped, determined stride.

Her whole life was about to explode.

July 26, 1947. Like riding dynamite — bang, a new Ruth — and the train wheels had the hot fizzling sound of a lighted fuse. Ruth watched the ocean and houses and thirsty brown hills roll by, picturing Frank's face, imagining a weekend of dancing and dinners and, if things went well, almost certainly a proposal of marriage. It was a life pivot, she told herself, one of those either-or moments that can turn things around forever. It was also a declaration of her own serious intent.

To keep things proper, and to protect herself, she'd be staying with her Aunt Elizabeth. Not the ideal situation, but at least the blast would be cushioned a bit: somebody to talk with, somebody she trusted and treasured. How long since they'd last seen each other? Three years? Probably closer to four. No matter, though, because they were like sisters, and time couldn't change a thing like that. In ten minutes they'd have their shoes kicked off; they'd be talking about their children and old times and the latest radio shows and the men in their lives. Mostly men. Mostly Frank. How she cared for him, maybe even loved him, but how in a funny way she was also apprehensive. How his words were always so beautiful and convincing, but how his behavior sometimes wasn't. How he'd sworn to be faithful to her, but how in the end she couldn't quite trust him.

Men.

She took several deep breaths, thinking, *Men.* They could blow you to pieces.

At four o'clock, when the train pulled in, Elizabeth was there on the platform, dressed in a red leather jacket and skirt, waving a feathered green hat. Same as ever, Ruth thought happily. The woman was sixty-seven years old but still lively, still slim and smooth-skinned and bristling with sharp arrowlike angles. Still eccentric, too.

"A drink!" Elizabeth yelled. "First a drink, then down to basics. Sex talk! Sex, sex, sex — nothing else!"

An hour later they were sitting at Elizabeth's kitchen table. A box of crackers, a bottle of sherry.

"Sexwise," Elizabeth said grimly, "it's chronic drought."

She pulled on a pair of long black gloves. Drinking gloves, she called them. With a grunt, sighing heavily, she folded her legs beneath her and spent a few minutes recapping her last several years in San Diego, the ups and downs. Almost entirely downs, she said. Maybe it was a function of age: after sixty, things drooped. In any case, up until recently her days had been massively and ferociously boring, pure drudgery. "The usual old-lady crud," she said. "Shopping, farting, teaching voice to little boys without penises."

Elizabeth burped and flashed a smile.

"Until *recently*, mind you." She winked. "Right now, just maybe, things might be looking up. Glorious things. Big hot ripe manly things, if you catch the innuendo."

"I do."

"Oh, I'm quite *sure* you do. Another drink?"

"Certainly."

"To manliness," said Elizabeth. "To firmness and solidity in all its enticing variety."

Ruth couldn't help smoothing down her skirt, grinning. "Immensity, too," she said. "Immense and exploding things, to be precise."

It was the sherry, no doubt — Ruth was shocked by her own tongue. She glanced down at Hale's wristwatch.

"Speaking of which," she said, "I'll be meeting someone over the marina this evening . . . and I'll need time to get myself . . . It's important."

"A *sex* appointment!"

"Not quite, but it's still —"

Elizabeth grinned and thumped the table with her fist. "No spice, no dice. Just cancel. Let the man squirm."

Ruth began to protest, then felt a smile come on. A postponement might give Frank a few things to ponder. "Right back," she said. She stood up, moved to the telephone, dialed quickly and left a short message with his secretary. It took only a moment.

As she sat down again, Elizabeth giggled. "Beautifully done. Elegant. You've got the worm wiggling."

"Not this one," Ruth said. "Anyhow, I'm free until tomorrow." She smiled at her aunt, uneasy, slightly tipsy. Her throat ached. "May I suggest one more round?"

"Indeed!" said Elizabeth. "Tiny nip, great big zip!"

By dusk they were feeling fine. Later, when full dark settled in, they found sweaters and moved to the porch and rambled on like a pair of teenagers. They'd forgotten about dinner. Old times, Ruth thought, that same togetherness. She raised her glass.

"Auntie," she said, "what if I told you I've been lonely?"

"Well, of course you have. And me too — more than you know." Elizabeth paused. "But what if I told you it can end?"

"And what if I asked how?"

Elizabeth smiled. It was a tender, wistful smile. "What if you did? And what if I were to say, 'Ruthie, there's something I've been dying to tell you, something beautiful'?"

"What if I guessed?" Ruth said. "What if I guessed love?"

"Ah, well. Then you'd win."

Elizabeth topped off their glasses and leaned back and explained that for several years a certain gentleman had been her constant companion, though till now she'd never mentioned it to a soul. Because the gentleman was somewhat younger than she. And because, frankly, there was still a great deal to be learned about him. At first they'd met only for lunch, or to go out to a show, but for some time now — was it appropriate to say this? yes, of course, they were both adults, weren't they? — for the past few months this certain gentleman had been calling on her most evenings, at home, and not always leaving before sunrise. Even so, it wasn't at all the way it sounded. Granted, the man had something of a reputation, and people might find his intentions with an older woman suspect, but in fact it was she who'd been avoiding any formal commitment. Especially after those horrendous experiences with Charlton and Stephen. Twice burned, forever shy, yes? So as a matter of course she was leery, to say the least, and always would be, but in recent weeks and months her opinion of men in general had been raised substantially. Ridiculous, she knew, but she was in love. Floating. Just like the happy young woman she'd been back in the early days. "Maybe it's old-fashioned prudishness," she said, "but the fact is, I've been too embarrassed even to talk about it. Not to anyone."

"Embarrassed?" said Ruth.

"Well, naturally. Your mother, for instance — who knows what she'd think?"

Ruth shrugged. "She'd be thrilled for you. Excited and thrilled." She gave her aunt's arm a squeeze. "So tell me. What if I asked his name?"

"Oh, I wouldn't dare say."

"What if I insisted?"

"What if?" said Elizabeth, and her eyes seemed to fill with something soft and youthful. "In that event, perhaps, I might be forced to confide in you. Mr. Deeds, I might say. Mr. Franklin Marshall Deeds."

Ruth's ears warmed.

"Frank?"

"Well, yes, exactly."

"Frank Deeds?"

"As in reeds and beads."

Ruth missed a breath. For a second her eyes blurred; her heart thumped so rapidly she feared she was having some sort of attack. She dug her fingernails into the palm of her left hand until it hurt.

"Whatever's wrong, dear?" Eyes narrowed, Elizabeth bent forward. "I hope you're not offended. Really, I was so sure you'd understand. And I *do* know you'd like him. Absolutely positive."

Ruth nodded. "You said Frank?"

"Precisely correct. Rhymes with sank."

Ruth attempted a smile, pushed herself up. "The sherry, it's making my head spin. To be honest, I'm reeling. I'd better lie down awhile."

Elizabeth stood and took her by the arm. "No problem, dear, just too much zip, I'm sure."

"Franklin Marshall Deeds?"

"You'll adore him."

It was a bad night. Odd dreams, odd shapes and colors. At one point she jerked up in the dark and found herself praying a laugh-aloud kind of prayer. She giggled and folded her hands. She said, "Oh, God." She giggled again. It occurred to her, almost surely for the first time, that even the most banal of human lives was ripe with the ingredients for some ongoing cosmic soap opera, coincidence teetering upon coincidence, absurdity upon absurdity, all the ludicrous episodes unfolding for the midafternoon delectation of a worn-out and dull-witted Housewife God.

Early the next morning, when Ruth arrived at the marina, the maggot named Frank Deeds was leaning against a wooden railing, back to the water, facing her. He grinned and reached for her arm. "I was worried," he said. "My God, when I got your message . . . I mean, hell, I thought you'd lost your nerve." He adjusted the sleeves of his blue worsted suit. "But hey, you look wonderful, better than ever. Which is lucky, because I've brought my camera."

"It wasn't nerves," Ruth said, "it was integrity."

"I don't follow," said Frank.

"Integrity. Exactly how the dictionary defines it, not that you'd know or care, not that you'd have the slightest little moral inkling." She almost laughed but didn't. When the absurdities were your own, humor was hard to locate. "Frank as in stank, Deeds as in weeds."

"Yes? I don't quite get it."

Ruth rebuffed that with her shoulders. She could not immediately say anything more — in fact, did not know what *could* be said — and so after a long vacuumed-out second, when Frank suggested they go for a stroll on the beach, she simply nodded and followed along. For several minutes they moved in silence. The beach was deserted, waves and rocks and white sand.

"A fact," she finally said. "I know about Elizabeth."

Frank smiled and reached for her hand, but she jerked away.

"Elizabeth. Remember her?"

"Well, listen, do you mean —"

"My *aunt*," Ruth said. "You're dating her."

"Dating?" Frank turned and grasped her by both shoulders, hard. "Now, come on, let's be reasonable here. There's a problem, I admit. I do admit that. You see? But then at the same time . . . Put it this way. Where there's a problem, there's a way around. An old lawyer's saw. Got a guilty client, you plead his ass, you try to settle, you do some bargaining and reduce the charges and try to . . . God, Ruthie, you're gorgeous when you're upset. You know that? Like a poor little kitten that's lost its ball of string." He chuckled and made a light purring sound. "Well, okay. Fair's fair — you know. But I wouldn't exactly call it dating. Plenty of other words."

Ruth stared at him. "My aunt, for God's sake. She's in love with you. And I thought —"

"There, you *see?* Reduced charges. It wasn't pure sex, nothing seamy."

"No," Ruth said, "it was sick."

"An improvement. Better than seamy, I'd say." He gave her earlobe a tug. "And like you said, she is *your* aunt. A wonderful family."

"Sick and disgusting — especially me. I almost believed in you, I almost did, and that's the sickest thing of all . . . I thought just maybe you loved me or cared about me or *some*thing." Ruth looked at him for an instant, then turned and walked over to a large black rock, where she sat down and dropped her face into her hands. The absurdities were multiplying. How could her instincts be so out of whack? She imagined that Housewife God looking on from her heavenly La-Z-Boy recliner — teary-eyed, no doubt — a purple housedress and curlers and a small midafternoon Scotch.

Right away, Frank hurried after her. "Don't be ridiculous, Ruthie, I do love you. Honest to God. A million times I told you that, maybe two million, but hell, let's face it, you've kept me waiting over two years. See the point? I've got — you know — I've got needs."

"Deeds, needs," Ruth muttered. "*Seeds.*"

"Right," he said, and grinned. "I guess that's the plain truth of it." He kneeled down in the sand. "Look, I'm too old for games. If you can forgive me, we'll put an end to all this silly waiting. Right now."

Ruth closed her eyes. She felt something move in her stomach, something moist and slippery. "How do you mean that?"

"You know."

"I don't. I don't know anything."

"There's this institution called marriage." He smiled a charming Frank Deeds smile. "First things first, though."

"That's my breast!"

"For sure," he said.

Later, when Ruth was sitting on the rock again, Frank took out his camera and snapped a picture. Gently then, he kissed her. "This is a solemn promise. I'll carry that photo right here in my pocket — right next to my heart — until you marry me."

2:24 P.M.

She was back at the entrance to the pool.

Her lungs ached, she couldn't catch her breath, then a pair of hammers seemed to crack against her temples. Damn, she thought, pushed too far, too long. Countless fingers seemed to seize her by the throat — they wouldn't let go. Her cane slipped away. A flood of white specks came down on her, like that TV static, and then she was falling. No chance to yell. Her right knee buckled and she toppled to her side and the sky went to a lovely shade of red.

Her eyes — open or shut?

There was still that gorgeous red in the sky, a shimmering spilt-paint red, and now it swirled into an animal shape. Like a rabbit, she thought, yes indeed, a rabbit in the sky, a giant red rabbit spouting up bright red foam. Where was everybody? Couldn't anyone see her from the pool yard? What about Kaji — wouldn't she notice and come running? Or had those goddamn gates locked them all inside? Suddenly, out of the red light, she heard a tremendous bang. And then a dog came racing at her, a wild red dog. It came storming out of Doggie Canyon, ears drawn back, and there were more bangs and more dogs and more rabbits and everything was blending with everything else.

She had loved to dance, and they were dancing *ladadada* . . .

and God! how she loved him

and she had never felt like this before, and she could not catch her breath, and her hands jumped all around . . .

Hale! she said

so full of love and yearning.

But then with Frank she had felt like that again

and who was this man anyway? and he most certainly was not to be trusted

but all the same

it was so much the same and Jesus! she thought this might just keep happening, and who knew where she'd end up.

But anyway he said he loved her

a widow alone and forty years old

while her hands twitched and waved

like one hand did not know what the other hand was doing

like one hand could not hold the other hand still.

The sky went blue, the swirling stopped. Her hands steadied, and she was able to open the silver locket at her neck, dumping out her pills onto the asphalt. One came to rest near her nose. She licked her index finger, pressed it down on top of the tiny white pill. It passed The Test.

She put it under her tongue. Her insides dissolved.

Some time passed — how much, she didn't know — and she was able to crawl to the steps that led up to the pool. She sat on the bottom step for a while, listened to the seagulls screaming from the ocean.

When her pulse slowed, she pulled back her shoulders and stood up.

She pointed the tip of her cane in the direction of number 24. Which was what she needed now, a Destination that mattered.

XII

XI   I

X   II

P A R T   T W O
~~~~~~~~~~~~~~~~~~~~~~~~~~~~~

IX   III

VIII   IV

VII   V

VI

3:10 P.M.

"WELL, I *did* it," Ruth was telling herself, "I overexerted myself, just walked too far." She sucked in a breath and eased herself down on the toilet. Her panty girdle and slacks lay in two wads on the bathroom floor, soaking wet. "Yes, yes, obviously," she muttered, "just too much for one day."

It occurred to her then that she had forgotten to take her third Cardizem. And here was the consequence. A horrible attack, which she'd survived, only to wet her pants the minute she walked through her own bathroom door.

For a moment she had the curious sensation of being watched. All those photographs on the walls, all those faces from her cluttered past. Quietly, breathing cautiously, she lifted her head and looked from one set of eyes to the next. Her high school graduating class. The entire Oil and Gas Leasing Division of the U.S. Geological Survey. Douglas's medical school class and her granddaughter's third-grade class. Walt and Lydia on the front lawn of their house in the Wilshire District; her own little Carter on a cliff above Woods Cove, flying a kite; Frank Deeds winking at her above his button-down collar; Hale grinning happily, decked out in Navy blues. And all the others. Nora at a sorority picnic. Cousins Margaret and McGregor building castles in a sandbox — Ruth herself standing to the side, face half averted, watching the children to be sure they wouldn't swallow sand.

A ghost gallery, she thought.

Hundreds of eyes looking on with dour pity at her wet pants and humiliation.

In a way, too, as Ruth squatted there, it almost seemed as if the eyes were regarding her with a kind of expectation: of mutual sympathy, perhaps; of a generosity far greater than any she was accustomed to feeling.

She studied the photograph directly in front of her, the one of her high school class. Lips pursed, head tilted back, she peered down her nose at row upon row of children standing quietly with folded hands, until, beneath her scrutiny, all their tiny white fingers began to pucker up and ooze and melt away like hot wax, the wrists liquefying, and then the arms, and then — Ruth was jittery now, breathing in quick gasps — and then the entire photograph began to bubble and go frothy like milk on a too hot burner, each small head dissolving before her, each little chin and mouth, and the ears too, and then whole sheets of flesh curdling and peeling back, until at last Ruth could no longer recognize a single face, not even her own. When she squinted, the figures in the front row went to fluid and dripped away altogether. Ruth removed her glasses. She rubbed her eyes, sniffed the air. A musty scent of smoke and wet soil and molten leaves filled her nostrils.

A warm breeze swished through the tiny bathroom.

What's this? a voice thought at her.

Ruth's glasses slipped from her hand and fell between her legs into the toilet bowl.

She spread her thighs and peered down into the water.

You, thought the voice, which was high and chuckly, *who are you?*

The chuckly voice then in fact chuckled.

"Why, it's me. It's Ruthie Caster."

Looking down, she recognized the liquid warp of her own reflection in the bluish water of the toilet bowl. She pushed up her right sleeve, pulled her legs farther apart, and reached deep down into the bowl, grunting as she stirred the water, until her arm was wet halfway up to the elbow.

You!

Ruth's heart did an acrobatic tumble.

"Well, of course it's me. Mrs. Ruth Caster Armstrong. Ruth Caster Armstrong Hubble." Her fingers brushed up against the glasses, which were down at the very bottom of the bowl, near the mouth of that mysterious black tunnel leading to the sea.

Ah, the little voice thought at her. *A mistake, then.*

Ruth grabbed the glasses, straightened up, and slid back on the toilet seat, telling herself to ignore this preposterous voice which she both recognized and did not recognize, which she had never asked to hear in the first place. One more intrusion. And in her own private sanctuary. She shook the water from her fingers, slipped the glasses back onto her nose.

Mistake, mistake, the voice thought at her again. *We're late, we're late! Important date!*

Ruth glanced furtively around the bathroom: every photograph was blurry and jumbled. Somewhere, somebody sniggered.

A bad fall, but falls ain't all.

"What the hell is this?"

She put her right hand into her hair, rubbed her scalp. Amazingly, her skin was warm and wet, as if she had a fever. When she lowered her hand to examine it, her fingertips were bright red. She blinked several times, unnerved, and rolled down her sleeve.

A chippery laugh filled the room.

Without thinking, Ruth again put her hand into her hair. She withdrew it immediately: an enormous blister, the size of a quarter, spread out across her palm.

Clock goes tick, just a nick.

Ruth felt a surge of real panic. "Excuse me. Please quit singing like that, I can't understand a word. Please just leave me alone."

The voice thought a little chuckle at her.

The voice thought, *Sorry to say, no luck today.*

"What?"

Hippity-hop!

"Now, sir, I'm not about to —"

The chuckly voice chortled. It thought, *That's the game! Hippity-hop! Time, Ruthie. Watch it. Zip ziiiip, zip ziiiip, zip zip ziiiip!* Another chuckle.

Ruth squirmed on the toilet seat. Briefly, it crossed her mind that she was engaged in a dialogue with some secret part of herself, the secret howling part, the blank empty desert part, the part that understood things that should not be understood.

She addressed this possibility.

"What do you mean, zip zip? What is this zip? What time is it, anyway?"

She raised her arm, glanced at the face of Hale's wristwatch. The numbers were so blurry she couldn't see a thing. "Now how am I supposed to read that?" she asked herself. She began to fiddle with the winding device, worried that some kind of damage had been done. Just then the image of Hale's face bobbed up before her. God, how she loved him! The joy of her life! She would put aside all other obligations, all routine endeavors, and devote herself to him; the universe, and time itself, would stand still in celebration.

Ruth pulled down her sleeve, fingers trembling.

Itty-bitty! Ruth's self-pity!

Getting late!

Surf's up!

The voice thought these things at her. A distinctly rabbity voice, for that matter.

Ruth once again directed her gaze to the photograph in front of her, which was blurrier than ever.

The voice thought at her, *Time goes ticky, don't be picky!* And then, *Nubby-hubby Henry! Compassion's the fashion! Karen, too, she's feeling blue!*

Ruth stole another glance around the tiny bathroom. Nothing at all except for that warm summer-seeming breeze. With a sigh she looked back down into the toilet bowl, where her own reflection gently swayed and stirred. "For God's sake," she muttered. "Almost a hundred years old."

An enormous guffaw came rolling at her from somewhere both close and far away.

Surf's up!

Ziiippp! Oh, where have you gone, charming Ruthie? A tisket, a tasket! Hippity-hop!

People steeple!

People here, people now!

Hear that chime? Now's the time!

Don't be cruel, off that stool!

Ruth put a hand to her forehead. When she drew it away, the palm and fingertips were still a bright blistered red.

"Well fine," she murmured.

There was a crackly, snapping sound like a telephone disconnecting.

Can't stop, gotta hop!

"Whiiiite Rabbit," called Luzma, "Whiiiite Rabbit!" and she swung the door open and stepped into the bathroom.

"Dios mío," she said, "poor Ruthie."

The girl used a foot to stir the wad of wet clothing on the floor. "Little accident, I guess."

Ruth looked up blankly. "Not at all," she said. "A damn big accident, obviously."

Luzma reached down and gave Ruth's shoulder a reassuring squeeze. The girl had on a bright yellow blouse, tight black jeans, spike-heeled sandals. She always wore the same jeans with that fancy designer label, which pulled up in little white lines from the zipper to her hips. The same red sandals, too, though Ruth could never understand why anyone would clean a house in heels. The yellow blouse was new. It was embroidered all over with small blue stars and topped off at the neck with sequined psychedelic flowers — some bright purple, some deep green, others a glowing sunset orange with shiny pieces of black plastic at their centers.

Latins, Ruth thought. Colorblindness seemed to be locked into their DNA. "Lovely, lovely blouse," she said. "Something new?"

A belt of red cotton snaked through the loops of Luzma's jeans, twisting over and over upon itself so that it barely reached around her waist. She'd tied it in a very small knot, secured with two safety pins. A yellow ribbon held back her long brown hair; her eyebrows were two upside-down V's.

Ruth shifted back on the toilet seat. "Dazzling, as always," she said, not quite snidely, but snootily enough to bring to mind the business about compassion. She tried to follow up with a generous smile. "And complex, too, I should add. The whole outfit today, it's dazzling and *very* complex." Ruth nodded to herself. That should be more than sufficient. "Now may I ask why you made that little comment?"

"Which little comment?" Luzma said.

"Just now, when you walked in here. 'White Rabbit,' you said. I heard it most distinctly. Maybe you noticed a . . . I mean, did you *see* something?"

"Dios mío," Luzma said again. "You sick, Ruthie?"

"I certainly am not."

"Well, I didn't see nothing. What's to see?"

Ruth smiled politely from the toilet, relieved. No doubt the whole episode *was* just a conversation with herself. Some peculiar symptom of fatigue. But that rabbity voice . . . the swirling animal visions just before her fall . . . She gazed down at her fingertips: they were red and bleeding.

"Hey, look!" Luzma said, bending over Ruth, grabbing hold of her hand. She reached for a piece of toilet paper, wet it on her tongue, and began to dab at Ruth's fingers. "What happened? You fall somewhere?"

"No pity required," Ruth said, dropping her hands to her sides. "That new doctor — Dr. Ash — he says I was born with my problems." Feeling embarrassed, she turned her eyes up at Luzma. The girl had probably seen much stranger things, what with all the old ladies' places that she cleaned, but Ruth thought of herself as different from those others — not better necessarily, just slightly elevated — and she treasured the notion that Luzma thought so, too. "Well, anyway, I'm perfectly spry, thank you," she said, her voice a bit wobbly. "I might've walked one loop too many, that's all. Let's just get on with things." Ruth nodded at the wet slacks, keeping her eyes averted from the watchful photographs all around her. "I'd picked those out because they match my blouse — a nice dinner outfit, I thought."

Luzma reached out toward Ruth's face and slid her glasses from her nose. "Soaking wet!" she said, as she wiped them on her own blouse. "I guess maybe you get caught in the sprinkler too?" She raised her eyebrows and looked at Ruth, but Ruth remained silent. Shaking her head, Luzma replaced Ruth's glasses, stepped back from the puddle on the floor, and leaned down for the wet pants. The girl made a grunting noise as she bent forward, and Ruth couldn't help noticing that Luzma had gained some weight in recent months.

"Don't you worry, I can rinse them out nice and fresh," Luzma said. "So what happened? Another dizzy thing?"

"Well, to be frank, I don't exactly know," Ruth said. For a second she tried to reconstruct the chronology of recent events, but the effort only made her more confused. Her left shoulder was tingling. "I did take a spill out there," she said, "but it's not worth talking about. An accident. No sense dwelling on spilt old bones." She leaned against the lid of the toilet and watched the girl fill the sink with water. After a moment it struck her that the faces in the old photographs were peering at Luzma, too.

"Stand up straight, dear. The walls have eyes."

"What?"

"The photographs. Haven't I shown you?"

"Oh, those. Yes, for sure, you showed me a thousand times." Luzma scrubbed at the pants with a bar of soap.

"Well, there's always an audience," Ruth said. "That's one thing I've definitely learned. Just a few minutes ago I was speaking with —"

Ruth's shoulder tingled again.

"Speaking with who, Ruthie?"

"Whom, dear."

"Yeah, whom?"

"Whom doesn't matter. Certain parties, let's just say. Enough said."

Ruth was frowning at her left arm, bending it in and out, monitoring the tingles that were now creeping down toward her elbow. It was a prickly, teasing sensation, an electric current that kept turning itself on and off, and Ruth worried that the problem might keep on spreading. When she clenched her hand into a tight fist — not a sissy fist, but with thumb bent across her index and third fingers, as her sons had taught her — her fingers did not feel quite right.

"Well, I guess those certain parties made you pretty mad," Luzma said. "Maybe you want to beat them up?"

"Of course not. I'm testing something."

"Oh, yes?"

"*Yes. And I'm fine.*"

"Okay then. Okay, good. But you still seem awful funny-acting."

Under normal conditions, Ruth would've had a snappy response ready, something to divert the girl's attention, but right now her reflexes were out of order. All her efforts seemed vaguely ridiculous. Still, she thought, it would be best to continue with her regular routine.

"Just a bit tired," she said. "Can you help me up? I want to go get the laundry while you finish in here."

"Sure, all right," Luzma said. The girl stood thoughtfully for a second, appraising Ruth's face, then turned from the sink and took a towel off the rack. "We'll wrap this around you till your pants are dry."

3:23 P.M.

With a towel of green terry cloth wrapped around her waist, Ruth opened the bathroom door and walked slowly across The Room. She was stiff from her fall. Luzma followed behind, a hand against Ruth's back.

"You don't have to do that, you know," Ruth said. "I'm no invalid, for crying out loud."

"Course not," said Luzma. "Just ignore me."

Luis, Luzma's son, was leaning against the stair railing with his head down, arms crossed, one ankle locked around the other. His black hair was matted, a few wispy tufts sticking up high in the back. The boy was in his usual foul mood, upset that he had to ride around on the bus with his mother on Saturdays while all his friends were out playing.

As Ruth approached, Luis uncrossed his arms and jammed his thumb into his mouth without looking up. Luzma reached down and pulled it out.

"Luis, Luis, such a grump," she cooed. "And too old for thumb-sucking." She scuffed up his hair with her fingers. "Come on, now, say hello to Ruth." She tried to pull up his chin. "Say hello to Abuelita."

"Hola!" Ruth said. She liked using the Spanish she'd studied at UCLA.

Luis said nothing.

"He'll feel better after a nap," Luzma said, and smiled at the boy. "Right, Luis? For now, you be a nice boy and stay with Ruth while I work. If something happens, something wrong, you come tell me."

"What on earth could happen?" Ruth said. "I'll just help with the laundry like I always do. Seriously, dear, let's not be making mountains out of molehills."

"Holehills what?"

"*Mole*hills."

"Yes?"

"An expression," Ruth said. "It's one of those idioms that refer to . . . Oh, forget it. Holehills — that'll do fine."

Each week Luzma did two loads of laundry, which Ruth and Henry collected and set aside in a yellow plastic basket. Now the loaded basket was waiting upstairs, on the landing of the third floor, between the two bedrooms.

Though Ruth still felt a bit strange, she was determined to walk up the stairs, retrieve the basket, and carry it down to The Room. There was no reason to disrupt the proper order of things. After Luzma returned to the bathroom, Ruth took several deep breaths and walked around Luis, who stood sulking, slouched against the stair railing — "Stand up straight, kid!" she said. "No hunchbacks allowed!" — and made her way up the first two stairs. Her right knee popped audibly. And now her entire left arm seemed to sizzle with electricity. She reached for the railing, pulled herself up another step. But once again she felt that sudden dizziness — so dizzy, in fact, she thought she might fall. She shut her eyes. Wavering slightly, she wondered if a doctor might be needed, but then shook her head. No doctors. She raised her left foot and struggled to pull herself up to the fourth step.

The walls began to close in. All at once the ceiling spun and everything went silver-white. Ruth felt herself teetering backward; she yelped and squeezed the rail with both hands. Marooned, she thought — she didn't dare turn back.

"Hey, Mamá!" Luis shouted. "Something's sick with Ruth!"

Luzma ran out from the bathroom. "You were supposed to stay with her!" she snapped, and grabbed Ruth around the waist, dragging her back down to the bottom of the stairs. "Better sit down, rest awhile," she said.

Annoyed, more with herself than with the girl who was trying to help her, Ruth pushed Luzma's hands away. "There's laundry to do, for Pete's sake. I can't just *sit* for the rest of my life."

Luzma reached out to straighten Ruth's towel, made a tsking sound with her tongue, and nodded. "Then take the elevator. Luis can go along, make sure you're okay." She nudged the boy, who had buried his chin again and was staring down at his feet. "Right, Luis? You go help Ruth bring the laundry to Mamá."

The boy raised his head slowly, rubbing his eyes with his fists. He looked from Ruth's sandals to the green towel wrapped around her waist. "I see those little blue worms under your skin," he said.

Ruth pulled back her shoulders. "Varicose vessels."

"Worms."

"*Veins.* You get them when you have babies. Just ask your mother. She probably has them, too."

"Yuck," said Luis. "You got no blood left."

Oddly flustered, insulted even, Ruth looked at the boy's mother. "What's this he says?"

Luis was poking Ruth's leg.

"Okay now," Luzma said, swatting him on the shoulder. "Enough." She smiled apologetically at Ruth. "One of his new ideas. His friend Tony told him . . . Anyway, it's nonsense. Sorry, Ruth. He's mad at everybody." She looked at the boy, shaking her head from side to side. "Another fight yesterday, some boy beating him up, and then his father yelling and —"

"White skin, no blood," said Luis. "Like a ghost." The thought seemed to please the boy, and he giggled and poked Ruth's leg again.

Drawing in a breath, Ruth decided to drop it. The child obviously had his father's temperament, which was not good, and how could she complain to Luzma about *that*? Anyway, Ruth knew that of all the old ladies Luis saw on Saturday, he liked her best.

They were longtime friends — he'd been coming with Luzma since he was just a baby — and the sullen moods didn't really matter. Ruth liked him, even loved him. Those huge, unblinking brown eyes; the way he could be so sweet sometimes; how he reminded Ruth of her own two sons when they were little boys.

"All right, white blood," she said, "no blood, whatever you want. I'm an old lady." She reached out and gripped Luis's shoulder, forcing him to straighten his spine. "Come on now, straight and solid. Elevator time."

She did *not* love the elevator. She hated it. The walls were lined with artificial cedar paneling and the space inside was cramped and tiny, like an old wooden coffin. It gave her a creepy, claustrophobic sensation to be shut up in a space so small and without windows. Today, though, she'd have to endure the ride. She smiled down at Luis.

"Come help your old abuela."

Luis glanced at his mother, who stood with her hands on her hips, tapping her toes. He frowned indecisively, nibbled at his lip, then nodded and grabbed on to a fold in Ruth's towel. Without a word, he pulled her toward the elevator, pushing open the flimsy, accordion-style door.

Luzma shut them in and they were off, jerky and slow. The overhead cables made a harsh jiggling noise; the lights flickered; Ruth blinked several times and tried to orient herself. For a second she couldn't tell if the confusion was located inside her body or outside or somewhere in between. It *was* a creepy experience. "Just another minute or so," she said, mostly to herself. "Fun, isn't it?" As they passed the second floor, the elevator made several sharp rumbling sounds and the lights flicked off again. Ruth gasped. She reached out for the safety rail on the door, only to find the wall much closer than she'd thought: her knuckles scraped up against something sharp. The darkness collapsed in on her. Suddenly, as if injected with poison, Ruth felt a rush of true terror.

"Fun!" she said.

Her voice, she realized, was pitched a bit too high. Images from recent nightmares popped up: gaping black tunnels, snake people wrapping themselves around her ankles, blood-red lips on the walls, unspeakable creatures with see-through bodies and revolving heads. An insistent gurgling rose from her chest. She began to feel along the walls for the emergency alarm, but then Luis took her hand in his own and wrapped his fingers around her thumb.

Ruth coughed. "Nice ride so far?"

Luis giggled and gave her thumb a squeeze. "Don't be such a scaredy cat."

"Nonsense. Who's scared? I thought *you* might be." She made a defensive throat-clearing sound. "What about worms, for instance?"

"Worms?" the boy said, his voice suspicious. "Why?"

"No reason. It's just that we all have our little bugaboos, if you see my point. Fat greasy worms wiggling out your eyeballs."

The boy didn't move.

With a final jolt the elevator began running smoothly again, and Ruth resolved not to mention her visions to anyone. What good could come of it? Henry would just gape at her, Nora would make a federal case of it, Karen would start in with all that new psychology mumbo-jumbo, analyzing Ruth's whole damned existence. God knows, you had to be careful talking with people about your private thoughts. They might declare you incompetent, like they'd done to poor Edith Tumay last year, or maybe even shut you up inside a hospital.

Gently, she pulled her thumb from Luis's grasp and reached for the safety rail. "Don't worry," she said, "it's just the dark."

Luis let out a nervous giggle. "Who cares?" he said. "I don't believe in bogeymen and all that stuff. They aren't even real, I bet."

"I wouldn't be so sure," Ruth said. "Sometimes I sense things. You know, like ESP and voices and so on. This old neighbor of mine, for instance —"

There was a quick sparking noise, and the lights came on. Luis was staring at her with his mouth open.

Ridiculous, she thought. Trying to prove her courage to a seven-year-old. When the elevator stopped at the third floor, she stepped out and shuffled over to her bed, then climbed onto her high mattress. She extended her arms behind her and leaned back for a minute, legs dangling.

A strange confusion had come over her. She didn't understand what had been happening lately — the dizzy spells, the visions and voices — and now, after her incapacity on the stairs and in the elevator, she felt awfully shaken. How would she keep up with the daily chores if she couldn't stand on her own two feet? Right now, for instance: Henry would have to take care of the laundry. No doubt he'd mess it all up, but there was no way on earth she could manage it herself, not feeling like this.

She pictured the old man hunched over his desk, caught up in one of those endless solitaire games.

"Henry!" she yelled.

She waited a moment, then tried again, more politely: "Henry?"

There was a dense silence. If he wasn't at his desk, Ruth wondered, where was he? She pushed herself upright at the edge of her bed, ran her fingers through her curls: they were stiff and oddly warm. Bizarre new thoughts filled Ruth's mind. What if something actually had happened to the old man? Who'd be there if anything went wrong while she was setting up her breakfast tray or getting undressed at night? Who'd bring home the groceries? Or carry up the mail and newspaper? But it was more than just that, Ruth realized, and she slumped. Henry had been there every day, no matter what, for thirty-six years. And day after day, month after month, he'd hardly ever complained. He'd never left her. He'd never died.

And that was something, wasn't it?

Yes, it was. A boob-something, but still . . .

Nervously, Ruth pushed the bobby pins around in her curls. Then she dropped her hands and pulled back her shoulders — she mustn't let herself be so foolish. She looked over at Luis, who was standing by the elevator door, kicking at the carpet. His silences, when he was tired like this, were more frustrating than his wildest bouts of mischief. "Luis," she said, "go find Henry for me. Tell him — ask him — to come in here."

Without a word, the boy nodded and walked out.

Ruth sat still a moment. The whole house suddenly had a hollowed-out feel. Barren and expectant, like an empty garbage bag. No doubt Henry was just asleep, dozing inside his closet with that silly radio earplug in his ear, blocking out the world. She waited, straightening the towel in her lap. Everything was going awry today, and the man had slept right through it all. In his *closet*, for God's sake.

Henry could sleep anywhere, anytime. In the middle of the day he preferred his overstuffed chair, the big blue one that was shredding at the arms. For years he'd kept the chair positioned next to his bed, until the day he'd resolved never to drink again. That very afternoon, after sweeping up the glass from his shattered booze bottle, he'd moved the chair into his walk-in closet. "It's more comfortable in here," he'd told Ruth. "A little nest — real cozy, you know?" He'd covered the worn-out seat cushion with a blue-and-red-striped beach towel. Then, sitting down, he'd screwed the radio earplug into his ear. "Cooler and darker," he'd said, leaning forward to fold the closet doors shut like a fan in front of her face.

3:53 P.M.

Ruth heard Henry holler "Leave go of me!" and a moment later she heard his feet, those deliberate, lumbering steps mixing with the boy's soft padding. She took a breath and exhaled slowly. In that instant, which seemed prolonged and significant, she felt a surge of enormous relief, even gratitude. Then Luis ran into the room, past her bed, and into the elevator, and Henry appeared in the doorway.

"Kid's a troublemaker," he muttered. He shook his head and looked at Ruth. He paused, his pale eyes flooding with concern. "Hey, you look kind of rotten. No offense."

Ruth's breath caught.

Nubby-hubby! Compassion's the fashion!

It was difficult, but she resisted the urge to retaliate. Instead, she frowned and watched Henry tug at the collar of his filthy shirt, which was bunched up like a brace around his neck, three or four buttons stuck into holes a slot too high. Finally, though, she couldn't stop herself. "Oh, right," she broke out. "You're no great beauty yourself."

"That's a fact," Henry said.

Ruth sighed. "Would you kindly bring the laundry in here?"

"Okay by me."

In a moment he returned with the basket, his mouth hanging open.

"Go ahead, put it in there," Ruth said firmly, gesturing at the elevator.

Henry nodded and turned like a big genial robot and placed the basket on the floor of the elevator. He ignored Luis, who stood quietly sucking his thumb.

"Now," Ruth said, "I'll need help getting into that contraption myself."

"What sort of help?"

"Well, you know, just like with the laundry basket. Put me inside."

"Body contact?"

The thought made her hesitate. "How else?"

"Righto," Henry said.

He reached up to play with his loose tooth, his eyes locked on the towel at Ruth's waist. It had been more than thirty-three years since he'd approached her bed with even the possibility of anything vaguely physical.

"But don't try —" Ruth paused again. The man was gaping. "Henry, don't *think* about it."

He grinned and opened up his arms. "Like old times," he said, and slapped his big hands against her hips.

"Not *there*," Ruth said. "My God!"

His hands slid up past her waist, almost dislodging the towel, and then settled into the flesh at her ribs.

"And not there!"

Henry took her under the armpits. He was wheezing slightly.

"Any complaints?"

"Well, I don't know," Ruth said. "Just don't wrinkle my blouse. And no more squeezie business."

With a low grunt Henry lifted her off the bed. He rested a moment, hoisted her up again, then trundled her over to the elevator and gently put her down. His face had become flushed; he stood panting, grinning like a schoolboy. "Felt pretty darn satisfying," he said. "You too?"

The man was deliberately provoking her.

"I didn't notice," Ruth said.

"No?"

"Don't be ridiculous."

The only way to be pleasant, she realized, was to ignore his absurdities. She took hold of his shirt sleeve, tried not to wobble as she stepped into the elevator. Once inside, she pulled away and clamped her arms across her chest. She looked down at Luis. "Still having fun, dear?"

Henry stood at the door. "Lots," he said.

"The boy. Not you."

"Him too?"

Henry flicked his eyebrows, made a kissing sound, then pressed the button to send them on their way.

"All these years," he said, "you're still my cutie pie."

4:02 P.M.

Ruth and Luis got out on the second floor, sending the laundry on to The Room by itself. "Coming down," Ruth yelled, though she did not know if Luzma would hear. She reached for the boy's hand and led him past the dining table and into the kitchen. If she moved slowly, she discovered, she could manage fairly well.

"Come on, amigo. How about a couple galletas?"

She opened the pantry and pulled out the foil-lined bag of Sweet Spot chocolate chip cookies.

"Now listen, I'll tell you a secret," she said. "If you put a match to one of these cookies, it'll burn like gasoline. Pure chemicals. Karen told me that — my granddaughter."

Luis eyed the sack of cookies. "My mom says not to eat sugar."

"Sugar? I told you, kid, these are *chemicals*. They'll scrub your teeth right up." She grinned at the boy. "Besides, they taste great."

Ruth dug around in the bag until she found two whole cookies for Luis — most had a bite or two taken out of them — and while Luis ate, she took a second bite from an already-bitten cookie. Delicious, if a little stale, she thought; everything was always turning soft from the moisture in the air. She ran her tongue along the chewed-off edge of the cookie, licking up the dark brown goo that oozed from the broken chips. Then she tossed the rest of it back into the bag, for later.

"Muy bien, hey?"

"I guess," said Luis, nibbling on his second cookie, one ankle locked around the other. He glanced up at her from the corner of his eye and said, "You're a weirdo."

Ruth grinned down at him, a smudge of chocolate on her bottom lip. "You too," she said.

When they'd finished their snack, Ruth led the boy out to the coffee table by the couch. She kept his crayons, paper, and scissors on top of the black-and-white TV at the far end of the table.

She got him set up, then walked over to her piano bench. It was the same thing each week. He'd sit on the floor at the coffee table, coloring and cutting things out while she played Beethoven or Bach or Chopin. The boy didn't mind the background music, and, for her part, Ruth took pleasure in performing for a live audience.

"So, Luis," she said, "what's for today's concert?"

Ruth opened her book of Chopin preludes and chose one at random, the Fourth Prelude in E Minor. Her left hand was still a bit cramped, so she played slowly and quietly, careful to keep her breathing steady. Except for one or two passages, she had the piece committed to memory, and now and then she glanced over at Luis, who was busy drawing figures with his crayons. Like her son Carter, the boy had a creative bent, a real imagination. He'd always begin by drawing the same three characters: Mr. Blue, Mr. Red, and Little Greenie. Mr. Blue was a fat, lumpy circle with a squiggle of a face on top. No arms or legs, but the kind of person you'd listen to anyway. Rather stern, Ruth thought, almost pompous-looking, but he could make you laugh. Mr. Red was tall (he did have arms and legs) and looked mean — the type who rolled his own cigarettes and pushed up his sleeves, a schoolyard bully, the guy who stole your lunch money and made you say thanks. Little Greenie had all his appendages, like Mr. Red, but he was tiny and very short, almost dwarfish.

As she played, Ruth watched the boy cut out the figures and begin stationing them here and there in his coffee-table kingdom. He was mumbling under his breath — "Now you go right up there, Mr. Blue" — he lay the cutout on a pile of magazines, where Mr. Blue could be in charge of things. "And you be good and stay in there, Little Greenie" — he wedged the figure upright into a dish of ivy. "And you, Mr. Red, you're stuck *there*" — he shoved the poor man into an ashtray, left over from Ruth's smoking days.

For five minutes or so everyone in the make-believe kingdom played his proper role, communicating peaceably as neighbors sometimes do. Little Greenie minded his own business in the bushes, a nice ordinary guy; Mr. Blue turned out to be something of a power-monger, greedily thrilled with the position he'd been given atop Magazine Mountain, which he knew he deserved; and Mr. Red was a bad seed through and through, who would've run amuck if he hadn't been ground into the ashes from the very start.

It was a small community, rather provincial, but Luis seemed to take joy in governing its affairs, like some all-powerful god.

For a time Ruth turned back to the piano. Eyes closed, she rocked with the music, feeling warm and calm, but as she neared the final triplet, all hell broke loose on the coffee table to her right. Someone was shouting at the top of his lungs.

"Get out, get out!" the voice shrieked. "Right now, before I burn this bush and everyone around it! Get away from here, you creepos. I mean it, scram!"

A tremor ran through Ruth's chest, bouncing down from her shoulder to her navel. Her left arm throbbed. She jerked back, looked over at Luis.

It would not have surprised her if Mr. Blue, the authority in the region, had raised his voice to settle a dispute. Or if Mr. Red had gone on a rampage, leaping from the ashtray, a mass murderer. But this was very strange. For it was Little Greenie who was crazed — the goody-goody mama's boy. "Asshole!" Greenie yelled, and when Mr. Blue tried to restrain him, he only shouted louder, "I mean it, buddy, scram!" His voice seemed tense and strained as he vented his anger on everyone around him. "Bueno, Blue, you asshole," he said. "Say hello to Abuelita. Say, 'Hello, Abuelita, scaredy cat in your stupid green towel. How are you on this shitty day today?'"

"Darling," Ruth said, "I wish you wouldn't —"

"You too!" Little Greenie screamed. "Scram!"

Ruth told herself to ignore it. Obviously, the boy was staging this demonstration for attention, still in his foul mood; just like her son Carter, his artistic expressions of identity were sometimes rather flamboyant. Anyway, Ruth mused, the boy had reasons enough to be frustrated — fierce poverty, to begin with, and an even fiercer father — and a little indulgence might do him some good. She turned to the piano again, though her arm and fingers ached. She pumped the pedals, banged hard on the keys. If it was a competition between Chopin and Little Greenie, Ruth was determined that real artistry, not mere self-assertion, should carry the day.

"Shit!" Little Greenie yelled.

Ruth played louder and hummed along.

A moment later, when the knocking began on the wall of 23, Ruth knew that Chopin had the edge: Hassan liked to compliment fine music, not nasty language. As she finished the prelude, there was a tremendous thundering of knocks.

"Super!" Hassan called through the wall. "Extra nice, Ruthie! You make that music super!"

Luis looked up from his game. "Hey," he said, "who is that? You'd tell *me* to shut up if I made all that noise."

"Otro amigo," Ruth said. "Hassan." She stood up from the bench and turned in triumph toward the boy.

Luis slouched at the coffee table. He closed his fingers around the cutout characters, tossed them all into a wrinkled heap in the ashtray, and scowled down at the wrecked kingdom. "I'm not playing anymore," he said, and he climbed onto the couch to curl up.

4:21 P.M.

Ruth picked up the little boy's feet and sat down with them in her lap. She removed his shoes, rubbed his toes and arches. In a few minutes he was fast asleep.

"Well, there," she murmured, "Little Greenie's better now."

Again, the house took on that scooped-out feel: a vast and enduring silence. She wondered what to do with herself. An unusual weariness had entered her bones, like a weight of some sort, or the utter absence of weight. Usually she'd follow Luzma as she cleaned, making sure things were done properly and thoroughly, seizing every opportunity to issue instructions in Spanish so as to practice vocabulary. But now her entire left side, from her index finger down to her toes, had begun to tingle. Her whole life, she'd never felt this way. Maybe this was how the man from 23 felt the day he walked down to Doggie Canyon and never came back.

She closed her eyes, tired and old.

"Hey there, White Rabbit," Karen said. "Thought you didn't believe in sleep."

Then a smacking sound.

Even with her eyes shut, Ruth recognized that wad of chewing gum. She wiggled to sit up straight.

"Quit that chomping," she said sternly. "Anyway, I'm not asleep. I'm trying to regulate my breathing."

Karen stood above her, bobbing up and down on the worn-out toes of her tennis shoes. Her legs were long and thin, the knees nicely formed. A good-looking girl, Ruth thought — took after her father, thank God, and not that mediocre mother of hers. The girl's thick blond hair, though, was still a mess. Too long and bushy. The roots, Ruth noticed, had gone to an amber shade of brown.

She pursed her lips and twisted sideways so Karen could kiss her cheek.

"I'm awfully glad you've —" Ruth hesitated. This compassion business was considerably more difficult than Chuckly Voice had let on. "I mean, thanks for taking some time out from your love life. It's so important —" She stopped again. Sympathy was one thing, syrup was something else. No need to overdo it. "So how was lunch with Count Dracula? Worth all the hurry, I hope?"

Karen pulled a strand of gum from her lips, bit it off, began rolling it into a ball. She was still bouncing. "Lunch was fine. I talked to Luzma, she says you're not doing too great."

"No worse than you, from the look of things," Ruth said. "Just what did Luzma tell you?"

Karen plopped down on the couch and rested a hand on Ruth's knee. "Didn't sound so good. How she found you in the bathroom, how you couldn't make it upstairs. Grammy, listen, you should've told me something was wrong. I would've stayed." She slid a fresh stick of gum into her mouth, rolled the used-up glob into the wrapper. Embarrassed, she cleared her throat and said, "Still trying to give up the smokes."

Ruth smiled an I-told-you-so smile.

"Well, kiddo," she said, "I did ask you to stay, as I recall. And, by the way, when I stopped smoking, after almost fifty-nine years, I managed it in one single day. Bam. Just like that. I remember vividly, in fact, how your Uncle Douglas explained what it was doing to my lungs, a very graphic description, so I just —"

"Have you taken a pain pill? I know you're supposed to."

"I most assuredly did *not* take a pain pill." Ruth adjusted her shoulders, straightened her spine. "And I don't plan to. I took a little spill on my walk — so what? — I made it back all by myself." Absently, she wrapped the fingers of her right hand around her silver locket.

Karen started. "Hey, what happened?"

She reached for Ruth's injured hand, but Ruth gripped the locket even tighter. The blister tingled on her palm. "Nothing," she said. She would keep up appearances, as she always had.

"Well, suit yourself. But let me take Luis upstairs. That way you can spread out here."

"No, dear, I do not *want* you to take Luis upstairs." Ruth looked down on the sleeping boy. "I like him to be with me. And I don't want to take a nap. I want to put on my pants, the ones I picked out to wear for dinner, and —" *People-steeple! Surf's up!* Perhaps she was being self-centered. "I don't suppose you'd like to stay and eat with us. Luzma and Luis always do."

Karen slumped back. "Can't, Grammy. Mike's waiting."

"I see. Love before blood."

"Come on, Grammy. Always making me feel so guilty. I'm twenty-nine — a grown married woman." She popped a bubble. Suddenly her eyes moistened. "Oh, Christ."

"Karen?"

"Forget it. Nothing."

Ruth leaned forward, pushing Luis's feet from her lap, and tried to stand up. She paused for a second, arms held out as if she were about to take a dive, then lost her balance and flopped down again. She glanced over at Karen.

"A Prince Charming problem?"

"I guess. Sort of."

Ruth took Luis's feet back into her lap, squeezed his toes one after the other. The boy could sleep and sleep.

"If you want my opinion, the problem's obvious," Ruth said. "This full-grown adult — a man who's supposed to be your husband — he leaves you for almost a year, then just happens to show up on your doorstep. You throw the doors open, he stays all night, God knows what else. Then he sneaks away again. He's a louse. Problem solved."

"It's not his fault, Grammy. Not now, I mean." She looked down at her hands. "And he's sorry."

"Sorry-schmorry," Ruth said. "Boob."

Karen released a quick laugh. "A pretty old-fashioned word, Grammy."

"And rude," Ruth continued. "He was rude with me on the phone. I suppose he's sorry for that, too?"

"But he's changed now, much more . . . more serious."

Ruth looked up at the ceiling. "Serious, she says."

"You know, settled down. It's hard to describe, sort of, but he's full of energy and new ideas and . . . I can really feel the difference."

"I'll bet you can," Ruth said. She moved Luis's feet down to her knees. She tugged at the towel in her lap, trying to close up the gap that ran between her legs. "Just how did you happen to cross paths with this creature again?"

"Does it matter?"

"Maybe so, maybe not."

Karen rubbed her eyes. "Well, a couple weeks ago I was out on assignment, this story about a third-stage smog alert — pretty awful. Went out to shoot the pictures, do the usual reaction stuff. Senior citizens, asthmatics, that sort of shit."

"Karen."

"Right. So anyway, I end up at this elementary school. Kids stuck inside, no recess, the red smog flags. That's when Mike trotted over."

"*Hot*, no doubt."

Karen only shrugged.

"Wonder of wonders," Ruth said. "And I suppose you were wearing the skimpy little outfit you've got on now? I swear, I've seen more cotton at the top of aspirin bottles."

Karen laughed and rolled her eyes. "No, just work clothes. You're not exactly interested in the emotional side of all this, are you?" The girl pulled another strand of gum from her mouth and chomped it off. "Anyway, Mike says he started teaching there last September — permanently, I mean, no more substituting — and he's doing pretty well. We got to talking. He likes teaching math best."

"X equals the unknown. The only thing I remember about math."

Sighing, Karen rolled the chewed gum into a ball, took out a fresh piece, and slid it between her lips. Each time she carried out this procedure, Ruth noticed, the wad in her mouth grew conspicuously larger.

"Not to interrupt," Ruth said, "but that's a very unattractive habit. Maybe gum's your problem. Maybe Prince Charming doesn't appreciate —"

The phone rang.

Karen threw her hands up as if electrocuted. "Don't let Henry answer it!" she shouted. "Or Luis!" She raced toward the phone table at the foot of the stairs, almost slipping on a small piece of yellow paper. There were dozens of them scattered about — little yellow scraps on the rug and floor. "God, what *is* all this?" she yelled, then snatched up the receiver. Her face had gone bright red. There was a pause before she sighed and lowered the phone.

"For you, Grammy. Nora Somebody. Calling to say White Rabbit."

"Well, for crying out loud," Ruth muttered.

Slowly, gloomily, it dawned on her that she had forgotten to White Rabbit Nora at the shop that morning, and now it was too late. The old bird had got her. So had Karen, for that matter, and Luzma. She could not remember a month when she'd been so unsuccessful with the game.

She squinted at Karen. "Who did you *think* would be calling?"

Karen shrugged. She was still holding the receiver in her hand. "I thought — Mike, I guess, maybe." She bent her lips into a weak smile. "I didn't want a man to answer."

"Mike? You just got here."

"Well, he's sort of — he's a little —"

There was a loud squawking sound. Even from across the room, Ruth could hear Nora's high voice through the receiver.

"Jealous," Karen said.

"*Jealous?*"

"Right! Jealous!" Nora shrieked over the phone. "You always were jealous, Ruth Caster, and you still are! But I win today, you hear? *White Rabbit!*"

Karen dropped the receiver back into its cradle. She seemed dazed, like a sleepwalker, the eyes not quite in register, and for a moment Ruth felt a mixture of indignation and pity.

"Excuse me, sweetheart," she said, "I believe that was a human being you hung up on. Not even a goodbye."

The girl didn't seem to hear. "Thing is, I have to be extra careful just now. We've been through a lot, you know."

Ruth snorted. "For Pete's sake, girl. What's happened to your dignity?"

Karen waved a hand in the air, as if the question were completely irrelevant. "He's waiting down at the beach for me this very second."

"At the beach?"

"Sure, right here."

"Here? At Paradise Lagoon?" Ruth's indignation grew as she realized he had not even stopped to say hello.

"So what he says," Karen went on, "Mike says he's ready to spend the rest of his life with me. Again. Do it right this time. Never be apart forever and forever and forever." Karen crossed the room and stood with her hands dangling at her sides, as if exhausted, as if she'd just dropped an enormous burden.

Ruth lifted her eyebrows. "And that's what *you* want?"

"I don't know."

"If it was, you'd know," Ruth said with authority, sounding much more confident than she had ever felt about such problems in her own life. "Kiddo, I hate to repeat myself, but Mike is exactly like Frank Deeds. Another smoothie. Always saying how happy you're going to be, how wonderfully and perfectly and beautifully happy. In the meantime, though, he's off God knows where, you've got headaches and diarrhea, you're jumping for the phone every time it rings — it's not healthy."

Karen sat down stiffly. She was silent for a few moments.

"God," she finally said, "what am I supposed to do?" She brought a hand to her throat. "All this time missing him, wanting him, feeling miserable without him, and now that he's back, none of it seems real. Like I've been dreaming about him for a year, and then now — I mean, just one *day* after he comes back, it's already . . . But I still love him, Grammy. God, I really do."

Ruth grimaced.

"Don't be ridiculous," a voice said.

It was Hale's voice.

Ponca City, 1935. She was twenty-eight at the time, even younger than Karen.

He hadn't been home the morning she arrived at his one-room house — already out at work in the oil fields — so, exhausted after the long train ride, she crawled into his bed to wait for him. How thrilled he would be to see her. God, how she loved him! She drifted off to sleep thinking strange, excited thoughts, picturing the young couple she'd met on the train: the tired eyes and tousled hair; her breast, his fingers; the impulse, the passion, the intense physical togetherness. *She* could be passionate too. She, too, could be impulsive. This visit to Hale proved it.

Yes, it did.

And in her dream, Auntie Elizabeth came to her, proffering advice about ice bags and yellow sashes and convenient magical powers; and Ruth smiled and lifted Hale's hands above his head; she removed his tie and wound it tight around his wrists; she unbuttoned his shirt and ran an ice cube over his chest.

Passion.

It rose into her throat. It was suffocating her.

When she awoke, the room was hot and stuffy and full of the dusty Oklahoma summer sun; her nightgown was covered with sweat. Hale sat on the edge of the bed eating a sandwich, staring down at her.

"Well?" he said.

His voice was uncommonly stern.

"Happy birthday!" she said, "Oh, Hale!"

She rolled over, lifted herself up, flung her arms around his neck. "Surprise!" she said, trying to pull him down on top of her.

He pushed her away and frowned. "Don't be ridiculous," he said. He took three bites of his sandwich, finishing it. Then he stood up, lifted his hat from a chair beside the bed, and moved to the door. "I have to get back to work." He turned to look at her. "And I always get home late."

"But Hale," she said, jumping to her feet and moving across the room to him, "I just arrived, I just —"

"I'm here to work, Ruthie. Not to honeymoon."

"But aren't you surprised? Aren't you even happy I'm —"

"Surprised?" His eyes widened. At other moments, better moments, those eyes had made her promises of faithfulness and love. "I'll say I'm surprised. Fellow works out at the fields spots you in the station this morning, asking total strangers for directions to my house." He glared at her. "Like a regular boxcar tramp." He placed his hat on his head with precision. "You should have warned me."

"*Warned* you? But Hale —"

"I don't like surprises, Ruth."

"But your birthday — I wanted — I — God, I *love* you."

"Don't be ridiculous." He opened the door. "I don't know what this is all about. I don't like irrationality. And I detest little games."

4:41 P.M.

Karen stood holding a messy handful of yellow paper scraps. She was saying something, her lips moving, but Ruth couldn't quite follow — she must have drifted off. It took a moment before sounds began to register.

"So it's all taken care of," Karen was saying. "Now you can lie back and —"

"What's taken care of?"

The girl squinted at her. "I just *told* you. I took Luis upstairs to Henry's bed. He's all tucked in, safe and sound. You can go ahead and stretch out."

"Thank you, I'll just sit."

"But you really *are* tired, Grammy — I mean, you blanked out or something. Right in the middle of our conversation." Karen shuffled through the wad of papers. "By the way, what are all these messages doing on the floor?"

"Mine," Ruth said. "They're private."

Karen rolled her shoulders. "Well, sure, but —" Then she read aloud from a few scraps:

"Henry — Bill about baseball game — 7/20/90.

"Henry — hearing aid ready — 10/23/92.

"Henry — Happy Hardware, radio fixed, pick up — 2/19/89.

"Henry — do you want hearing aid or *not?* — 2/1/93.

"Henry — Bill says Happy Seventy-ninth — 11/18/86."

Ruth held up a hand. "All right, you've made your point," she said. "You can just put those back where they belong."

"All over the floor?"

"Obviously. If that's where you found them."

Karen shook her head. "Well, I suppose, but poor Henry doesn't seem to *get* these messages. On the floor, I mean. He doesn't even seem to look there."

"Is that my fault?"

"But if —"

Ruth huffed. "Near the phone is certainly a proper place to deposit any such messages. They're doing just fine where they are." She stretched her numb hand out toward Karen. "Sit back down here next to me, please, dear."

The truth — not that it was Karen's business — was actually quite simple: Henry's hearing was bad, therefore Ruth took all phone calls. This in itself was no problem. After all, she was a trained receptionist, graduate of the Sawyer Secretarial School, and it was only natural that the phone should be her responsibility. Whenever calls came in for Henry, she was careful to write down the important details, names and dates and subject matter, and over time she'd developed an equally meticulous four-part Delivery System: (1) If Henry was nearby, she'd jot down the message and hand it to him in person. (2) If he was within shouting distance, she'd yell at him to come fetch it. (3) If he was out of range — on another floor, for example, or on his way to The Pig Pen — she'd leave his message beside the second-floor phone, on the table at the foot of the stairs. Henry was to check the table occasionally to see if anyone had been trying to reach him.

Almost always, in fact, the System functioned without flaw. There was only one exception: when she took calls in her bedroom upstairs. On those occasions, delivery became difficult. She'd first try System Parts 1 and 2. But if Henry was beyond shouting range — at the grocery store, perhaps, or preparing their coffee in the kitchen — the System threatened to break down under the weight of serendipity. She was not about to roam through the place in her nightgown, walking downstairs with God knew who peeping at her through the windows. Instead, she'd slip on her bedjacket and step into her slippers and walk to the landing above the stairs. There she'd pause, taking aim at the table below, then flip the message over the banister. This was Delivery System Part 4.

The Scrap Pile, she called it. If Henry chose not to pick up the messages, well, that was his problem.

4:53 P.M.

"Earth to Grandmother, Earth to Grandmother," Karen said, waving her hand in front of Ruth's eyes. A hunk of moist gum went flying from the girl's fingers and dropped through a gap in the towel that covered Ruth's lap.

"Well fine," Ruth muttered. She lifted the towel and began searching between her legs. "My God, girl, what if I'm gummed *shut?*"

Karen prodded Ruth in the arm, gently. "Stop daydreaming! No kidding, I'm beginning to think you're on your own private planet — someplace like Mars, not enough oxygen in your tanks. And you say *I'm* not healthy."

A loud cry filled Ruth's ears, like the shriek of some ravenous animal, and a pain shot through her chest. She bolted up straight.

This time it hurt. Not a little — a lot.

"You okay?" Karen said.

For a moment Ruth was dead silent. Then she said, "Of course I am. Mars, I was thinking about Mars."

Karen took Ruth's arm and slid a toss pillow behind her back. "Look, you better take one of those pain pills. And probably a tranquilizer, too. Let me run up and get them."

"Never mind."

"But you can't just wait for —"

"No," Ruth said.

She wanted to say more, but the words wouldn't come. Her popping knee and jaw, her infrequent headaches, even her bad eyesight — these were problems she could discuss and analyze; they had a solid, well-defined quality, they were things a doctor might diagnose. But she couldn't find language for the discomfort she was suffering today, the dizzy spells and tinglings, the quick stabbing pains in her chest, the bizarre voices and visions, the vague sense of dread. Especially the dread. Besides, to articulate all this would only overwhelm Karen, shattering the girl's own fragile fears. Better just to leave it alone.

She leaned forward a little, continued to dig between her legs for the gum. "Mars, Mars, Mars," she said. Then, "This man of yours, Mike. We were talking about Mike."

"And?"

"You tell me."

"I don't know," Karen said. "It's complicated."

"Complicated." Ruth located the wad of chewed gum, began rolling it between her fingers. "And since when is desertion so complicated? Or an extramarital affair?"

Karen glanced away. "There was never any proof of that. No real evidence. Just a thought I had, for a while."

"Yes, you were once capable of it."

"Excuse me?"

"Thought."

"Stop it, Grammy. That's cruel. Really, you can be so insensitive."

Ruth frowned.

"Anyway," Karen said, "there were lots of reasons for the separation."

"Separation!" Ruth snorted. "Since when was it a separation? The man walked out on you, for God's sake. Don't start pretending you had any say in it."

For a time Karen sat motionless. Then she snatched the chewed gum from Ruth's fingers, dropped it in the ashtray on top of Luis's cutouts, slid a fresh stick into her mouth. "Look, let's drop it. I'm married, remember? I'm twenty-nine years old. The biological clock. Enough said?" Karen pulled her feet up on the couch and sat leaning forward, arms cradled around her knees. "Anyway, Mike was . . . I mean, he was terribly depressed."

"Oh, I see, depression. Funny how in my day, depression was no excuse for —" Ruth put her hands into her hair; she removed them immediately, fingertips burning. *Surf's up! Time goes ticky! Don't be picky!*

There was some silence. Ruth took the occasion to clear her throat. "Well, okay, depression."

"Down on himself. You remember those big dreams of his, all those ambitions, how he wanted to be a spy."

"An actor, last I heard. A movie star."

"No, the last you heard, he wanted to be a spy. I told you all about it."

"Nonsense."

"I *did.*"

"A spy?"

"Close enough," Karen said, and laughed without humor. "You know, join the Secret Service or the FBI or something. Jump on presidents. Save their lives. He even wrote away for application forms — I *told* you all this, remember? Those stupid night classes over at USC. Forensic Science. Apprehending the Criminal Mind. It got to the point where he . . . I mean, all of a sudden he seemed so caught up in it, always daydreaming and stuff . . ."

A thin coat of moisture had formed on Karen's forehead. Her eyes, too, seemed a little damp.

"Honey?" Ruth said.

"Huh?"

"Are you so sure depression's the real issue here?"

"What are you trying to say?" The girl's voice went tight. "That Mike and I don't really love each other? That you're the only person on earth who ever really loved someone?"

Ruth blinked at her, perplexed.

"No, no," she said, "not at all."

In truth, Ruth had no idea what she was trying to say. "But I *love* you," she told Hale on that day in Ponca City, lifting his hand to her breast and squeezing it. She stared at him, dumb with romance and desire, struggling to think of the right words: "Honey," she tried, but the word stuck on her tongue; "Darling," she said, and "Dear," but they did not sound quite right either. "Silly girl," he said, moving his hand to her head and patting her like a child, "don't be ridiculous. You *know* I don't like little games." With Frank Deeds, of course, the dynamics had been very different — "That's my breast!" she said, as she slumped back against a rock, her toes curled in white beach sand; "For sure," he said, squeezing until it hurt — but the results had been nearly the same. All her painful deliberation, her desire, her love or lack of love . . . finally these things had mattered only to herself. Mere details. They had not affected circumstances.

"Grammy, what are you *saying?*"

Ruth blinked at her granddaughter.

There was a slight tremor about the girl's lips, and for an instant Ruth felt worried. Had she revealed something shameful? She was relieved when Karen made an angry, jerking motion with her shoulder.

"You don't listen. You don't hear a word I say."

Ruth took a deep breath. "Not true," she said. "Mike. I've heard every word — been hearing it for years." She readjusted the towel at her lap. "Now, what I want to know is, how much time have you spent with him lately? How well do you really know him?"

Karen blew a bubble. "Well, last Tuesday I went along on a field trip out to the La Brea tar pits — you know, where they have all those preserved fossils. His whole fourth-grade class was there. Not exactly romantic, I guess, but it was fun. Mike's good with kids, I never would have —"

"Fossils!" Ruth said. "Listen, I can't stand it. This whole business, this *change* business, it's the oldest story in the world. You *can't* change a fellow in one afternoon. And even if Mike has transformed himself, which I very much doubt, he certainly can't turn into a completely different person. You sound just like your Great-Aunt Elizabeth on her second time around, with that big religious boob Stephen MacLeod. *He* was supposedly transformed too. And look how it ended up."

"This is different," Karen said. "Elizabeth was stupid."

"Hardly. You think she was so stupid to fall in love with Stephen? Everyone did — you should have just seen him! They started out very hot and passionate, just like you and your dreamboat. So she marries him. Has two children by him." Ruth paused for a moment. That was not strictly accurate. "In any case, two fine children and then disaster. He gets some crazy, jealous notion in his head and blows her father's brains out."

"Oh, brother," Karen mumbled. "Not this again."

"*Father.* Jonathan was Elizabeth's father. *My* grandfather."

Downstairs, the washing machine made a loud thumping sound, then clicked into the rinse cycle. As the machine swished and whirred, the sound of Luzma's voice drifted up the stairs — a happy song about bumblebees and summer afternoons. Ruth and Karen sat still for a while, listening. Then Karen made a sudden, violent motion with her arm.

"Mike isn't Stephen," she said fiercely, "and he's not Frank. Really, Grammy, you're so stuck on these old stories. You make everything seem so horrible and hopeless. I mean it. You've practically given up living."

Ruth pulled the towel tight around her legs as if to protect herself. "I *am* a full century old," she said.

"You're not. You're eighty-eight."

"Quibble, quibble."

"No, it's not."

Ruth hesitated. She felt frail and hurt. "Well, I'm very sorry if you don't enjoy my stories. I was trying to help."

Karen sighed. "I didn't mean it that way — stories are fine. All I'm saying is, people have to care about the present, too. And the future. The world's full of *new* stories."

Ruth nodded. The girl seemed very, very young.

"The future," Ruth said. "I'll keep it in mind." Down inside, though, she felt a familiar hardness in her stomach, as if it were full of wet sand, thick and solid, and there was simply no room for anything new. It wasn't a question of right or wrong. She recognized Karen's meaning; she even approved of it. She'd felt the same way a long time ago, when there was still space inside her, still openness and hunger, back when newness was truly new.

Karen sat up quickly, as if jolted awake. "My God, what am I doing here? On and on about myself, when you're feeling sick." She shook her head. "Anyway, about Mike and me, it's not so bad. Not really." She nudged Ruth. "One thing's for sure — we've still got chemistry."

Ruth nodded.

"Chemically speaking —" Karen giggled. "Scientifically, I'd have to say we're . . ."

Ruth lifted the edges of her mouth into a smile.

Chemistry. Like the time she and Edith Tumay went skinny-dipping in Santa Monica, the summer before their junior year in high school. A warm, moonlit night, and Little Boy Mackelroy was there, the one who drowned in a riptide later that summer; his older brother Chester was there too, with a friend of his from college; and Tom Snelson and Ricky Gwynn and Henry's brother Bill. Henry might have been there, she supposed, but that part she couldn't remember. So, yes, a warm summer night, and she and Edith had been so modest, crouching behind that big white boulder, waiting for the boys to dive under a wave before they stripped off their clothes. They kept their naked shoulders beneath the water at all times, and didn't splash, and later, when Little Boy Mackelroy stole their skirts, they stayed in that freezing ocean for almost half an hour, maybe longer, waiting for the coast to clear. Finally, almost numb with cold, she and Edith made a wild naked dash for the shore, shrieking and hugging their own shoulders and snatching their clothes back from Little Boy Mackelroy. The memory made Ruth smile. So many years ago. And what stuck with her most vividly — more than the cold water, more than the ensuing pneumonia and those weeks she'd spent recuperating in bed — was Little Boy standing there buck naked on the beach, big and bold, waving two skirts at the moon, and how, in one glimpse, she'd understood where he got his foolish name. "I think I'm in love," Edith had said as they dressed in the dark, "I really do, I think Little Boy's my big, big man." A month later Little Boy drowned in the riptide off Seal Beach. Chemistry: it was not reliable.

Upstairs, there was a loud clattering noise.

"Help!" Henry yelled. "Save me!"

5:16 P.M.

They stepped out of the elevator, hurrying through Ruth's bedroom and across the landing to Henry's door. Just inside the doorway, Karen jerked to a stop.

"Wow," she said, "what *happened?*"

Ruth was panting, rushing to catch up. She nudged Karen aside and entered the room.

Henry's top desk drawer was wide open, and empty; the contents lay scattered across the rug — pencils, paper clips, a Scotch tape dispenser, a pencil sharpener, memo pads, a broken pair of scissors. And strings, too. Dozens of long white strings. Like fishing lines, Ruth thought, each attached to an item from the desk. The strings snaked across the floor and disappeared into Henry's walk-in closet.

"Mother of virgins!" he was yelling. "Help!"

Tentatively, Ruth picked her way through the debris and peered into the closet, waiting for her eyes to adjust.

"Judas Priest!" Henry squealed. "Get me loose!"

It took some time for Ruth to make sense of it all. The man sat wiggling in his overstuffed chair; a band of strings was wrapped around his forehead like a pauper's crown. Struggling, he yanked his neck back, which set off a chain reaction: the strings went taut, there was a clattering sound, and a procession of desk items came scooting across the rug. A small plastic ruler slithered up to his left foot.

Henry's eyeballs made a long, wide revolution in their sockets.

He sat tied firmly to the chair, yards of string winding around his wrists and chest and knees and ankles. The King of Trinkets, Ruth thought, strapped to his throne. She stepped into the closet and switched on the overhead light.

Luis peeked out from behind an old overcoat, a ball of string in his hand.

"Help!" Henry yelped. "One minute I'm sleeping like a baby, next minute I lift my head, I'm hog-tied. And every damn thing in my desk comes flying out." He tried to blow a string off his nose. "Kid's nothing but trouble."

"He was snoring," Luis said. "I can't sleep when he snores."

Ruth nodded grimly. "*That* I can understand."

With a quick laugh, Karen moved into the closet and began to undo the maze of strings.

"Angel of mercy!" Henry said, and grinned stupidly. "Karen — darling — God bless you!"

Ruth watched for a second, then shook her head. "If I were you, Karen, I'd just leave him be. Let Mr. Solitaire figure his own way out." She put a hand on Luis's shoulder. "Go on, amigo, run on into my room and I'll come tuck you in." She smiled at the boy as he left, then turned to Henry. "Hurry up, now," she said. "We're going down to the beach."

Karen looked at her grandmother, astonished, then continued to disentangle Henry.

"What?" the man hollered.

"The beach," Ruth repeated. "Mike's waiting."

"For Chrissakes," said Henry. "I got this damned plug in my ear, can't hear a friggin' word."

"The beach!" Ruth yelled.

A bright, almost playful glow of pleasure came into Henry's face. "Swimsuit time!" he said.

He began to struggle against the strings with renewed vigor.

Ruth leaned over, yanked out the radio earplug, and said, "Good luck. We leave in fifteen minutes."

Back in her own room, Ruth shuffled over to the space heater next to the TV. She picked up her sleeping bag and, when Karen arrived, handed it to the girl. Luis lay at the foot of Ruth's bed, sound asleep.

"If you're done helping the old geezer," Ruth said, voice slightly bitter, "you can do a favor for youth and zip this boy in for a proper nap."

Karen pulled the sleeping bag from its plastic sack and sniffed at the nylon. "Thing's filthy," she said. "You should let Luzma wash it or else sleep between the sheets like a regular person. And, by the way, if you'd ever turn that radio off," she said, nodding toward Ruth's bedside table, "you'd be able to hear the ocean from your bed."

Ignoring the girl, Ruth bent down for her sit-up pillow. A sharp, painful jolt shot down her spine. She grabbed on to the TV antennas for balance, squeezing with both hands, but even then she couldn't steady herself. The makeshift rabbit ears had been molded from strips of tinfoil — like holding on to air — and after a second she teetered backward, scattering the pile of catalogues at the foot of her bed.

Karen dropped the sleeping bag and reached out to catch her. "Jesus, Grammy, I'm really worried. No kidding, I think we'd better call the doctor. Right now."

"Don't *touch* that phone," Ruth said.

With effort she pushed herself upright, stood with her feet widely separated. Even so, she felt like a cattail in a brisk wind.

"When I talked to Dr. Ash about my knee two days ago, he said I was born with my problems. Some genetic nonsense. So if I've made it this far, I'll be just fine today."

"But you can't —"

Ruth covered her ears with her hands. She smoothed her hair, brought her arms to her sides, and walked around the TV to her chair. "Well, I'll rest here for just a minute, if you can handle that sleeping bag properly." She tugged on the towel at her waist, moving the flap to her left side, then tucked in her blouse and sat down. "But I won't be idle for long."

Karen groaned. "You're impossible," she said, and lifted the sleeping bag, carrying it over to Ruth's bed. She paused at the nightstand, turned the radio down low. Then for several seconds she stood very still, as if distracted, or as if contemplating some hidden internal puzzle. "And this old pillbox, too — you've had it as long as I can remember. How about if I get you a new one for Christmas?"

The box *was* a sad thing, Ruth knew, chipped and dirty, like everything else in the bedroom. But still, it seemed odd how the girl kept poking through the pills, sliding a hand down toward the pocket of her shorts.

"I hope you realize," Ruth said, "that those drugs are prescription. People can't just swallow them willy-nilly."

"Swallow what?" Karen said.

"Whatever's in that pocket."

"Oh, that's —"

"Listen, I know you're upset, dear — this Mike business — but if you need to calm your nerves, I'd recommend a nice cup of hot milk. Not tranquilizers."

Karen seemed relieved. She smiled and said, "Well, thanks, but I'm afraid you're seeing things."

"Perhaps so," Ruth said. She adjusted her glasses. "Lately I've been . . . Just remember, though, you can't medicate your life."

As Karen spread the sleeping bag over Luis, he grumbled in his sleep and said, "Shit!"

Karen looked at her grandmother. "What's with him?"

"Oh, nothing new — fighting at school, that ferocious father of his, you get the picture."

Karen looked personally wounded. "Really, Grammy. The things you say sometimes."

Ruth let out a small snort and looked down at her stiff bony fingers, folding them in and out. "We all have our troubles, Karen, but I certainly don't go constantly complaining or chewing on pills every time a little predicament pops up. Just stick to my routine and hold my head high and keep marching on, no matter what."

She looked up.

Karen was gone. A soft purring sound drifted through the bedroom, and for an instant it seemed the girl had been sucked away by an invisible vacuum cleaner. Then Ruth noticed the tip of a tennis shoe bobbing on the floor near the bedside table. Partly hidden, her back against the bed, Karen had sunk down to the carpet. She was holding her head in her hands, weeping.

Ruth felt quite helpless. "Come on now," she finally said, shuffling over to the side of the bed. "Self-control, Karen. Keep yourself together."

The girl's sobs only thickened. "I'm *trying*. Except it feels like my whole stupid goddamned life is . . . Don't you realize these things are hard for some people? Maybe not for you — it doesn't even seem like anybody matters very much to you."

Ruth stared. How could Karen, of all people, say that? It didn't make sense. Just like that Mr. Chuckly Voice with his flippant reprimands. Briefly then, as she looked down on the weeping girl, she felt a bizarre heat radiate up through her body, a kind of visceral comprehension. Her granddaughter, for all her complex rationalizations, was terribly frightened. This boy Mike had set her head spinning; she'd lost her internal compass. Her hair dyeing and gum chomping and fast car and glamorous job — these were mere breakwaters, bulwarks against the shifting demands of ordinary human uncertainty. Ruth recognized herself in her granddaughter. And down inside, where the sand was, she felt the same shifting ambiguities, the same terror.

She waited for a moment, one hand grasping the bedpost, then lowered herself to the floor. Her knee popped; her entire left side tingled. "There," she murmured, "there now." Hesitant, she reached out toward the girl. "I'm sorry."

Karen bent her head against her grandmother's chest. "Mike and me — I mean, *me*, I guess — I was so in *love* with him. I thought we were so absolutely, perfectly *made* for each other." Her shoulders heaved. "God, it's like —" She pulled a wad of gum from her mouth, wrapped it up, and tossed it feebly in front of her. "I don't know — I guess you're right, Grammy. I guess he *doesn't* really love me." Her voice wavered. She pulled in a heavy breath.

Awkwardly then, aware of the tension in her own body, Ruth reached out and put an arm around her granddaughter's shoulders. For a long time she simply cradled her. "Sweetheart, sweetheart," she said, but then her breath caught. A sudden thought struck her. Not a thought, exactly: a picture. Karen as an eight-year-old, Carter dropping her off to spend a weekend in Laguna, the first of many weekends she was to spend at Paradise Lagoon during her parents' bitter divorce. Despite all the sorrows at home, Karen was a happy child. Always talking a mile a minute. Always laughing. Ruth remembered how at night they'd sleep in the same bed, how they'd build blanket-forts and make things snug and lie there telling each other bedtime stories. Yes, and how they'd play that game called Lost Spider. "Where's my web, where's my web?" Ruth used to whisper, and she'd run a finger along Karen's tiny ear, tickling, then pulling away. "Where's my web?" she'd keep saying, and she'd bring the finger closer to the ear's opening, hovering there, making spirals, maybe retreating for a moment — "Where am I?" — and then slipping the finger down Karen's arm with a touch so light that the skin would turn to gooseflesh — "Hurry up, Grammy! Hurry, hurry!" — and then, at the last instant, Ruth would plunge the finger deep into Karen's little belly-button — "I'm home!" Now, cradling the girl, Ruth could still see all this. She could hear it, too, and feel it, how Karen kept squealing and giggling, and how later they'd curl up together, side by side, dreaming.

"There now," Ruth said. She paused for a moment: one's options in life were so horridly limited. "I didn't mean to imply he doesn't love you." She thought of Mr. Chuckly Voice and tried to insert some cheer into her words. "All I'm saying is, he needs to get his priorities in order. You know, his people steeple." She nudged the girl. "And you need to remember your dignity."

She waited for a reply.

"Isn't that right?"

Karen made an effort to straighten up, toyed with the laces on her tennis shoes. "I'm just so tired," she whispered.

"I know, honey. I know *exactly* how you feel."

And then for a long while they sat together on the floor, feeling the closeness.

The distant sound of shrieking gulls came through the open window. A cool breeze filled the room as the late-afternoon shadows moved like spilled oil across the dirty white carpet.

Ruth brushed a wisp of hair from her granddaughter's cheek. "Aren't we a pair?" she said. "Two lost spiders."

5:42 P.M.

They walked hand in hand to the elevator. Ruth pushed the button to bring it up, and a minute later, when the door slid open, Luzma stepped out with Ruth's slacks and panty girdle. She was eating a chocolate candy.

"Here's your things, Ruthie, good as new." Luzma wiped her mouth on the back of her hand, tossed her hair behind her shoulders. "I mopped the bathroom floor and put in the second load of laundry. Nothing more to do, really, till it's ready for the dryer."

"What about the dusting?"

"Already done," Luzma said. "Last week, remember?" Her eyes twinkled. "Mike's here, out on the balcony. Says he waited over an hour at the beach." She beamed at Karen. "Muy guapo, as usual."

Ruth looked at Karen, pulled her into the elevator. "I'll dress on the way down," she said.

The elevator was cramped with three passengers, barely enough space to move, and it was a struggle for Ruth to slip the panty girdle over her sandaled feet. She bent down, nudging Karen sideways, then cautiously straightened up again. The girdle still dangled at her knees.

"You want help?" Luzma asked.

"No," Ruth said, "I do not."

"Just turn around, I'll yank it up real fast."

"*Please.* I'm fine."

The elevator cables jiggled. Ruth lunged forward, and then backward, and then waited a moment before reaching down again.

"Perfectly fine," she muttered. Discreetly, one elbow clamping the towel to her waist, she wrestled the girdle over her hips and up to her stomach. Her breath was coming hard. Bad air, she thought — like getting dressed in a casket. She pulled on her slacks, hooked them shut, and draped the green towel over the safety rail.

"Eighty-eight years old," she said to no one in particular, "but I can certainly find the wherewithal to dress myself." She felt strangely loose inside. Her thoughts were rattling around like coins in a large dark piggy bank, and it took effort to focus on the simplest practical details. "You finished everything?" she asked Luzma. "Polished all the silver?"

"Sure, Ruthie, six times in the last two months."

"Good. One more won't hurt."

Luzma glanced at Karen as if to inquire about something, then reached out to tuck Ruth's blouse into her slacks. "What about this dizzy problem?"

Ruth pushed Luzma's hands away. "Never mind. You're still planning to stay for dinner, aren't you?"

Luzma looked at Karen again, raising her painted eyebrows,

and Karen nodded. Luzma patted Ruth on the back. "Sure," she said, "I'm staying."

"I'll stay too," Karen said. "Mike too."

With a jolt, the elevator landed at the second floor. Luzma gave Ruth one more comforting pat, then pushed her way out and lifted the silver tea set from the phone table and headed straight toward the kitchen, whistling. Ruth shuffled to keep up with her. Briefly, she thought of Mike waiting out on the balcony; at the same time, however, she pictured Karen's teary eyes, and decided the boy could use a lesson in patience. "Henry bought some nice frozen turkey dinners for tonight," she said to Luzma. "And I'll make salads. Of course, with Karen staying, and Mike, we won't have enough to eat."

Karen reached out for Ruth's elbow. "Hold on, Grammy," she said. "Please quit rushing, you're not up to it. Anyway, those dinners take thirty minutes to cook." She pointed across the sitting room, past the piano, to a spot where tightly closed drapes hid the sliding glass doors that gave access to the balcony. "Go on out and talk with Mike for a minute while I pop the dinners into the oven."

Ruth looked suspiciously at her granddaughter. "Why on earth would I greet him alone?"

"Come on, he's *waiting* out there."

"Splendid," Ruth said. "Waiting's tonic for the soul." She gave her granddaughter a sly little smile and sat down in her place at the dining table, the only spot that was cleared of old knickknacks and mail. Karen hesitated, glancing toward the balcony. "Well, I guess," she said. "Rest up a minute while I take care of things in the kitchen, then we'll go out and greet him together."

The kitchen, Ruth knew, was a mess. There were piles of used napkins on top of and behind the toaster oven, greasy paper plates stashed between the bread box and spice rack. Grime in every crack, dirty dishes in the sink and drainer. Five or six burnt-out light bulbs — which Ruth had inscribed in permanent black ink with the date they had ceased to function — were lined up along the kitchen windowsill. Several boxes of chocolates, which Ruth had wrapped in plastic freezer bags, were stashed away in half-open drawers, some of the boxes years old.

As Ruth watched, Karen took one of the freezer bags from a drawer and pulled out a heart-shaped candy box. She peeked inside and selected a candy.

"Well, help yourself," Ruth mumbled.

But just as Karen put the chocolate to her lips, she paused. She held the candy up and examined its bottom, which was gone, the cream center entirely scooped out.

Luzma laughed. "Join the club," she said. "Some days it takes me hours to find a whole one. Our little Ruthie, she's got some weird habits."

Ruth smiled to herself. "They *are* my candies," she said. She looked down at her hands. The palm of her right hand was still blistered; her left hand was still cramped and numb. Damn, she thought. Painfully, she clenched and unclenched her fists. With a sigh, she shut her eyes to rest. She could hear the girls chatting in the kitchen. Luzma, as usual, was complaining about how she had to ride the bus to work six days a week, and how every Saturday for the past five years, since her husband got a job at Margarita Haven, she'd had to bring Luis with her. Together they rode the bus, Luzma said, and together they visited every kind of house California had to offer, like a cheap version of those mansion tours in Hollywood.

"One thing for sure," Luzma was saying, "I'm tired of all this driving around to other people's places. I got my plans. Go to classes, learn real estate. Start *selling* houses."

Ruth opened her eyes and peered out toward the kitchen. Karen was standing beside Luzma, one hand gripping a salt shaker, the other crammed into the pocket of her shorts.

"Well, great idea," Karen was saying. "Lots of women and young people in the business. I hear we're in a down market, but there's only so much California. Things are bound to turn up." She pulled her hand from her pocket, glanced over the counter toward Ruth. "Luzma, could you help me with something? You know how . . ." Karen's voice became curiously quiet, and though Ruth strained to hear, the words seemed to fade in and out. "When those dinners are done, make sure that . . . and plenty of salt so she won't . . ."

"What are you doing in there?" Ruth called. People didn't seem to realize she knew what went on in her own house. That very morning, for God's sake, she'd twice caught Henry red-handed, right in the act.

Karen turned to face her. "Oh, nothing, Grammy," she said. "Discussing real estate."

"Well, don't go rearranging things. You may think I'm old and crazy, but I can still spot a conspiracy when I see one." She felt too tired to say anything else. And, though she'd already rested so many times today, she was having trouble keeping her eyes open. She stretched her arms out on the table in front of her.

"I can *hear* you, too," she mumbled.

5:55 P.M.

"You awake?" Karen asked. "Dinner's in the oven." She lifted a ring of keys from the table; when she jostled the pieces of metal in her palm, they made a light tinkling sound, like sleigh bells. "Mike's still waiting out there."

Hesitating, Ruth lifted her head. The world seemed to have gone blurry during her snooze, a fluid melting at the edges of things; she felt the need to reestablish some solidity. Slowly, with real effort, she stood up and moved to the foot of the stairs. She gathered some oxygen into her lungs.

"Henry!" she yelled. "Come on, man. Visitors!"

Karen took an indecisive half-step toward Ruth. "Look, I'm sorry you're not comfortable with this. I mean, I know you're under the weather."

"Don't be silly, dear. I was willing to go the whole way down to the beach to greet the man, wasn't I?" She kept her eyes fixed on the landing of the stairs. She wanted very much to talk to her granddaughter, but what of any real significance could be said? She glanced over at the girl, who was bobbing up and down, sliding a new stick of gum into her mouth.

"Does it hurt much?" Karen asked.

"Oh, probably."

"Probably where?"

Just then Henry appeared at the landing, bits of string trailing behind his shoes as he lumbered down the steps. Ruth's eyes wandered across his shirt, which was still not buttoned properly. His wispy white hair was matted into strange shapes. With a thump, he came to rest at the bottom of the stairs. "Beach time," he said, and grabbed Ruth's hand.

Ruth allowed her hand to remain in Henry's. To her own surprise she even shuffled toward him, leaning forward a little. "No, Henry, the beach is off. Mike's *here*, out on the balcony. You remember Mike — Karen's alleged husband."

"Oh, yeah, the spy. Good fellow."

"You're entitled to that opinion," Ruth said. "Anyway, he's here for dinner." She lowered her voice to a whisper. "I don't know what he'll eat, though, because we only bought the four turkeys." And she started across the room, pulling Henry along after her like a fishing line heavy with bait.

6:00 P.M.

Henry reached into his back pocket, pulled out his baseball cap, placed it squarely on his head. After a second he sank down into a wicker chair opposite Mike.

"So look here," he said earnestly, "how's the spy business?"

Ruth couldn't help snorting. She took a seat beside Henry and crossed her legs.

Off to the west, beyond a row of pointed condominium roofs, the sky shone with a purplish blue glow like the inside of an abalone shell. A cool, salty breeze swept across the balcony.

"Spy business?" Mike said slowly. A narrow crease formed between his eyes as he slung his feet up on Ruth's glass-topped coffee table. "I'm not sure I follow."

"Hey, mum's the word," Henry said. "State secrets and all that."

Mike shot a quick, accusatory glance at Karen, who stood beside him, leaning against the wooden balcony railing. "Afraid you've been misinformed. I'm no spy."

"Course you ain't."

"Seriously, I'm a teacher."

Henry snapped off a crisp military salute. "Cat's got my tongue. Couldn't even torture it out of me, no sir. Call me Silent Sam."

"Well, thanks," Mike said.

"You guys still use them fingernail-yanker things?"

Ruth waved a hand at the air. "Henry, *listen* to him, he's a schoolteacher."

"I'd just like to take a little look-see if he's got —"

"Fourth grade," Karen said.

"Gotcha." Henry lowered his voice. "Maximum deep cover."

Again Mike glanced at Karen, who found an excuse to fix her gaze elsewhere. The girl's fingers flitted along the railing like nervous butterflies.

Ruth opted for mercy. "Look, I don't know where this spy stuff came from," she said, "but I recommend we change the subject. Nice evening. Typical California December."

"Very," Karen said.

Mike gave her a last sharp look, which promised future discussion, then turned to Ruth and summoned up a pleasant smile. He had excellent teeth, large and very white. A good-looking specimen, all in all. Almost handsome, in a boyish sort of way: freckled and sandy-haired and playful around the eyes. He was wearing one of those fuzzy outdoorsman's jackets, with faded jeans and tennis shoes like Karen's.

There was an uncomfortable silence before Mike smiled again and said, "So here we are."

Then came a longer, denser quiet.

Ruth eased back in her chair, eyes fixed guardedly on Karen, listening with half an ear as Henry began filling up the silence with a spray of baseball chatter. In his own way, she thought, the old man knew what he was doing. Even that relentless spy talk, it was a method of deflection, using his own buffoonery to cut through the awkwardness and tension among them. He was annoying, true, but he also had a generous, well-intentioned manner that she couldn't quite deny.

After a time Karen visibly relaxed, and Mike too. The sun was low on its journey toward Japan.

"Don't get me wrong," Henry was explaining, "I ain't against progress, but these new feminine-style uniforms, they strike me like something you'd see on a bunch of ballet dancers over at the . . ."

Ruth tuned out again as the old man soared off into soliloquy. The descending sun caught her eye, fierce and bloody as it moved below the balcony railing, highlighting her granddaughter's thin figure, and for an instant she found herself overwhelmed by a powerful sense of her own aliveness. She thought of Frank Deeds on that morning forty-some years ago when he leaned cockily against an almost identical wooden railing at the San Diego marina; she thought of Hale, too, how hot his skin had been on the night he died — the way he'd called out that word "Time!" — and how his death, when it came, had seemed an act of pure and ferocious desire.

For a few minutes she sat quite still, hearing nothing, trying to gather up her emotions. She almost felt like crying.

Various obscure thoughts revolved inside her: the notions of youth and age, the fragilities and resiliences of the ordinary human spirit. At one point she lifted up her aching leg. So pretty, she thought. Her mother's legs, too, and her granddaughter's. The promise of happiness was always so rich and infinite, the reality so abridged.

Quickly then, with a jerking motion, she stood up. "I've got to fix the salads," she said. "You coming, Karen?" And she exited the balcony.

6:23 P.M.

Ruth trudged through the sliding glass door, humming to herself, trying to ignore the shifting sensations in her stomach. All this commotion — it was overwhelming.

In the kitchen, Luzma had set the TV dinners on top of the stove and was peeling back their plastic wrappers.

"I hope those things don't cool too quickly, I still need to make our salads," Ruth said. This was a matter of vital importance, she told herself. After all, there was still living to be done; you couldn't eat an old lady's musings. "Of course, we don't have enough turkeys," she said. "I guess Henry and Luis can have bologna." She reached for the refrigerator handle, bending slightly, and suddenly lost her balance. She grabbed Luzma's arm.

"Okay?" Luzma asked.

"Yes, fine."

"You're sure?" Karen asked, coming up from behind.

"Perfectly," Ruth said, but a great black exhaustion seemed to fill her body. Maybe these girls were right, she shouldn't be moving around so much.

"Look," Karen said, helping to open the refrigerator, "I'm not hungry, Grammy. Just salad for me. Henry can have his turkey; I'll make a bologna sandwich for Luis."

Ruth peered straight ahead into the refrigerator. "That's fine. If you want to be anorexic, refusing to eat, sucking noses, I certainly won't stand in your way."

"Sucking noses?"

"Oh, you know." Ruth inserted a healthy dose of authority into her voice. "You know exactly what I mean. I get around. I've seen all the kids doing it. Go ahead, join them if you like. Just don't ever forget it was germs that killed your grandfather."

Karen sighed. "I have no idea what you're talking about." She pulled the packet of bologna from the meat drawer and moved over to the counter.

Ruth continued to gaze straight ahead. Five open quarts of milk — three nonfat and two whole — took up most of the space on the middle shelf; each carton was wrapped in a plastic bag and clothespinned at the top. Tidbits of chicken and other leftovers were sealed in zip-lock sandwich baggies and crammed onto the top shelf between yogurt cartons and margarine tubs. A glass coffeepot, the automatic-drip-machine type, and an old percolator stood side by side on the bottom shelf.

Ruth pushed the percolator aside and reached in for her salad makings.

"Well, well," she said. "Something's amiss."

Luzma laughed. "The famous Refrigerator Rules."

"Don't be smart with me."

"No chance, Ruthie. Rules are rules."

Ruth let the girl's sarcasm pass. Right now there was the problem of getting to her cottage cheese and pineapple: her wax-coated muffin bags were blocking the way. And the bags had clearly been tampered with — Henry's doing, almost for sure. Ruth groaned and shook her head. Muttering to herself, she passed several waxed bags over to Luzma, then reached down for her salad makings on the bottom shelf. When she turned around, Luzma was leaning over the garbage bin, about to throw the muffin bags away.

"Hey, I'm saving those!" Ruth snapped.

"Por qué?" Luzma looked startled. "You kid me, right?"

"I am not a kidder. Those are valuable." Ruth straightened up quickly, arms bent sharply at the elbows, a cottage cheese tub in one hand and a pineapple tin in the other.

Luzma held the bags out in front of her, looking with disgust at the refrigerator. "But why so much old crud in there? It's too hard to get at things."

"Don't say 'get at,' Luzma. Just say 'get.'"

"Yeah, okay, but all these stinky old bags, you catch yourself a disease or something."

Ruth sighed. "Listen, dear, I sincerely believe if you'd been around in 1930, back when the Depression began —"

"Filthy," Luzma said, her voice tight. "Unhealthy. Health hazard."

"Not in the least. They're waxed."

"So what?"

"Moisture resistant, I might add. Extremely sanitary. No germ on earth could wiggle through, not even those evil little villains that took my Hale away. I don't believe I've ever told you how he came down with that terrible —"

"You told her, Grammy." Karen was buttering a piece of bread.

"I wasn't talking to you," Ruth said. She looked at Luzma. "Did I tell you?"

"Dios mío. A lot of times. Remember?" Instantly, Luzma's eyes went soft with compassion.

"Yes, well. To be sure." Ruth nodded at the counter. "Clear me a space next to Karen there, please."

6:32 P.M.

Ruth lumped two tablespoons of cottage cheese into each of six tea saucers, which she always used for salads. She placed four pineapple chunks on each cheese mound, and a spoonful of coleslaw at the side, for roughage. When these operations were completed, she asked Luzma to clear the table — "Keep my papers in their separate stacks," she warned, "and be gentle with those cardboard envelopes, they happen to contain my fortune" — and then she carefully transported the salads to the table, one by one.

As Ruth placed a salad at what was always Luzma's place, at the end of the table beneath the window, a sudden shower of sparks crackled along her neck and spine. Like a lightning bolt, almost, and it sprayed out from the back of her skull and across her forehead and down toward her left shoulder, where it paused to gather new voltage, dividing into two halves and sizzling down her left arm and left leg. The world went null-white. She lost touch with her own whereabouts; consciousness was just a distant tapping amid the electric buzz.

For a few twinkling seconds she felt utterly powerless. Like loving someone too much, or losing him, or waking in the middle of a dream.

When her vision cleared, she was surprised to find herself still standing there, clutching the back of Luzma's chair.

She felt a vaguely familiar pang.

"So *that's* it," she murmured. She stretched her arms, took a few hesitant steps away from the table. Half smiling, calmed by a sense of recognition, she adjusted her glasses and watched with a kind of prideful curiosity as her pretty old legs carried her back to the kitchen. "Yes, of course," she said. "What else?"

Surf's up!

Time chime!

Ruth nodded to herself. She watched Karen carry the last salad dish to the table and arrange the silverware and water glasses. They would all drink ice water, except Luis, who'd have milk.

When things had been orchestrated to her satisfaction, Ruth moved to the stairs and called up to Luis: "Come get it, amigo! Dinner's on." In a moment the boy came tripping down, barefoot and still groggy with sleep, and plunked himself into his assigned chair at the table, between Ruth and his mother. Ruth tucked a napkin under his collar, smoothed it down, then moved out into the sitting room and shouted toward the balcony. "Come on, Henry! Right now, man, dinner's ready!"

Luzma giggled from the kitchen. "Sounds like you're calling a dog," she said. "Here boy! Here boy!"

"Perhaps so," Ruth said crisply, "except most dogs are trained to obey." She shouted again, "Henry!"

Karen drifted past and opened the sliding glass doors. "Okay, boys," Ruth heard her say, "soup's on."

Ruth returned to the table and slipped into her place. She watched Luzma carry the TV dinners out two at a time, placing them on paper plates to catch spills, the way Ruth liked. "This one's yours," the girl said to Ruth.

Across the table, Mike and Karen sat down beside each other. Henry slumped into the chair to Ruth's left, at the head of the table. He pulled over his dinner. "Jeez," he said, "what a day. Trussed up like a damn Thanksgiving turkey." He gave Luis a suspicious, almost fearful stare. "Kid's a bundle of laughs." He tugged on the visor of his baseball cap.

Luzma took her seat. "You're a good sport, Henry. And it's nice to have you down here for a change, not eating all alone up at your desk."

Henry beamed. He'd had a crush on Luzma for years, sneaking peeks at her bottom whenever she happened to bend over. "Well, it ain't often we got guests. I figure it's my job to keep things on the up-and-up." He tucked his napkin into his collar. "Looks like you've prepared a pretty good feast here, Lucy."

"*Luzma*," Luzma said, and laughed. She undid the top button of her jeans to make room for dinner.

Henry's eyes bulged. He tugged at his baseball cap and forced himself to turn toward Ruth. "So how'd business go this morning? See anybody downtown?"

"Just Nora," said Ruth. "She has a new boyfriend. It appears there's no rest for the weary."

Beneath the table, one of Mike's feet nudged up against Ruth's ankle. He didn't apologize. In fact, Ruth noticed, he was conspicuously quiet, prodding at his meal with his knife. Men, Ruth thought. Masters and enforcers of silence. She felt furious. She *would* hear this boy explain himself. "You know," she said to Karen, anger rising in her voice, "for all your lectures about new stories —"

"Dinnertime!" Henry cried.

Ruth sighed and directed her attention toward the man as he grasped his fork and scooped up a mound of mashed potatoes. She wagged her head: his habits were so ridiculously predictable. He wouldn't go for the turkey immediately; it might be too stringy for his gums. He'd avoid the dressing altogether — too crunchy. First the mashed potatoes, then the cranberry sauce, then the peas. Finally he'd screw in his loose tooth and chew as many bites of meat as he could manage, until Ruth came to pick up his plate. Pitiful, Ruth thought. In some ways the man was more helpless than a baby.

"Delicious entrée," Henry said. "I'd have to rate it a genuine gourmet delight."

He drooled a little as he forked the mashed potatoes into his mouth. Then he noticed Luzma sitting across from him with her head bowed; he drew back his fork, staring at her wide-eyed for a moment. Ruth couldn't help smiling. The girl was simply scraping some excess salt off her turkey, Ruth knew, but Henry obviously thought she was in prayer. Henry's first wife, Eleanor, had been Catholic, and he still loved all the rituals and Hail Marys and elaborate hand actions. It made him feel "cleanly," he used to say.

Now, hands folded, he began to mumble a prayer of his own. Luzma blinked and glanced over at Ruth; Ruth blinked too, and stared at Henry. It went on for almost a full minute, then Henry crossed himself and raised up his water glass. "We have a lot to be thankful for," he said. "À la salud."

"Oh, Jesus," Ruth said.

Beside her, Luis made little farting sounds.

Mike continued eating, his movements stiff and deliberate, but Karen giggled.

Luzma said, "Amen."

Ruth studied her TV dinner. Turkey was by far her favorite, much better than the enchiladas or the meat loaf. Diligently, making sure she hadn't been cheated, she took stock of the items in each plastic compartment. All the old-fashioned trimmings were there. Gravy and home-style dressing and peas in seasoned sauce. Cranberry with . . . She leaned forward for a closer look. Instead of deep red cranberry sauce, this stuff had strange pale hunks in it.

She made a sour face and looked around the table. "Is this someone's idea of a joke?"

Luzma shook her head. "Apple-cranberry. So what?"

"Okay by me," Henry said.

"Puke," said Luis, and began to dissect his bologna sandwich.

Ruth frowned, lifted her fork, dipped it skeptically into the sauce. Well fine, she thought. Always fiddling with basics. She tasted it. "Unusual," she muttered, and continued to take inventory. God knows what they'd done to the mashed potatoes: probably laced with tofu. And no dessert at all, not even a piece of apple crisp. Here she was, eighty-eight years old, looking forward to just a little something sweet at the end of her meal, and what did these cheapskates give her? Not a thing. Back when the dinners had been covered with foil — and even more recently, since they'd started using that plastic wrapping you had to peel off or poke holes in — back then, the dinners had *always* come with apple crisp. This new development struck her as positively sinful.

"Karen, Mike," she said, "why do you think —"

And what was *that* on her turkey?

She closed one eye and bent forward over the dinner. A white powdery substance, almost like chalk, had been sprinkled over her entire entrée. For a second she wondered if it might be a defect in her vision, another wave of those blurry white speckles. She poked at the stuff with her fork. And then the truth came to her: cheese. Parmesan cheese — nothing else could look like that.

She turned to Luzma. "Dear," she said crossly, "you *know* I don't like Parmesan."

"Parmesan?"

"Here! See here?" She was raising her voice. "Right here on top of my turkey!"

Henry leaned over. "What's that you say?"

"Parmesan!"

"What?"

"Take your nose out of my dish," Ruth said. "What I *say* is, there's cheese on my turkey."

"Sounds gourmet to me," Henry said, and beamed at Luzma. "Never tried it, now, but Eleanor used to fix turkey with yams and marshmallows on top, and sometimes peaches, and I liked all that pretty fine."

"Yuck-a-doo," said Luis. "Pooh-pooh, too."

"I'm quite sure Eleanor was a fine cook," Ruth said, "but I don't believe that's the issue right now. Luzma, I *despise* Parmesan."

The girl seemed nervous. "Just salt, Ruthie."

"Calm down, Grammy," Karen said, "it's on everybody's dinners. See, look at Henry's."

At that very moment Henry was sprinkling salt all over his apple-cranberry serving.

"Salt my eye," said Ruth, her voice loud. "This is what I call cheese. What do you all think we're eating here? It's supposed to be turkey, just basic regular-style turkey!" She licked her index finger, preparing to Test the tiny white flakes, except she couldn't quite get her fingers to separate. Oddly, this complication had a calming effect on her temper. Never mind, she thought. Maybe the cheese nonsense was some ancient Mexican custom; she certainly didn't want to hurt Luzma's feelings. With a sigh, Ruth gave the girl a sidelong glance, looked down at the dinner, and sliced off a small piece of white meat. There was a first time for everything. She lifted the meat to her mouth and started to chew.

"Not so bad," she said. "Not bad at all. Very Latin." Strange, though, it didn't taste like cheese. Surely not Parmesan. "Very interesting. South of the border, so to speak."

"There's this kid," said Luis. "This black kid named Tony — he's my friend — and he used to scare me all the time on purpose. Like, whenever I walked to school in the morning, he hided himself at that liquor store on the highway. Right behind that big trash can there, and then —"

"That's a dumpster," said Henry. "Next to the Spigot. Used to know the place pretty well myself."

Luis nodded. "Yeah. So this kid Tony, he always hided there, and every time I walked by, he jumped out and yelled bad stuff. 'You're so white,' he goes. 'You're as white as a whale's behind.'"

"Luis, please," Luzma said, "let's everybody just enjoy eating, before it gets cold."

Across the table, Karen sat observing the boy. She looked worried.

"Yeah, but he kept doing it all the time," Luis said. "So I decided to kick his ass."

Henry's mouth hung open; a pale hunk of apple dropped to the table. "Atta boy," he said. "And you let him have it?"

"Henry!" Karen said. "Don't encourage him. Kids are violent enough."

"That's right," Ruth said. "All those knives and guns and gang murders." She patted Luis on the head. "Revenge is never proper, dear. Don't take out your frustrations on others. Just keep a stiff spine. You know, backbone!"

Luzma rapped the table with her knuckles. "That's enough, everybody. I have something important to talk about." She placed her fork beside her plate and turned to Ruth. "Something I want to tell you about. I got this plan. Make a future for myself — right? — don't want Luis riding around on the bus his whole life. Anyway, now that things are going good for Enrique, settled down a little, I want to get my own profession. Like I was telling Karen —

go into the realty business. I read all about it in these brochures, and I . . . Are you listening?"

Ruth was in no mood to answer. As she was stabbing the last bite of her meat, she'd noticed something else on top of it, something pink.

"Just one question," she said grimly. "What kind of salt comes in pink?"

"No kind," Henry said, "and that's a fact. Which reminds me, today I went up to the bakery section —"

"What reminds you, Henry? Pink salt?"

"No, the thing Luzma said a minute ago, about the bus."

Ruth made a growling noise. What was it with this man's selective hearing? He made strategic use of his ears, to be sure — just like his legal blindness and sporadic buffoonery. She put a hand to her stomach. Patience.

Henry smiled affably. "So today I go up to the bakery section for Ruthie's muffin, right? And there's this young kid working there who says, 'I know, one oat bran muffin,' and I says, 'Who the devil are you?' and the kid says, 'We've known each other for two years, Mr. Hubble,' and I say, 'Hey, I know all the girls who work here. I never seen you before in my whole life.' So the kid says, 'I'm no girl, Mr. Hubble' — it's a guy, see — so he says, 'I'm Steve, and I've been giving you muffins here every weekend for the past two years.' And I says, 'Weekend? What day is today?' and he says, 'Saturday,' and I says . . .'"

"Jesus," Ruth said.

Karen giggled.

"Just listen a minute," Henry said. "My little story gets pretty dang interesting."

"*Your* story?" Ruth looked around the table. "What I want to know is, what culture on earth eats pink cheese?"

Henry coughed suddenly and spat a wad of turkey onto his plate. Eyes watering, he ran his tongue across his gums, muttering to himself, then picked up the meat and began pawing at it with his fingers. He plucked a yellow tooth from the meat, said "Bingo!" and dropped the tooth into his water glass.

Ruth nearly gagged. "Henry, I'm warning you, there'd better be some point to this. You interrupted Luzma, you know."

Henry dipped his spoon into his water glass and scooped up the yellow tooth. He spun it between his fingers, getting the angle right, and jammed it back into the opening in his gums.

"I didn't interrupt the lady," Henry said. "You did it first, all your harping about green cheese. Anyways, if you don't mind, I think the señora wants to hear the end of this one, even if you don't." He smiled at Luzma. "So I says, 'Saturday? My God!' And the bakery kid says, 'Hey, Mr. Hubble, come on out back and see how I revamped my old van.' And he takes me out to the parking lot — you know, the one for the employees — and he shows me this big van he's got. Honest to God, he has that thing decked out sweet as can be, wall-to-wall carpeting, indoor plumbing, the works. So I check it out. I look at how the faucet's got hot water, how the bed folds out, and this kid says, 'I bet an old guy like you's got a billion stories to tell,' and I says, 'My God, how old you think I am?' and this bakery punk says —"

"Pink!" Ruth yelled. "I want to know who at this table has ever *once* ingested pink cheese!"

Luzma and Karen were both giggling now, and even Mike had a smile on his face. Luis said, "Asshole, Tony, *you're* white."

Mike turned angrily to the boy and spoke. "Excuse me, young man," he said in a schoolteacher's voice, "I *resent* your racist comments."

A white streak ricocheted across Ruth's field of vision, bouncing from object to object, off the table, up to the hanging lamp, over to the window; when it bounced back onto the table, Ruth recognized the very same creature she'd seen in the Postal Connection that morning. Yes indeed, a furry little white rabbit. She blinked several times. She felt a pain in her head and put her hands up to her temples and said, "Just stop!"

"Hey, qué pasa?" Luzma said.

Ruth straightened up in her chair and looked around the table: nothing out of the ordinary. So fast, she thought. She drew in a breath to settle herself. "Never mind. Go ahead now, Luzma, your plans."

"Ruthie, you look kind of —"

"Please. Let's hear it."

Luzma squinted at her for a moment. Then she looked around the table and cleared her throat. "Well, you know, I just want to improve myself. Real estate's the classy profession these days, especially around here, and you don't need college or anything to get a license. Just go to this class, or even do it by mail. A correspondence course, that sounds good to me."

Ruth put down her fork. Maybe it was Henry's story, or the pink cheese, or Mike's stubborn attitude, but she'd totally lost her appetite.

"So you'll quit cleaning, just like that? Do this correspondence business, then leave?" Ruth stared down at the napkin in her lap.

"Well, I'm thinking it's cheaper that way, by mail, but I could always take night classes."

"No," Ruth said. "What I mean is, it appears you're about to abandon us."

She lifted her head. Across the table, a furry white rabbit was rooting through Karen's salad, snorting and sniffling and thumping its paws. It glanced up at Ruth. It wrinkled its little pink nose. It wiggled its ears. Then, quick and sprightly, it hopped down from the table and out of sight.

"Please —" Ruth's breath caught. Was she going completely insane?

Turning in her chair, her guests momentarily unseen, she gazed past Luzma and out the dining room window. The sky was black. Her head was throbbing. The entire cosmos seemed to press against her temples.

What was this rabbity vision?

The creature of her habits come to life?

Something buried beneath those habits suddenly surfacing?

Something half forgotten, something never completely known, like a pebble lodged somewhere in the deep folds of her brain?

She could feel her heart beating.

All the hope and longing and regret in the world. All the expressions of love, and all the things that passed for love.

She shook her head. Enough.

But she continued to stare out the window, past the lighted tennis court and belt of green grass. Life, she thought, was so incredibly temporary. Nothing ever lasted, nobody ever stayed. But then she pictured Henry bumbling home across the highway with her groceries in his arms, so small from the vantage of this dining room window.

"You know, it's remarkable," she heard herself saying. "How we come to need each other. How we *become* each other."

The others looked up at her — Henry and Luzma and Karen and Mike — but also Hale and Elizabeth and Stephen and Frank and all the others, their faces uniting into a palpable human thereness.

A people steeple: *these* faces, her faces.

"It's hard to explain," Ruth said. "All of us here — we're not just ourselves, we're everyone. All the people we've known." Her eyes came into focus on the young couple across from her. "Like Karen. It's not just that she's my flesh and blood — my daughter in all the ways that matter — she actually helped to make me who I am."

Karen smiled.

"Very profound, Mrs. Hubble," Mike said. "Truly profound and amazing."

"Mike, please," Karen said beseechingly. She looked nervous again.

Ruth cleared her throat. "A teacher, young man. You must know the importance of respect for elders."

Mike rolled his eyes.

"God knows it's never simple," Ruth said, determined to continue. Her dinner was stone cold. "Marriages can be like zoos, I know that. Always that wildness inside the cage." She turned to fix her eyes on Henry. She felt oddly calm and articulate. "This old man and I — we have our ways of doing things, you know, ways of getting along. But it's more than that. He's *part* of me. I'm *part* of him. The things we remember, the things we've done — just circumstance and coincidence and habit, you might say, but —" She broke off abruptly.

"Anyway," she said, "one of life's little ironies, I suppose." She reached over and touched Henry's bony elbow. Then, beneath the table, she brought a foot down on top of Mike's toes — not hard, but not soft, either. "So what about you?"

"Yeah, what *about* me," Mike said, placing his napkin on the table. "Look, I don't know what you're trying to get at. All I know is, we're here to visit you. Doing you a favor. I don't want the third degree."

Henry nodded. "Hey, mum's the word!"

Mike struggled to free his toes. "Anyway, Mrs. Hubble, we agree about Karen. We both care about her. Personally, though, I don't need your approval for my actions."

"But I do," Karen said.

"Right," Luzma said, chiming in. "Me too."

Ruth felt confused. "Yes, yes, approval's fine," she said, staring intently across the table at Mike. "But I'm talking about something else. About faithfulness. Respect for human intimacy. We're not only responsible for our own lives. Sometimes we lead other lives, too."

Mike stared at her blankly.

"Understood?"

He frowned. "Whatever."

"That's it? That's all you have to say?"

Mike sighed. "Look, think what you want, I was never trying to . . . Could I have my toe back?"

"In a moment," Ruth said. "What *were* you doing?"

"Look, I don't know — that *hurts.*"

Henry nodded soberly. "Real fingernail yankers."

"Go on, young man," Ruth said, her voice stern. She released his foot and leaned back, crossing her arms in front of her chest.

"Okay, right, we've had our problems, just like everybody else. But we're working things out." For a fleeting moment, the boy looked truly pained. "God, I don't know . . ." He winced. "Sometimes I just feel like screaming."

Ruth turned her eyes toward the dark window. "And that justifies desertion? Abandonment? You feel like screaming, so you just . . ." But the rest of the thought drifted away.

Somewhere in her mind it was 1945 and she was driving down an empty desert highway, alone, towing along all her own dead dreams in a Mullen's Red Gap trailer. Innocence and hope and romance: all of it packed away in cardboard boxes. And then that long savage howl from the bottom of her lungs. Maybe at the center of every human being, she thought, there was some sort of unique and enduring noise — like a fingerprint — the secret wailing sound of the soul.

When she looked up, Mike was leaning forward, his freckled face very close to her own. She felt something approaching affection for the boy.

She turned to Karen. "A man's feelings, dear. You can't predict them. That's one thing I've definitely learned." She cleared her throat. "Maybe the problems start when you love a person too much. I guess if you're too enthusiastic, they just —" Abruptly, she thought of her experience in the downstairs bathroom that afternoon, all those people in the photographs melting and oozing away. "They just disappear, maybe, burning up like fire, melting away into nothing . . ."

"Not me, Ruthie," Henry said, reaching out for her hand. His voice was agitated. "Not me and you."

Ruth gave him a weak smile. Gently, she pulled her hand free.

Mike glanced at Karen, apprehension in his eyes. He was still leaning forward. "Listen, Mrs. Hubble, please don't get all worked up. I'm sorry, I really am. I made a few mistakes, agreed, but I've also made some progress since then. It's all in the past now. Really. I'm back for good."

"Except for parachute missions," Henry said.

Mike nodded. "Right, except for that."

Ruth stared at her granddaughter. Almost imperceptibly, a small fold of skin twitched beneath the girl's right eye as she leaned over to kiss the back of her husband's neck. "So there we are," Karen said. "It'll just take some time."

"Time," Ruth said quietly. "I suppose."

"That's a blessing?"

"No, dear. It's complicity."

For a few moments no one spoke. Then Henry gave a decisive tug to his baseball hat. "Well, hey," he said, "I guess we got things pretty well figured out here. Men and women speaking, it's always a tussle. Like today, for example. Ruthie and me, we barely say a word to each other all these years, then bingo, right out of no-where she up and wants to play cribbage. And then bingo again, this afternoon she lets me pick her up and waltz her over to the elevator. Right by the armpits. The whole nine yards. Crazy. I'll tell you something, though. I don't complain. Just count the mir-acles."

Ruth blushed and turned away.

"God," she sighed, "what a hammerhead."

After a few minutes Mike and Karen both stood up. "Take care of yourself, Grammy," Karen said. "I'll call you in the morning." The girl started to say something else but then stopped and gave Ruth a coded look that went woman to woman, partly thanks, partly the collusion of survival. "Better run," she said.

"Yes," Ruth said, "and don't stop."

When Henry and Luis had excused themselves, Ruth turned to Luzma. "Well, we'd better do the dishes," she said. Then she looked down and began to tug at the hairs on her left arm. "Correspondence," she said softly. "With complete strangers."

"Oh, come on, it's not like I'm gonna leave, Ruthie. No way. You do the correspondence stuff at home. I could even study right here."

Ruth didn't respond. From the corner of her eye, she watched the girl stand and gather the silverware and carry it out to the kitchen. Watching, in fact, was all she could manage. She watched Luzma fill the sink with water. She watched her return to the table for the glasses and trays and plates, her face hazy at the edges, everything unwinding in a jerky slow motion.

After a moment Ruth forced herself to speak up. "Now listen, don't throw away those paper plates, they're perfectly fine. Just put them there next to the breadbox, on the counter, in between the —"

She stopped because her eyes had filled with tears. She certainly didn't mean to cry, hadn't realized it was coming, but somehow it seemed the right thing. It felt good, in fact. She hadn't cried in years, maybe decades. With Luzma leaving, whom would she talk to on Saturdays? And who would accompany her to her dental appointments? The doctor's office was nearby on the Laguna bus line, but not the dentist, and how in the world could she ride alone to *that* part of town? She put a hand to her eyes. The crying wasn't loud at all, just a soft spilling sound.

"Right, I know," Luzma was saying, "five inches from the sink. I'm not some crummy amateur, Ruthie." She rinsed the silverware, cheeks glowing with happiness. "So what I'm thinking, Ruth, I try to hook on with the Perpetual Prestige Agency. They hire minority types like me. There's this Vietnamese guy I heard about, could hardly speak English, but he walks right in there out of the gutter, says his family's starving to death, says he needs money bad. So Prestige hires him. That same year, he's top sales-man for March and May. Two years later, he's taking in more than a hundred thousand. A true story, Ruth. I saw him once from the bus — guy's driving a Mercedes."

Ruth wiped her eyes. She didn't say anything.

"Well, he's rich now. Prestige gives their agents this six-week training program, free. Lots of possibilities, too — they got escrow companies, mortgage companies, all kinds of things."

The girl sounded so different, Ruth thought. Where had she learned to talk like this? Again, Ruth pulled at the hairs on her arm. In a dim way, of course, she was pleased for Luzma, going off to follow her dreams. But she couldn't help feeling that strange emptiness inside.

"Well fine," she finally said. "I guess maybe I'll just go to the dentist all by myself. You'll probably be too busy. Probably too famous."

One tear, which her eye-wiping had not erased, slipped down her cheek and dangled at the edge of her jaw. She waited for it to fall. She counted to five, slowly, then to fifteen. She resolved to let it drop of its own power.

Luzma walked out from the kitchen and sat down beside Ruth. "Now, come on, don't be a silly goose," she said. "You won't go all by yourself to the dentist. We'll still be friends, won't we? It's not like I'm moving to Alaska — I'll still always go with you. And I'll come over on the first day every month, no matter what. Fair enough?"

She bent to look into Ruth's face.

"Come on, Ruthie. I know you're glad deep down."

Five minutes, Ruth thought, and that tear was still stuck there on her jaw, like an icicle. Maybe the laws of gravity weren't what they used to be.

Luzma made a tsking noise with her tongue. "You should be happy for me, it's like a happy story. You're the one always telling stories. Always sharing the same old stories, right? Like the one about your father coming to California, remember? And like my dad in Mexico, too, working hard so he could raise a family right. Nothing to be scared about."

"Sure," Ruth said, "okay."

Luzma persisted. "Only thing new is, girls have careers now. Not like when you were young. We're more ambitious. You know, be your own boss. Take charge of things."

"I *was* a professional secretary, if you care to remember," Ruth said. "Anyway, you and Karen — your big careers — I mean, when Hale died . . ."

She fell silent. Her attention was now entirely on that mutant tear. It seemed immune to the stern laws of science — like Henry, who refused to understand the rules of the house — and Ruth was determined to teach it a lesson. She wouldn't wipe it off, or shake it off, or anything. Just wear it down. Make it hang there and suffer until it *had* to drop.

"And for me," Luzma was saying, "it'll be lots of fun, I bet. Especially in Beverly Hills, where I wanna work. I got connections there. Girls who clean houses, you know? They find out first when a place is up for sale, they keep their eyes open, they see if the husband's been in bed with the wife or if he sleeps on the couch or if he's not in the house at all. You follow my thinking, Ruth? They can tell me if it looks like a divorce is coming. Lots of divorces in Beverly Hills, lots of bucks for somebody like me."

Ruth started to raise her head, cautiously, so as not to disturb the adhesive tear.

"One or two sales, I'm rich," Luzma said. "Those places in the Hills, they cost a bundle. The commissions must be amazing. No joke, I could buy a new BMW and drive you to your appointments. No more bus trips for *us*."

"Well, yes, it sounds splendid," Ruth said. She gazed directly into the girl's eyes. "Listen, dear, do you know anything about gravity?"

"Sorry?"

"Gravity," Ruth said. "Like why apples fall, that sort of thing."

Luzma shook her head. "Houses, Ruthie. I'm selling *houses*. It'll take a while to start, though — I don't got all the information yet." She stood up. "You sit there awhile, let me finish with the dishes."

Ruth reached for Luzma's hand. "No, that's all right. Just leave them. You and Luis were my guests tonight. The least I can do is finish tidying up. Enrique will be home soon and he'll wonder what's keeping you."

"Well, I guess. You feel okay?"

In fact, Ruth realized, she felt considerably better: the tingling had died down and the pains were entirely gone. She opened and closed the fingers of her left hand. "Much better," she said. "All I needed was your dinner company, Karen's nice little visit — that's all, not Dr. Ash and his pain pills. I did get the whole way back here from the pool by myself, you know."

Smiling, Luzma tucked in her sequined blouse and buttoned up her jeans. "I'll just put the laundry into the dryer."

"No, leave the laundry too," Ruth said. "Don't worry about anything."

"You sure?"

"Completely."

"Well, if you say so. And it was nice for us, too. Mike back and everything — really super." She called her son in from the living room. "Give Ruthie a kiss goodbye, Luis."

The boy looked up into Ruth's eyes. "So long, Abuelita," he said, and pecked her on the edge of the jaw, taking the tear away.

"Now here's somebody who knows physics," Ruth said, reaching out to straighten his shoulders. "Don't forget, kid. No hunchbacks in *this* clan."

When she heard the front door close, Ruth pushed herself up from the table. Luzma was so optimistic, she thought — just like Karen, just like she herself had once been.

She piled the glasses into the kitchen sink, leaving them for morning, then moved heavily out to the living room. Luis had left the TV on, and *Wheel of Fortune* was just now coming to a close. Absurd, she thought. All these poor souls cheering a half-naked hostess, everyone wild-eyed and gluttonous and ripe for disappointment. Ruth sat down on the couch and pulled off her sandals.

Spin the wheel: there was Frank Deeds.

So many fine shining promises.

True love, he kept saying. He'd be faithful to her always. But though she knew Frank cared for her in his own unique way, which was a careless caring, Ruth couldn't shake off the suspicion — the intuition — that the man would remain a philanderer forever.

It was not passion and anxiety she wanted for her middle years. It was peace. Not surprises, pleasant or otherwise, but certainty.

Romance had died with Hale. Simplicity and practicality, these were the fallout, and so one day she composed a short note to Frank, explaining that she never wanted to see him again. They could exchange letters if he liked, but nothing else. She signed the note "Yours truthfully, Mrs. Ruth Caster Armstrong."

So lose a turn.

Spin again.

She cut her hair short, stopped wearing perfume. She worked long hours at the doctor's office in Los Angeles, filling up her days like a leaky bucket, often staying late into the evenings until everyone else in the building had gone home. For fun, she resumed piano lessons. She grew vegetables and flowers. With her savings from work she bought herself a car, a sleek yellow Studebaker, and on Saturdays she drove herself down to the beach at Laguna, to lie in the sun.

On one of those empty afternoons at the beach — it must have been in the late summer of 1956 — she happened to run across Nora Gretts, who had just recently returned from Europe. Predictably, the two of them had little in common anymore, except for heartbreak and their days at UCLA, but there was enough to get them through an hour or two of conversation under a merciless California sun. In the end, they agreed to meet for lunch the next day, which led to more lunches, and eventually to something not far removed from friendship.

Nora worked regular hours at Intime in those days, and when fall came, and it became too cold to go to the beach, Ruth began spending her Saturdays down at the shop. Just a way of passing time, refilling the leaky bucket that had become her life. Still, there were pleasant moments. Nora's idea of fun, Ruth came to realize, was more than a little odd; in fact, Ruth would've thought the woman a perfect floozy if she hadn't been a longtime witness to Nora's ostentatious declarations of identity. Even then, though, the woman was sometimes hard to stomach. But Ruth needed to distract herself, needed to occupy the hours, so on those Saturday afternoons she'd talk and laugh with Nora, for old times' sake, and together they'd page through tattered back issues of the *Daily Bruin* and sing sorority songs. When no customers came in, they'd smoke cigarettes and eat brownies for lunch behind the counter. And after lunch Nora would model a new camisole or negligee, dancing down the aisles while Ruth hummed Perry Como tunes.

Ruth stretched and yawned and reached for a toss pillow.

She blinked in surprise: her arm didn't hurt. She lifted her left leg, and that too was feeling better: numb, as if she'd been shot full of novocaine.

She pulled both legs onto the couch and curled up.

·   ·   ·

And so, yes, it was one of those Saturdays — March 1958, almost for sure — and Nora was strolling through the shop in a purple strapless bra and a pair of beaded blue underpants, and Ruth was doing her best to affect an air of amused indifference — "It's definitely *you*," she was saying, "a match made in heaven" — and at that instant the door swung open and a tall, skinny, vaguely familiar man sauntered in off the street. Nora fled for the bathroom; Ruth turned and stepped behind the cash register.

The thing to do was to behave normally. A salesperson, polite and efficient. She pushed her glasses up on her nose and watched closely as the man moved about the store, sometimes muttering to himself, sometimes pausing to finger an article of clothing. Again, she felt that inexact sense of recognition. For five or ten minutes the man roamed up and down the aisles with a heavy step, the top of his gray-streaked head bobbing above the racks.

Ruth finally summoned up a crisp clerical voice, calling out to ask if he needed help.

"Help how?" he said.

"Well, the usual. Advice or whatever."

"Guess not, cutie." The man was behind a rack of half-slips. "No thanks for now. Just having a general all-around look-see."

It was the voice that seized her memory. A Hubble voice. Bill or Henry — she prayed it was Bill — but she hadn't seen either of them since high school. She leaned over the register. "Billy Hubble?" she said. "It's *me*, Ruth Armstrong. I mean Ruth *Caster*, to you."

The man peeked around the half-slips. It was Henry.

"Well, holy-moly, I'll be hanged and danged," he said, and he walked over to the register. "Ruthie Caster. What's you doing in a joint like this?"

Ruth flushed. Something in his manner, maybe the awkward way of talking, made her conscious of the enduring singularity and unity of a human life. All that Hubbleness. All those years. In the standard ways, of course, he'd undergone the changes that come with age, yet at the center of the man there was something stone-hard and permanent that made her warm inside, that made her touch her curls and smile and explain with a slight nervousness that she was simply helping out an acquaintance for the day.

"I mean, I have my own job during the week," she said. "In a doctor's office."

Henry nodded. "Hey, I'll bet you do. Always the sophisticated lady. Just like the song."

"I was?"

"Right as rain."

Ruth felt herself blushing again. "And you're still a stockboy over at Simpson-Ashby?"

Henry slapped his leg and laughed. "Oh, hell no, I haven't been in produce since I was eighteen. I'm at Bullocks now, moved into housewares. Head buyer."

"Splendid."

"Yeah, I guess I'd have to agree with that."

He took a step forward, sliding a hand across the counter toward her. Ruth removed her glasses. It was an involuntary gesture, utterly unwilled; nor could she wipe off her nervous smile, nor stop herself from reaching up to freshen her curls again.

"Well, good for you," she said. "I always suspected you'd do fine, even if you did drop out of school during that nasty influenza epidemic. Back when so many of my friends were *really* dying."

Just then Nora came out, more or less clothed. It was a relief for Ruth to step back and make the introductions. "Pleased as punch," said Nora, and offered her hand. "Call me Lady Soirée, please do. Mind if I call you Hank?"

"Mind if you don't," he said.

"Well, there we are, Hank. And what brings you here to Intime? Looking for anything special?"

"Not exactly, Lady Sorry. Sort of browsing."

"*Browsing?*" Ruth said. "Aren't there some hardware stores in town?"

Henry lifted his eyebrows, sliding his hand toward Ruth again.

"Hardware's just hardware, Ruthie. I figure to myself, I figure like this, a man's got to expand the old horizons. You know, learn about things that please the ladies. Anyways, I'm passing by this fine establishment here, I spot them artistic dry goods in the window and I say to myself, I say clear as a bell, 'Henry' — Hank, I mean — 'Hank, you best step inside and see what's what with the ladies these days.' All in the line of duty, eh? Customer taste."

He rocked back on his heels, then forward. The hand came to rest a few inches from Ruth's right breast.

She took a step sideways.

The hand followed.

"But aren't you awfully far from home?" she asked. "Why, I heard you somehow managed . . . That is, I hear you have a lovely place in San Marino."

"Well, hey, I don't live here in Laguna, if that's your drift, but I like to come down on Saturdays, to get away. My wife passed a few years back, see, and I have an awful time knowing what to do with my weekends."

"Isn't *that* the coincidence!" said Nora, throwing out her chest, dropping a hand on Henry's arm. "Ruth here, she lives up in Los Angeles, not too far from yourself, Hank, and comes down to visit me on Saturdays. And her own dear spouse also died recently. Well, not so recently, actually, but you know how some women are. She's still in mourning, Hank. Note the clothes. She certainly doesn't follow the latest fashions."

Ruth couldn't help glancing down. Her gray shirtwaist dress *was* a bit dated — she'd seen no reason for fancy clothing since Hale died. Still, she thought, Nora was off base on this one. Out of bounds, too. Ruth clenched her jaw and dragged her finger across her throat like a saw.

Nora took no notice.

"I guess our darling Ruthie just has difficulty getting on with things. Needs to take her own sweet time. But look, Hank, that's a mighty interesting tie you've got on — are those by any chance trombones? — I'll bet a guy like you could show our sad friend here a swell time."

"Nora, for God's sake."

For an instant, a familiar image filled the air in front of Ruth's eyes: Hale slipping a tie around his neck, knotting it with elegant precision, moving to examine himself in a mirror. Handsome and graceful and dignified, the image of perfection. Ruth stared at the man before her. Why, he couldn't even make a proper knot — the tie was pinched into place with a shiny safety pin — and the trombones were positively shameful. Quite unexpectedly, Ruth felt a measure of compassion for this unkempt, uncouth widower, this Henry Ho-hum Hubble.

He winked at her. "The idea suits me fine. Might just show this cutie a trick or two." A flash of yellow teeth appeared in his bright pink face, and he reached into his breast pocket, passing a business card across the counter. His hand brushed up against the front of Ruth's blouse. "Give me a call this week. We'll plan ourselves a jaunt down here together next Saturday. I'd be proud as a plum to make the ride with you. Course, I don't drive or nothing." He flashed his teeth again. "In the prime of life, you bet, but already blind as a bat."

Nora patted him on the shoulder. "Don't you worry about that, Hank. Ruth here has her own Studebaker. She'll just pick you right up, won't you, darling?"

Ruth did not answer.

Henry shrugged. "Well, can't miss my bus," he said, setting his card on the counter. "See you next week, sweetheart. I'm pleased as can be."

"At least you could've offered him a ride home," Nora said when he was gone.

Ruth was furious. "What the hell did you do that for? I haven't even laid eyes on the man in thirty-five years. Walks in here like some pervert — snooping through cheap lingerie, for God's sake

— and now we're supposed to have a date? And I drive? No thanks."

Nora picked up Henry's business card and slipped it into Ruth's handbag. "Cheap lingerie, you say?"

"Well, I wouldn't call it —"

"Who here knows about quality, me or you? Lady Soirée, who spent her entire prime in France, or you, who's been sitting around at her parents' house, crying her life away for years? Anyway, Hank's a splendid male specimen. Lonely, that's obvious, but you can't beat the male part." Nora studied her long red fingernails for a moment. "Look, honey, take it from me, a gal who's been around and back. You won't do better. No great shakes, I'll admit, but at least he's a gentleman."

"Oh, for God's sake," Ruth said, and she took the card from her purse and dropped it in the trash.

That Monday, when Ruth was back at her desk in Los Angeles, busy helping a blind patient fill out a medical history form, Henry telephoned her.

"Hear you're free on Friday," he said, "and I'd sure like to take you out for dinner."

"Free?" Ruth said. *Kill* Nora, she thought. Strangle her with that purple bra. "I am not free," she said. "I will not be."

Henry laughed. "Haven't changed a bit, have you Ruthie?" He made a loud phlegmy sound in his throat. "Listen, I've been pretty lonely these days." He made the sound again. "Real lonely."

"Well. I don't think it's possible."

"Miserable lonely."

"Oh, for Pete's sake, where's your dignity?"

"Too darn lonely for dignity. Lonely like to bust."

Now what could she do? She sighed and glanced up at the blind patient. The man was grinning, head cocked, enjoying this end of the conversation.

"All right," she said at last. "But I'll tell you something. It's pure charity."

"Okay by me," Henry said cheerfully.

Ruth dreaded it. All week, in fact, she tried to think up excuses. Polio maybe. Trapped in an iron lung. But when they walked into the restaurant that Friday evening — a noisy steak house Henry had picked out — she was pleasantly surprised. His posture, for example, was erect and confident. Of course his skin had gone a bit nubby, but she liked the way he moved. Very slowly, with a measured gait that conveyed — she sincerely believed at the time — a firm and manly self-possession. Later, less charitably, she would come to refer to this walk as "lumbering."

Once at the table, she placed her napkin in her lap and asked about his parents.

"Oh, they passed a few years back," he said. He tried to smile at her. "Hear yours are still with us."

"Oh yes, they're just fine," Ruth said. "Well, you know, tuberculosis. But other than that."

Henry shifted in his seat.

"Hale, that was your husband's name, I hear."

Ruth froze. "You hear quite a lot, Henry, don't you?"

He frowned and licked his lips. "I guess that's right. Maybe when the eyes start to go, the ears . . . Anyways, I know he was sick, Hale, before he died." He tried again to smile. "One thing I understand," he went on, "it's sickness. You see, my own Eleanor was sick a long time, too, before she passed. Well, ten years, just about."

"Ten *years?*" Ruth stared.

"About that, I'd say."

"My God. I'm sorry, Henry."

"Well hey, look now. Never did have any kids, that's the killer. But all in all I've been pretty lucky." He smiled weakly. "She was a Catholic, did I tell you? An honest-to-God living saint. I swear. I was so proud of that woman." His lips quivered. Like waves, Ruth thought, forever gathering themselves up into frothy smiles, forever crashing down again, defeated.

"Sure do miss her."

Ruth sat in silence, looking down at the napkin in her lap, thinking. She felt sorry for the man. He was kind — Nora was right about that. He was sensitive. And at times he could even be charming. Really, she was not at all ashamed to be seen with him. He looked a lot better than he had as a boy, now that his tomato-red hair had turned gray, and he seemed much more self-assured. On top of all that, he had that beautiful house in San Marino. An elegant Victorian house, she'd been told; nothing like her parents' little bungalow or the flat old Caster ranch house out in San Diego. To an extent, Ruth felt guilty thinking such thoughts, but it occurred to her that she wouldn't mind living in San Marino, she wouldn't mind at all. It was near her parents' place, and near the first house she'd shared with Hale, and San Marino was one of those ritzy areas she'd always had an eye on. All in all, not a bad bargain.

"How's your ribs?" Henry asked.

"My ribs?"

"Your dinner, cutie pie, how is it?"

Cutie pie! Clearly, Ruth thought, the man would require some extensive training. But there was something in his voice that struck her as dependable, something firm and unchanging, something that promised she would never again have to worry about being alone. The object, after all, was no longer perfection. Certainly not joy. And there was much to be said for that singular and enduring Hubbleness now gazing across the table at her. In a way, like a kind of cement foundation, it seemed to offer support to her own fragile Ruthness.

"Well, as ribs go," she said, "they're not bad. Quite the barbecue, in fact."

7:37 P.M.

Jeopardy! had started. Ruth blinked once — a contestant was explaining how his career as a butcher had been "born" on his father's farm in northern Idaho. She blinked again. Her eyes fell on those paper characters that Luis had cut out — a spirit world full of spirit people — all of them heaped into the ashtray. Little Greenie seemed to be at rest.

Valentine's Day, 1959, and Ruth Caster married Henry Hubble.

"Hale, I'm sorry," she'd said the night before. "I loved you. I loved and loved you. Hale?"

They were married at the courthouse in Pasadena, and that evening there was a small reception at Henry's house — which was now *her* house — in San Marino. By and large it was a fairly pleasant gathering. Except she couldn't stop whispering things to herself: "God, I'm sorry, I *loved* you, Hale."

At one point, she recalled, Henry found her standing alone in the kitchen.

"Hale," she was whispering, "I'm sorry."

"My new bride," he said, slapping her bottom. "Helluva day, but the name's Hank."

"Fine," she said.

Just then Douglas and Carter arrived, both late. Douglas had been performing emergency surgery, and Ruth smiled with pride as he came into the kitchen to meet Henry. Not yet thirty and already a successful doctor, the boy had made quite a name for himself in Hollywood and Bel-Air. Carter was late because of thunderstorms in Caracas, Venezuela, where his plane had been delayed. In this case, too, Ruth felt the stir of pride. Barely twenty-six, president of his own commercial-design firm, traveling all over the world. His expensive and conceited new wife, Melinda — who would later be Karen's mother, and later still, the obese and conniving financial ruin of Carter — pressed herself against him like a case of chronic hives.

Ruth cast a cheerless smile on her boys and said, "Don't Mr. Hubble and I have a beautiful house here?" She glanced at Henry. "My boys," she said. "Hale's boys."

Henry said, "Righto." He clicked his teeth and held out an unsteady hand.

Right then, Ruth felt a rare surge of anger. At herself, partly, and at this bargain-basement marriage, and at the man standing before her, this husband who now reminded her of a soda jerk in some tacky Hollywood drugstore. His jacket was white and his shirt was white, and his pants and belt and shoes and socks. His face, and the wilted carnation in his buttonhole, were a ghastly shade of red. Like a drunken ghost, Ruth thought.

She couldn't stop the rage from bubbling up. "What in God's name," she whispered, "were you thinking? Meeting my sons for the first time, dressed like that, like a giant maggot!" She made a fist, trying to control herself. Then, by chance, she noticed his tie. It was a tie she had given him just two weeks before — an elegant Brooks Brothers red-and-blue-striped silk tie, a beautiful tie. She reached up to Henry's neck and adjusted the knot; a quiver of tenderness passed through her fingers. For a moment, she stood just smiling up at him.

Then Henry tossed back a shot of tequila. It was easily his sixth or seventh of the evening.

"Sons," he said, "I've worked long, hard hours all my life. Saw my share of success, carved out a niche for myself in housewares, clobbered the competition. But even though it looked like I had everything, I was always asking myself, 'Hubble,' I asked, 'what's it all for?' Well, now I know." He threw an arm around Ruth's shoulders, almost knocking her down. "Your little mother here suits me just right, and I know I'm gonna make her happy as a clam."

Henry kissed Ruth's cheek, then Douglas's, then Carter's and Melinda's. "Call me Hank," he said.

Later that evening Ruth shut herself in her bedroom to write a final letter to Frank Deeds.

Valentine's Day, 1959

Dear Mr. Deeds,

    I regret to inform you that I have been married.

    I am quite content. I have a perfect house. I have every

convenience a woman might desire, and am only a forty-five-minute drive away from my parents. Things are very, very, *very* fine. The sun comes up peacefully; the sun goes down peacefully. And every night, when I go to bed, I know what will happen the next day.

I hope you will be happy. Please never write to me, and try never to think of me again.

Cordially and Even Fondly,
Mrs. Ruth Caster Armstrong Hubble

A week later, Frank sent Ruth the snapshot he'd taken of her at the San Diego marina, inscribed on the back with the words "You will always be close to my heart." He also sent a large, flattering portrait of himself and a letter declaring his lasting love.

She stashed the photographs in a drawer of her roll-top desk.

She disposed of Frank's letter.

She never spoke to him again, never saw him again, never regretted it.

On occasion, though, especially in the hours before bedtime, it came to her that she had been offered the risk of a second chance, which was something in itself, and that by declining she had willfully and freely chosen to become the Ruth she was, the Ruth she would now always be.

7:48 P.M.

She rolled onto her side. Curious white shapes were drifting through the air again, moving slowly from place to place: they seemed distant now, almost unearthly. A kind of laziness trickled through Ruth's body, like sweet warm milk, or like one of Dr. Ash's no-need-to-suffer medications.

Surf's up!

·   ·   ·

Ruth and Henry passed many years together in the San Marino house. Then, in the summer of 1973, shortly after Henry's retirement (Ruth had long since quit her own job), the inland heat and the demands of caring for such a large house began to wear on Ruth's health. Both of her parents were dead, and her own life batteries were weakening. No more spark: her skin had dried up, her curls began to flatten and thin out. Idly at first, then with resolution, she and Henry visited several condominium sites along the coast, and after long discussions (with Douglas offering frequent counsel) they eventually reached the decision to move to Paradise Lagoon. They made a down payment on number 24 and contracted to take up residency that winter.

Over the next several weeks, Ruth spent countless hours sorting through her belongings, discarding much, packing up only the essentials in cardboard boxes and plastic trash bags. The compelling notion of ruthlessness had taken hold of her. Partly literal, partly a pun: less and less Ruth. One morning, only a day or so before the move, she had just begun to sort through a shoebox full of trinkets when she heard the mailman at the front door. She rose from her spot in the back corner of the living room, where she was sitting Indian style on the shag rug, and squeezed her way through the boxes and bags to the door. The mailman handed her a letter from Margaret, Aunt Elizabeth's girl, whom Ruth had often taken care of as a child down at San Diego, and who was now a waitress in Las Vegas.

The mailman tipped his hat and hurried down the sidewalk. Ruth opened the letter.

"Dear Cuz," it said, "I am sorry to be the one to tell you that my mother has died. I know you were close to her in the past, and I'm sure the news will come as a great blow to you, as it did to me. Mr. Deeds is also deceased. They were found at the table in Mother's kitchen. Heart attacks in both cases — pure coincidence, I'm told, though no official investigation was done."

Oddly, Ruth felt no great emotion. She stood for a while in the doorway, aware of her own breathing. What eventually impressed itself upon her was not sorrow, but rather a wide and shallow melancholy.

Ruthless, she thought. Just less and less.

She had been prudent. She had risked little. She had lost little. She had chosen correctly — sound judgment, sound instincts — and here was the validation. Sadness without sorrow.

"Well now," she said.

Back in the living room, Ruth stared absently at her boxes and bags. At one point she almost cried, but did not permit it. She concentrated instead on the reward of unfelt pain. All those untold lies. All the foreclosed misery. The frustration and broken promises and suspicion and excuses and betrayal — none of this was hers. It would've ended exactly as it ended: Elizabeth and Frank at a breakfast table. A bad wager from the start. She had known this all along, even while hoping otherwise, and what she felt now was the dull ache of her own good sense.

"Poor us," she murmured. "*All* of us."

For a few seconds the tears were very close by.

Then she shook her head. She crossed the floor to her roll-top desk and pulled open the drawer full of old photographs. There was Frank in his bow tie and con-man smile, making an attempt to look earnest. And there was Ruth herself — a younger Ruth, an almost happy Ruth — blushing at the camera with what now seemed the last faint glow of passion.

Yes, a bad risk.

She sat down at the desk. With two pieces of Scotch tape, she carefully attached the snapshot of herself to the back of the larger portrait. "Ha!" she said. Then she took a frame down from the wall, removed the photograph of Carter deep-sea fishing in the Bahamas, and inserted the pictures of Frank and herself, Frank's facing out.

A souvenir of sorts. A tribute to good sense.

She put the frame into one of the boxes destined for Paradise Lagoon.

"Ha," she said again. "There."

When she and Henry had settled into number 24, after unpacking and arranging the furniture, Ruth devoted herself to the problems of household decoration. Paradise Lagoon: this far and no farther. Except to the cemetery, there would be no more moves. She displayed her paintings and Oriental scrolls in the third-story bedrooms and second-story sitting room; she repapered the living room walls, installed new linoleum in the kitchen, purchased lawn furniture for the balcony. As a final act, with something like devotion in her heart, she spent a long and quiet afternoon arranging her gallery of photographs in the tiny bathroom by the front door. An old lady's monument, she thought. Her own little people steeple.

The last picture to go up was Frank's. She placed it above the sink, at eye level, where visitors might take notice as they glanced up from washing their hands. And behind Frank's face, hidden there, was the shadow of her own.

As she stepped back, something seemed to swing shut inside her.

Just an old friend, she'd tell Henry if he asked. An old, old acquaintance.

But Henry never did ask.

8:00 P.M.

Ruth opened her eyes and sat up straight, holding her shoulders back. She felt tired. Enough of Frank, she thought. Enough of Elizabeth. Just a stew of worn-out memories, and what good had they done her?

She bent down to put on her sandals. Her toenails needed clipping, she noticed; they were yellow and looked more like horns than toenails. She stood and walked toward the elevator.

On the radio in Ruth's bedroom, a Brahms piano concerto was coming to an end.

. . . and in just a moment we'll be back with more here at The Golden Age, *Southern California's only truly classical hour of programming . . .*

Ruth stepped from the elevator and, pausing briefly, switched off the radio. A great silence filled the room, pressing up against her ears. Then the sound of distant waves washed through the air around her.

Ruth glanced in the direction of the window: all dark.

She walked past the bed to her chair. She undid the hook-and-eye clasp on her pants and had just started to pull down the zipper when she reminded herself that undressing from the top down would leave her body exposed for the shortest span of time. So she released the pants' zipper and, crossing her arms above the wrists, took hold of the bottom of her vest. Starting with her right hand near the left hip bone, her left hand near the right hip bone, she raised her elbows in front of her and up to her chin.

"Skin the rabbit!" she whispered, and lifted her hands high to pull off the vest. Years ago, she used to say those same words to her boys as she undressed them, and before that, her own mother had used the expression with her: Here we go, Ruthie, skin the rabbit!

She gave a final tug, uncrossing her hands, and the vest popped off. She placed it on the chair. Absently, she undid the top buttons of her blouse and began to skin the rabbit once again. She crossed her wrists, grasped the blouse, lifted her hands high above her head. Except this time something went wrong — a tight pinching at her throat. It took a moment to realize that the cord of her silver locket had twisted up; it was attacking her neck.

"Oh, criminey," she said, "just what I need."

She gave her shoulders a shake. She wiggled her arms and

head, twisted at the waist, but the locket wouldn't budge. The thing had somehow snagged on the button of a sleeve, winding around itself, and the long cord was squeezing her throat like one of those weird African snakes.

Blouse over her head, the stupid locket almost strangling her, she couldn't see a thing. She took a couple of steps in what she supposed was the direction of the door, but almost immediately her pants slithered down around her ankles. She yelped and stumbled; her feet wouldn't work; she couldn't move more than two or three inches at a time.

Still wiggling, arms pinned by the blouse, she began to shuffle forward. Suddenly things got darker.

"For crying out loud," she muttered. She'd ended up inside her closet. She felt the hangers against her arms, the skirts and dresses swishing all around her. A person could vanish, she thought, in a place like this.

For a moment she stood perfectly still.

Disappear, she thought.

The idea was seductive.

It was also disconcertingly familiar.

A streak of white light pierced the pure, black background of Ruth's temporary blindness. Was it a mistake to nurture fantasies of how things should have been? Ruth swayed to the side, then stood motionless again. Life without illusion. Might it have been more bearable, more meaningful, more kind?

Nineteen thirty-six, Washington, D.C. — Hale sequestered in his study with Frank Deeds — and she was listening to the low, conspiratorial hum of their voices from the kitchen, where she stood waiting for the coffee to finish percolating. One more misfortune in the Deeds household, she thought. No doubt something Myrna had done. Poor Frank — she pitied the man, she really did. And Myrna, too. How lucky she was to have Hale. God, she loved him.

Shaking her head, Ruth poured out three cups of coffee. She placed the cups on a tray and then crossed the hall toward the study.

"If only *I'd* married her," Frank was saying.

Ruth paused. She lowered the tray to her left hip and inched toward the door, which stood ajar.

"Charming," Hale said.

She heard an odd chuckle, high and artificial.

"You should have just *seen* her, last year out in Ponca City. Such antics. Such desperation. Just the thought of it sickens me." Another chuckle. "I mean all of it. This marriage."

"My God, man, she's the loveliest woman alive." Frank's voice, ordinarily smooth and commanding, sounded almost bewildered. "And she's crazy about you. Thinks about nothing else."

"Certifiable myopia. Lucky, lucky me."

"Enough, shut up," Frank said.

For a while there was silence.

Then Frank said, "You want to know, I'm jealous as hell."

"Charming once again." Hale's voice was not his own. "Christ!" he said.

There was another brief silence.

Hale said, "Thing is, I adored her."

Then, after a moment: "Couldn't get enough of her, be with her enough. But Christ, I hardly knew her, only six *weeks* before we married, and now . . . Well, now my whole goddamn future . . ." Something hot entered Ruth's throat; somewhere down inside her, the pain of a lifetime was gathering force. "So much *time!*" he said. "I swear to you, Frank. It's killing me."

An angry, hostile silence.

And in that silence, which Ruth would not allow herself to remember for almost sixty years, her heart lost its natural rhythm. Ownerless and free, it floated for a time through the cold, shapeless mass of the universe.

She stepped forward into the room, mumbled something about coffee.

When Hale turned toward her, his features revealed no trace of treachery, nothing at all; he looked just as he had looked every day since she'd met him. The same small, well-formed mouth and crooked nose, the same glowing green eyes with those beautiful flecks of brown. Such splendid eyes.

Frank stood up and reached for the coffee tray. "Now, what was I saying? Ah, yes. Ruthie, my darling, I was just telling Hale how happy any man on earth would be to have you for a wife."

He smiled.

A cocky Frank Deeds smile, yes. But she saw the compassion too. And the pity.

After Hale died, Ruth devoted herself to the watch he had given her, regulating her actions according to its stern requirements; her heart took up the rhythm of that strict metronome; all harmony, all melody, slipped away.

It wasn't betrayal exactly. Maybe not even inexactly. He had only shaken her from a dream, a silly romantic dream.

All that time, he'd said. His whole sad future.

Alone in her closet, Ruth thought of those tapes of airplane pilots screaming "Mama!" as they made their brain-bending surrender to gravity. She thought of Hale's last syllable. "Time!" he'd yelled — part proclamation, part question — the sound of one human voice adding itself to the great electric buzz.

The heat began to rise in her throat — her own electric clamor, her own indelible Ruthness releasing itself to the universe — a vulgar and desperate and angry scream that she'd somehow managed to swallow back all these years.

"Gehr," she said, blouse wrapped around her head, lace collar pressing up against her mouth and nose.

"Gehhhrr!"

A moment later, incredibly, Henry entered the bedroom. She heard him lumber over to the bed, heard him rustle her pillow and sleeping bag. There was some silence, then the sound of drawers opening.

She tried to clap, stretching her arms high, but all she could manage was a muted little pat.

His hand touched her shoulder.

"Well, hey," Henry said, "what's this?"

He fingered her blouse, reaching beneath it to touch her belly, then ran a hand up to her armpit. When he spoke again, his voice seemed full of wonder.

"I'll tell you, Ruthie, we've been married all these years, but I never figured you for a closet person. Shows we're made for each other." His hand moved to the side of her breast. "Like I said once to Douglas, I says, 'Closets are a darn good place to hang out, sort of collect your thoughts and — '"

Ruth spat away some fabric.

"Okay, okay," Henry said.

He took her wrist. He unhooked the locket from her sleeve, pulled the cord over her head, lifted off her blouse.

"Fiend," she said.

"Hey, I just —"

Ruth snatched the blouse from his hands and yanked up her pants. Henry stood gaping. "All *right*," she said, "you saved me, that's no excuse for a peep show." She walked around him to her chair. "Hope you're satisfied."

"Not bad," he said, and smiled at her. A goofy smile, partly, but also calm and tender. It made her glance away.

"Well, anyway," she said. "Thanks."

"That's what I'm here for."

Ruth reached up to smooth her curls. "So I guess you'll be going to bed now?"

"Right," he said. "Guess so."

She waited a moment, almost looking at him. "First, though, you'll set up my breakfast tray? The usual way. I think you know how I like it done."

"Oh, sure," Henry said, and kept smiling. "Quarter cup of bran, no milk till morning. Don't want the stuff mushy." He crossed to the chair and placed the locket on the cushion, still smiling, his mouth wide open. He reached for his tooth, twisted it a couple of times, then turned toward the door.

"Call if you need me," he said.

When she was certain Henry was downstairs, Ruth took off her pants and struggled to hang them underneath her blouse and vest on the hanger. She lay her garters, panty girdle, and camisole over the back of the chair, slipped on her flannel nightgown, stepped into her slippers, and pulled on her bedjacket. Stooping to lift her silver locket from the cushion, she made her way into the bathroom.

Methodically, humming quietly to herself, she lay the locket on the table by the toilet, next to a stack of old bills, then turned to the counter where her laxative was waiting. She picked up the spoon she always used and dipped it deep into the jar to pull out a heaping teaspoonful of brown pellets. She chewed them thoroughly for a full minute — a few dropped to the tile — and while she chewed, she idly took stock of the items around her sink.

Too much, she thought.

Seven bottles of moisturizing lotion were turned upside down, leaning against the medicine cabinet mirror. Their faded labels said "Moondew." Ruth picked up a bottle and pumped its top, but nothing came out. She tried another one, then several more — all empty. Most certainly, Karen and Luzma were right: all the old clutter should be thrown away. Next week, she tried to convince herself, she'd find a place for these bottles in the trash.

The phone rang.

Ruth licked her index finger, popped the fallen laxative pellets into her mouth, and hurried out from the bathroom and over to her bedside table. Wheezing slightly, she reached for the receiver.

There was silence at the other end. Then a shallow whisper: "White Rabbit."

The voice startled her. "Who is this?"

"It's me." There was a quick, high chuckle. "I meant to get you earlier."

"Nora?"

"Not quite."

"Carter? Douglas?"

"Well, no, I'm sorry."

Absently, Ruth sat down on her bed. The voice seemed familiar now.

"Elizabeth? Uncle Stephen — it's you!"

The voice chuckled.

"Frank?" she said. She paused and adjusted her glasses. "*Hale?*"

On the other end there was a delicate, almost feathery sound, not the wind, not the sea, but something in between, something cool and breathy and weightless.

"Who?" she said.

Again, for an instant, she detected that odd feathery sound, then came a sad little sigh.

"Just me. White Rabbit."

Ruth reached for her pillbox. She picked out a Cardizem, studied it for a second, then washed it down with water. Enough, she thought. No need for Tylenol or Naprosyn or pink tranquilizers. She set the box on her bedside table.

She didn't bother to clean her face. She didn't bother to turn out the lamp, nor to take off her bedjacket, nor to pull the bobby pins from her hair. For a few minutes, perfectly still, she listened to the waves whisper through her open window.

Well fine, she thought.

She unfastened her digital watch and put it aside. Then, staring straight ahead, she also took off Hale's wristwatch. She held it firmly, as if to contain time in the palm of her hand, then eased back slowly against her sit-up pillow.